Book I

The Southern Lights

Amanda Townsend

Cover design and illustration by @Zukellogs

ISBN 978-1-7635625-1-6

House of Dumbrell Pty Ltd
26 River Avenue
Chatswood NSW 2067
Australia

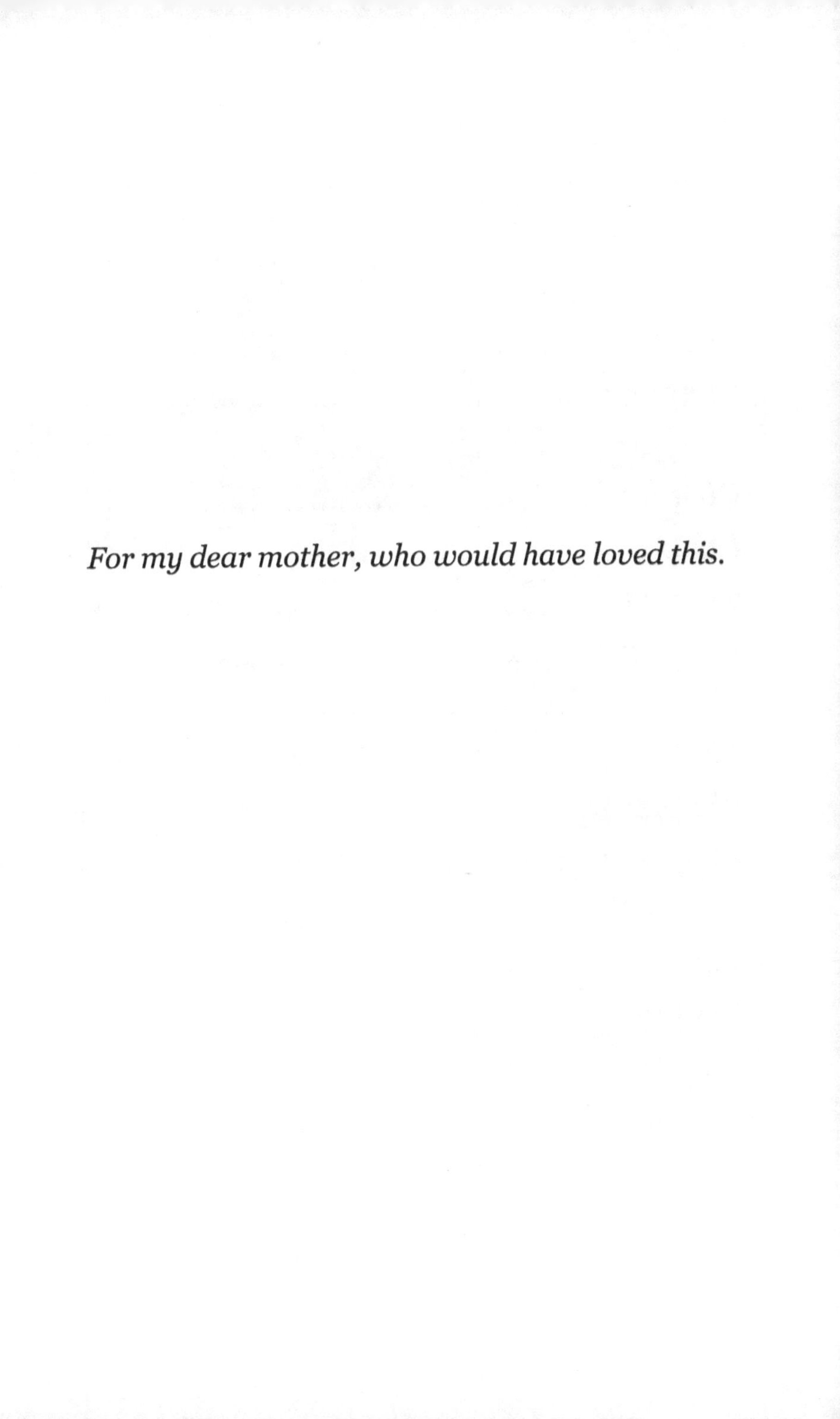

For my dear mother, who would have loved this.

Table of Contents

"You can never be overdressed or overeducated."
— Oscar Wilde

So here it was, the start of yet another chapter in her life, another beginning, another new school, although this time it was different: this was technically not school, it was university, and this time was the last. No more new schools, she only had to do this one last time. She was also new with hundreds of others, so she should be much better at it than most; she'd had practice, she reasoned. It would be a level playing field for once... hopefully.

Her father came down with the last of her bags to finish packing the car. He considered packing to be an art form and nobody wanted to get in between him and his arrangement of the car. It was currently full and he was pulling that face, "the grimace", her sister Lanna had dubbed it. He wore that face a lot; four kids and all. He thought she was taking too much.

"Aurora, you can't possibly need all this? What's in this box?" he inquired, shaking his head, frowning.

"Dad, it has my ornaments," she replied.

"Ornaments for what, is that another word for jewellery?"

"No, ornaments for my room, Dad. I need them for the atmosphere, to give my room the right vibe," she answered with some attitude.

"Your room doesn't need to be ornamental, you're there to study." Her dad was a practical man.

"Dad, I'm decorating my room, I'm taking that stuff," she insisted, positive everything she was taking would be necessary.

"What's in this, it's heavy?" He was opening another box now, checking for himself.

"Books, just the ones that are important to me."

He continued moving bags and boxes around, mumbling to himself and continually propping his glasses back on top of his head as they fell down, but dutifully packing everything she wanted into the family Discovery.

Her mother issued last-minute instructions. "Okay, kids, remember to put the dog out just before bed and make sure the cat is inside, it's getting too cold for him to be out now it's autumn. Little one," she turned to Aurora's youngest sister, Evie, "make sure you brush your teeth."

"Sebastian," she called out to her son, "she has to be in bed by 9 p.m., watch her and take her phone away!" Bas was just starting his gap year, so responsibility was not high on his list of priorities. "And absolutely no fighting with Lanna, Bas."

"No, Mum, I've got this," he said resolutely.

"Me and my bro are gonna hang," Lanna said, lifting her curly head up while raising her eyebrows suggestively to taunt Sebastian. She was always trying to get a rise out of everyone, especially her older brother, and she drove him crazy. He had never learnt to ignore her.

"I'm gonna hang you out of an upstairs window," he threatened.

The dog was running around the Discovery, hoping to be invited into the back of the already full car. "Sorry, boy," her dad said, "not this trip. Your job is to mind the children." It would soon dawn on him that he wasn't going and his head would drop. Ajax the Doberman was big, too big for the breed standard, more like a large black-and-tan hound as he was quite lean with a lovely broad head he insisted on laying in your lap. Aurora would miss him terribly.

"Right then, that's that," said her dad, slamming the boot shut. "Look after each other, kids. Ajax you're in charge." He patted the dog's head fondly. "We're done, honey, let's go, we're late getting on the road as it is, I wanted to get away an hour ago," he called to his wife.

"You always say that no matter what time we leave," her mother said absent-mindedly, checking that her enormous handbag, bulging from all the last minute necessities, had her phone in it. It was a normal, everyday sort of comment, but Aurora could hear the emotional tension it was hiding.

Her mum gave an exasperated look at the over-packed car, then took a deep breath and let out a sigh as she collected herself. They were used to this, used to change, used to new chapters and packing.

Aurora was dreading this part. She hated goodbyes, there'd been too many. She thought of the different countries and companions she'd left behind, so many goodbyes, and now this one. Evie came and attached herself like a leech.

"You look after Ajax for me while I'm away," Aurora said to her. "He'll need you to run him down to the river in the afternoons, you do it on your bike, okay?"

"Okay, I will, and I'll look after your bedroom too." She thought she might as well go for broke while her big sister's defences were down.

"Ahh no, just the dog, Evie, the room will be fine."

"Bye, Rory," Bas said, easily wrapping her up in a hug with his broad shoulders. "You'll get on fine," he assured her quietly, sensing her anxiety. Born just over a year apart, they had always been good buddies.

Lanna hugged her without any words, tears welling up in her green eyes. The family dynamic would be forever changed after today and Lanna, the most sensitive of the Bond children, was well aware of this.

Three hours later they slowly made their way past the gate posts with a nameplate that proudly announced they were entering Tudor Hall. The name reflected the fondness Queen Elizabeth I had for Bristol and its St Mary Redcliffe Church, which she called on one of her progresses "the fairest, goodliest and most famous parish church in England".

The old building was stately and grand. It was the sort of place you could imagine young nobles and novelists discovering friendship and heartbreak. For Aurora, it would be like stepping into a foreign world. An old weeping birch tree stood blowing in the breeze out the front as parents stood in line with their children waiting to receive their room allocation. She tried not to stare as she assessed her new peers.

Her room was on the top floor. The blocks were staggered boy/girl, and the bedrooms arranged over the three floors, with nine in a block. Aurora found herself on the top floor, looking out over the lawns that swept down to tennis courts and gardens. "Well, it is quintessentially British," her mother stated, "and very pretty. It's got everything you need, and the shower is just down the hall. It's good," her mother said simply.

"I love the view." Aurora stared out the window over the rooftops below, wondering what a year in halls would be like, then she turned around and studied the room.

For student accommodation, it was generous. On one wall was a fireplace that obviously didn't work, but gave the room a focal point. The furniture was basic, the standard issue wardrobe, desk, bed and bedside table all in the same dark oak, but the beautiful mullioned windows framed the view of sky, town and lawns below. She would be okay, she kept telling herself as she looked around her new home.

"Just girls in the block, so your father will be pleased. Come on, let's help your dad unload."

Another girl came out of one of the rooms as they shuffled down the stairs and smiled at Aurora. Aurora returned the smile.

She and her mother then attacked the task of unpacking. Her dad was hanging her clothes in the wardrobe, which was going to be woefully inadequate for the purpose.

"My God, Aurora, how many clothes do you have? Have you left anything at home?"

"Yes, Dad , most of my summer wardrobe is still at

home," she said, laughing.

"You have too many clothes then," he said mildly, as he awkwardly hung up a blouse.

"There's no such thing, Dad."

"I didn't sanction all these purchases." He was looking at his wife, attempting to sound authoritative.

"No, honey, you didn't, but as you do almost anything to get out of shopping, you probably were not present," she reminded him. It was really the fact that, as an actuary for an insurance firm, he worked long hours and many weekends. Her dad was an easy-going man, generous in all ways and was a soft touch where the women in his life were concerned.

For their first evening there was a mixer in the bar and Aurora was dreading it. As her mother and father helped her unpack, she could feel herself tightening up, could feel she was preparing and steeling herself for the initial, inevitable first contact. There was no getting away from it, she had to go through it.

Her mother interrupted her reverie: "You will be okay," she comforted her. "Let's hope for the best." She filled a pillowcase with a new fluffy pillow as she finished making the bed.

"Doesn't the saying continue with 'but expect the worst'?" Aurora was a cynic by nature.

"I don't like that part so much, so I leave it out."

"I know, Mum, I just get tense," she admitted. Trying to be herself when she was anxious and nervous was always a struggle for her. She had to force herself to be bubbly and engaging when she really just wanted to withdraw and observe.

"I know, I can see you seizing up before my eyes, but it's just the thought of it, remember reality is never as hard as we project it will be, it's never what you expect. You always make friends and you cope well with change. Just stay in the moment and put one foot in front of the other and you will get through it," her mother assured her. She was a psychologist and was always passing on lessons in life. All Aurora could do was nod.

It was getting close to being time for her mum and dad to leave and she didn't want to cry; her mother would, she was sure. Samantha Bond was an emotive person by nature. If she was angry, you knew it, if she was happy, you knew it; emotion poured out of every pore. They couldn't watch a sad film without her crying, even if she had seen it a hundred times.

They finished unpacking and Aurora urged them to go and check into their hotel so they could enjoy the rest of the evening alone. Besides, she wanted to organise her room herself and just get on with it all. It was time.

"You guys go now, I'll do the rest," she said.

"You know we are only a phone call away, and we will be here until lunchtime tomorrow if you've forgotten anything," her mum reminded her.

"I know, I'll be fine," she said bravely, wanting to allay their fears, convincing herself in the process.

"Bye, beautiful, I'm really proud of you," her dad said, cuddling her.

"We're all behind you," her mother said as she embraced her with tear-filled eyes.

"I know, Mum, I love you."

The door closed behind her parents.

She took a deep breath, opened her first box and unpacked her books, hugging a collection of Oscar Wilde plays close to her heart like an old friend, willing the wisdom and humour on the pages to infiltrate her psyche and grant her courage. After a moment she put it on the bedside table and reached in again to pull out the scrapbook in which she had placed close to a hundred pictures and cuttings from magazines. Many had been stuck to her wardrobe at home and she was transferring them to uni. Her support crew until she had new friends.

Aurora was suddenly jolted out of her solitary activities by a knock on the door. Had her parents forgotten something? She opened the door and the girl she'd seen earlier was standing outside.

"Hi, I'm Paige. I'm in the room just across the hall," the girl said, pointing to her door.

"Hi, I'm Aurora." She stretched out her hand to shake the other girl's warmly, taking in the thin frame standing opposite her. Aurora wasn't tall at 5'3 but the girl facing her was tiny.

"Wow, that's such a cool name, where are you from?" Paige was all smiles, chirpy and friendly, keen to engage.

"I'm from a little village outside Cambridge. What about you?" Aurora smiled shyly, pleased this girl had reached out so soon, it was a good omen.

"Oh my God, I'm from Hertfordshire, so not far from you," she exclaimed enthusiastically.

"When did you get here?" asked Aurora, consciously forcing herself to be more effervescent.

"Yesterday and I've been so bored," Paige said, rolling her eyes, "everybody else is moving in today it seems."

"Wow, so it was pretty quiet here yesterday then?"

"Yes, it was, but my boyfriend Cameron is here too."

"Well, it must be nice to have someone you know starting too," Aurora said, envious that Paige had such support already.

"I know lots of people coming to Bristol, I went to Cheltenham and there's a few of us. I know girls from Malvern, Marlborough, Stowe, and Cam knows some guys he used to play football with, so I'm not worried about that. Where did you go to school?"

"Oh umm, well, I went to sixth form in Cambridge. Before that I was at school in Asia, but I was born in Australia."

"Cambridge? Let me think; I know some people there. Was it The Perse or The Leys?" queried Paige, ignoring the overseas references.

"No, not a big private school, a smaller independent one."

Confused or bored, Paige moved on rapidly. "Oh my God, you're so pretty," she gushed at her, "and you're Australian, that's so cool."

Aurora was pretty, but not in an obvious way. Unmanicured and unadorned, from her honey-coloured skin to her long, wavy, dark hair, she was naturally beautiful. Her classmates often used the term "exotic" to describe her. Her parents were both from Australia but her father was half English and Dutch, her mother French Polynesian and Māori. She was a mix of cultures and ethnicities, a DNA melting pot. Her eyes were almond shaped and green from the Dutch influence, and she had a small button-like nose and naturally full lips. Perfectly proportioned and shapely, her figure was one of her best assets.

"Thank you, you are too," Aurora responded. Paige was petite, with very tanned skin, almost orange, which Aurora figured came out of a bottle. She had bright blonde hair and an aquiline nose with protruding, round eyes.

Aurora found herself mesmerised by Paige who was exceedingly bubbly and excitable, reminding her of a tiny bird, flitting here and there.

"Well, we're, like, going to have so much fun, I can't wait for this week. It's going to be party, party, party! We have to meet the other girls, come on," she said, dragging Aurora out of the room.

"Oh, but I was just going to fix my room up ..." Aurora trailed off, as she stood in the doorway looking longingly back into her room, keen to make it a warm, comfy nest.

"You can do that later, we have to go and meet everyone," Paige insisted, walking down the hall. "It's going to be such a full week!"

Downstairs the girls were in a feverish state. Paige was the loudest by far with a high-pitched, shrill quality to her voice, and her enthusiasm for the upcoming activities was evident. "I simply must join the Shooting Society."

Another girl, Sophie, was responding in like fashion, equally animated. "I shoot too. Mummy is from Scotland, so we go up to their family estate all the time, but we live in Hertfordshire."

"You don't?" said Paige emphatically.

"Yes," nodded Sophie, "I do!"

"That's amazing," countered Paige with wide eyes, "I'm from Hemel Hempstead!" she announced triumphantly.

"I went to Berkhamsted!" Sophie squealed in excitement.

The other girls all seemed to know what that meant, but Aurora was struggling to keep up. Anxiety was making her feel delirious now, she was having an out-of-body experience, like she was underwater and the rest of them were all safe above the water line breathing air. She rubbed her gold 'A' on one of the chains around her neck nervously.

Eventually she struck up a conversation with another girl called Annabel, who was quieter like herself, and they chatted about courses, schools and backgrounds. Before long it was time to get ready to go to the Tudor bar for the mixer.

Paige wandered into Aurora's room and started looking around. "Why do you have so many Oscar Wilde books?" she asked as her eye caught sight of the books on Aurora's shelves.

"I don't know, I like his wit and wisdom, I guess." As Paige inspected her room, Aurora, already self-conscious, felt herself tense further.

"I think I did one of his plays at school," Paige recollected as she continued to scour the room, her opal eyes searching the desk and alighting on the scrapbook which she opened. She turned a few pages before moving to the wardrobe and began flicking through the coat hangers, oohing and aahing at her eclectic clothing collection. Aurora had collected a lot of her clothes from vintage and charity shops as well as from her travels with the family.

"Okay, well I'm going to take a shower now," she said, hinting to Paige that she wanted to get undressed.

"Yeah, good idea." Paige carried on, oblivious. "Do you think I could borrow this dress for the Friday event in town?"

"Sure, no problem, but right now I need to get undressed."

Paige got the hint the second time. "Oh, okay, I'd better start getting ready too." Aurora guessed it was going to be like living in a commune.

Eventually, all ready, they found their way into the bar. They were late and the room was full and buzzing as students ran around signing each other's shirts. The mission was to write one nice thing about each person on their white T-shirt or just sign your name if that was too hard, a sort of icebreaker. The tension and anxiety radiating off the new recruits generated an atmosphere of mild hysteria. The music was loud and thumping and the beer and cider were flowing from the taps behind the bar. The idea of Freshers was to bond with people in your halls by drinking solidly for a week, embarrass yourself and therefore lose all inhibitions. If everyone participated, there was total acceptance, whatever lines were crossed.

Aurora and the girls ploughed in and joined the ranks. It was wild, and got wilder as the night went on. As she stopped to sign an Asian boy's shirt, it hit her that apart from herself and one other guy, he was the only other person of colour she'd seen. There didn't appear to be very much diversity in Tudor.

Sophie came rushing up to her at some point. "I just met the most gorgeous guy, OMG he was so fit! I'm going to look for him again."

Later the girls regrouped and Annabel pointed at the back of Aurora's shirt, where many had written their adjectives, and started reading them out. There were lots of positives about her appearance. She didn't see herself as the rest of the world did. She had struggled with her weight through her teenage years. She was a butterfly, but didn't feel it. "You're kidding?" she said, surprised.

"No, she's not, she's telling the truth," Paige said flatly.

"Well don't go near the beautiful boy I like. He's tall

with beautiful hair," said Sophie, "and I saw him first."

"Okay, girls code," Paige said, looking serious and authoritative. "We all respect that, hands off the fit boy Sophie has seen."

"It's okay," Aurora said, putting her hands up in surrender. "I'm not touching any boys tonight."

The following Friday, Aurora headed out with the girls to the Freshers Fair on the Downs, the sprawling blanket of green dotted with trees that covers the high part of the city. Though it was constantly used by dog walkers, runners and the sports clubs of the university during the day, it was an area to avoid after dark. Everyone was warned not to walk through it alone after the sun went down.

The sun was out, but it wasn't warm, a cool breeze swept over the park as the seasonal change made itself felt. The trees were all turning, and the colours of the leaves ranged from pale yellow to dark crimson, and the first fallen leaves blew across the Downs like they were being dragged against their will. It was beautiful and Aurora was reminded of how much she appreciated the changing seasons, having never lived in a country that truly had four separate seasons before.

She wasn't sure what sports and activities she would join, but was looking forward to seeing what was on offer at the fair. She thought she might follow in her parents' footsteps and play ultimate frisbee. She was also thinking she might sign up for lacrosse with Annabel, who said she was utterly hopeless at it, but needed the exercise. Aurora was never sure when girls said that sort of thing if they were actually useless or just being modest. Annabel with her round, full face, soft features, and thick, shoulder-length chestnut hair seemed genuine enough, though. She reminded Aurora of apple crumble: honest, reliable, but not too fancy.

"Now, girls, I'm meeting Cameron here with some of his mates," Paige said, tossing her long hair as she strode along at speed-walking pace, looking left and right, scouting for him, "and while my girls always come first, we've hardly seen each other this week and I'm beginning to feel separation anxiety. Besides, I need to remind him of what he's been missing."

"Oooh does he have any friends for us?" Sophie whispered conspiratorially. She was always on the prowl and had apparently struck out with "fit boy" at the ice breaker.

"Sophie, you've gotten with a different guy every night this week," Annabel said tartly. Sophie was gregarious and flirtatious. She exuded confidence when it came to the opposite sex. She was busty with tight, blond, bobbed curls and knew how to dress for her figure. She didn't have the most beautiful face but she giggled and beguiled. Boy mad, she was clearly enjoying her newfound freedom away from parents and boarding school, unfettered and free to pursue any impulse.

"Cameron," Paige trilled, running up to a nice-looking boy standing by a fish 'n' chip van in a group of three.

"Hey there!" he said, hugging her and acknowledging the girls behind with a nod of his blonde head. He was dressed in full Adidas tracksuit with white Nike Air Forces. His straight hair was cropped short, faded at the sides.

"These are my girls, Cam ... Sophie, Annabel and Aurora. We're all in the same block, which you will see when you come and visit me," she said pointedly. Clearly Cam hadn't stayed over yet and his absence had been noted.

"Hi there, how has your week been so far?" he said generally to all of them. Aurora noted his accent was different to Paige's.

"Well, we have had so much fun, it's been full-on crazy," buzzed Paige.

"We've hardly slept," said Sophie.

"Well, *you've* hardly slept," corrected Paige with a knowing look.

Sophie laughed. "No, don't say that, what will Cam think of me?"

"Nothing anyone else isn't doing," he said. "This is Flynn and Will, we're all in Leigh Hall."

They exchange greetings with the girls. Cameron wasn't what Aurora was expecting. He seemed like your average guy, maybe a bit of a lad. According to Paige, he was mad for football and liked hanging out with his mates in the local pub. She wondered what he and Paige had in common. She seemed like an uptown girl, next to his downtown boy. She certainly seemed besotted with him, although maybe he wasn't quite as responsive.

"Where are you girls heading to now?" he asked.

"Oh my God, I have to join the Shooting Society! My parents would kill me if I didn't. Will you come with?" Paige pleaded with Cam, tugging on his arm.

"We're just off to football right now, I'll come find you after."

"Oh okay," she said, pouting. "Let's go to the pub together later, okay?"

"Sure, sounds good," he replied.

Aurora smiled at the boys as they departed. Flynn smiled back at her. "It was nice to meet you," he said as she went to walk away.

"You too." She nodded, following Paige, who was again leading the way. Sophie was giggling and whispering in her ear as they walked along.

Eventually they found their way to a stand emblazoned with "University of Bristol Clay Pigeon Shooting Society". Standing out in front was a dandy young man dressed head to toe in tweed with a Barbour jacket and flat cap. It seemed a little formal and weirdly conservative for the Freshers Fair. The president, George, was handsome in a classically clean-cut British way. Aurora could imagine him striding out across Balmoral with the young Windsor princes. The other girls signed up and he turned to look at Aurora with eyebrows raised questioningly, but she resisted. "I've never even held a gun before," she said, shaking her head. "I don't think it's really me."

"It's fun, we're just shooting at clay discs, nothing gets killed. It's shooting for vegans," teased George.

"Really, shooting for vegans?" Aurora returned quizzically.

"Oh come on, join us, we'll have such fun," pleaded Paige.

"Yes, it's good for the environment. Each week you get a break from the city and head into the countryside," George continued, coming around the table to stand closer to them all.

"I wanted to do ultimate frisbee, though," said Aurora, looking away from their intense scrutiny.

"You could do both," Paige pressed.

"Oh all right," Aurora conceded, worn down by the badgering, "but I'm just trying it."

"Excellent!" said Paige, clapping her hands and bouncing up and down. "We're all together." And together they remained.

"Some cause happiness wherever they go; others
whenever they go."
— Oscar Wilde (attributed to)

As Freshers week drew to a close that evening, they were in the Old Royal Lounge, a room downstairs at the front of the Tudor building, stately, intimidating and grand, to sign up to run for a Junior Common Representative position on the committee before heading to a club. Paige was desperate to be on the JCR. "We can organise everything just how we want it when we are on the committee," she had said bossily. She was ambitious to be vice president and Sophie, Social Secretary. Annabel and Aurora were happily keeping them company.

In the Old Royal Lounge there was a fireplace where a roaring fire was lit and the room was bathed in a warm glow as the sun went down outside. Students sat in various deep armchairs and sofas, and the walls were lined in oakwood panelling with portraits from eras gone by. In the corner of the room was an old grand piano that someone was currently playing.

Aurora heard him well before she saw him. She heard the soft English brogue, the playful teasing banter, the confidence complicit in the conversation. It was effortless and easy, no struggle involved, almost like a spider spinning a web around an unsuspecting insect. He was talking to a girl and the object of his attention was being drawn in while he wasn't even flexing a muscle.

Aurora got all of this just eavesdropping on the conversation as she looked through the list of roles available on the committee. She couldn't see the couple in question, they were sheltered by the tall wingback chairs they sat in, cosying up by the fire and facing away from her. She could see they had drinks on the small coffee table between them. The sign-up sheets she was looking at were on desks near the entrance of the room, and students filed in slowly, filling the room as they registered their interest in JCR or not. The other girls were doing the same, and so while she looked through the options, she continued to listen in on various conversations coming from the many different seating areas:

"What school did you go to?"

"Oh, I was at Winchester."

"You must know Patrick Martin?"

"Actually, I played rugby with him. Did you hear what happened to his mate Tuffers?"

"Borrowed one of his old man's Porsches and crashed it into the Rectory? Good job it wasn't vintage so he had an airbag."

They had only just met but it was like listening to old friends familiar with each other's company, a casual relaxation that Aurora found alien. She had witnessed many of these conversations in her first week at Bristol. She felt like an outsider. Moving around was her normality. These people, whoever they were, had probably lived in the same manor their entire lives.

The voice she was interested in didn't engage in that sort of conversation to promote himself. He gave nothing away personally, just flattered and engaged the object of his attention with question after question about herself. Interjecting with, "I'm sure you were in the first team. I've only been talking to you for twenty minutes but you have me wanting to watch netball now." Aurora recognised the type. She'd been burned before, lured in by a guy with all the right words, she wouldn't make that mistake again.

He was the player: smooth talking, confident, not necessarily intelligent, but the confidence was the clincher. That was intoxicating, she'd learnt, and the most successful predators just drew their prey in. He was clearly on a mission tonight, she didn't need to see him to know that. They were the same the world over.

Perhaps she would put herself up for a position after all, it was good for the resume and another way to meet people. Her mother always said it was good to have friends in lots of different baskets, but she didn't usually put herself out there this early. She asked some questions regarding what was involved as the outgoing reps were on hand to highlight the upside of the experience and answer questions. She looked through the positions and wrote her name down to run for International Rep.

Having finished that, she turned and looked for her girlfriends, who she found were sitting with a few boys they had struck up conversation with. The girls were sharing an old chesterfield, two of the boys sat on each armrest and one stood in front doing most of the talking. Aurora headed over, willing herself to relax, taking in deep breaths on the way. Trying to bond with people you had only just met, she was hopeless at it. Paige was holding court, and going through her checklist. She could have had a clipboard and been ticking off her requirements: prestige school, family name, holiday home. She was, however, affable and pleasant throughout the process. Aurora walked up and introduced herself as seamlessly as she could.

The boy standing was Winnie and the two sitting were James and Harry. All of them spoke beautiful English, which seemed to be a prerequisite for finding yourself in Tudor, but they were charming and witty with no airs or graces. They were a breath of fresh air. James, it turned out, had met Sophie before as they had mutual friends.

Winnie offered Aurora a glass of red wine, but she only drank white, upon which he dashed back to the bar and returned with a bottle of white and more glasses.

"Aurora, isn't that Sleeping Beauty?" he said, handing out glasses.

"Are you named after Pooh Bear?" she asked lightly.

Winnie smiled before answering. "Winnie is short for Winston, but I don't think it really suits me." He shrugged his shoulders and smiled warmly at her.

"Aurora as in the Aurora Australis, not the princess," she replied self-consciously, taking the proffered glass. She was used to this sort of comment. Now she was older, she sometimes felt a little ridiculous having the same name as a Disney princess.

"Ahh right, the Southern Lights. Your accent isn't entirely Australian, though, is it? I can't make it out."

"No, I grew up moving around, born in Australia, moved to Singapore, then the Philippines and now here, so it's more of an international school accent and this is sort of what you end up with," she replied.

"So your name is very appropriate, you hail from down under?" He began pouring wine, starting with the other girls.

"Yes."

"Still, you don't look Australian?"

"Yeah, my mother is French Polynesian and Māori, and Dad is Dutch Australian."

"Well, that explains it then."

"Explains what?" She was aware of the slight edge in her voice, she wondered where he was going as she watched him pour wine into the glass she held out.

"Your beauty," he said, looking up as he finished. He said it matter-of-factly, without artifice, and continued to look directly at her. It was slightly cheeky, but genuine and not provocative, maybe a little flirtatious. She blushed, she was sure, but it would be hard to see under her olive skin, and she had no other response to offer. He just smiled and turned to James next to him, passing on the information he'd just learnt. Out of the corner of her eye she could see Paige looking somewhat displeased and stony faced, but then Sophie asked her what she thought her chances of being voted Social Secretary were and they were off talking about campaigning. Perhaps it had nothing to do with Winnie's comment.

With the break in conversation Aurora took the opportunity to glance around the room. It looked pretty full now and soon they would all head out into town to a club. It had been a long week and she felt wrecked before the night had begun. She knew the wingback chairs were behind her, about four metres away, and curiosity had gotten the better of her, she just wanted to check out the pair she had been eavesdropping on earlier.

She angled herself to the side, pretending to look into the fire, and glanced in the direction of the voice, looking casually to her right, only to discover the guy in question was already looking at her. She felt she'd been caught out, but of course he couldn't possibly know she'd been summing him up in her head. He just continued staring, looking right through her, brazen, bold given that the girl he'd been chatting up for the last half hour was still sitting next to him. Aurora wasn't able to look away, and neither did he. He was lazily slumped in the chair next to the fire, seemingly at ease, in command. In command of what, she wasn't sure, but just in command.

Winnie noticed them looking at each other and called out, "Hey Teddy, come and meet the Southern Lights." God she hoped that name wouldn't stick.

That broke the deadlock, it felt like she'd been staring at him for a full minute. She could see why he was so confident now. He was "that guy" alright, but she had to give it to him, he was very beautiful. Tall and lean but well muscled, his broad shoulders making his T-shirt hang off him just right. He had sandy blonde, tousled hair with the most striking denim-blue coloured eyes. He came over with his hand outstretched to shake hers with a bemused look on his face.

"Hi, I'm Teddy."

"Aurora," she said, shaking his hand, which was smooth, tanned and engulfed hers.

"Where are you from?" he asked.

"That's hard to answer really, a bit of everywhere."

"So you've been around," he said, smirking.

Rude, she thought, but decided not to respond to this remark and let it pass.

"The clue is in her name," Winnie interjected.

"Okay, Princess." She inwardly cringed. "I can't totally place your accent. It's a mix of things, could be Australian, but sounds a bit American," he said, thinking and furrowing his brow. He looked up at the ceiling and then back down again to continue staring directly at her. "Which is probably misleading."

She met his gaze, trying to give him the benefit of the doubt, but her judgement had already been passed and his conversation wasn't helping to change her mind. She tried not to feel self-conscious under the microscope of his piercing gaze as he continued to almost mock her.

"Southern Lights," he mused, "we're talking about the Southern Aurora then, so I'm going to go with Australia."

"Well done," she said, smiling as she took a sip of her wine.

"So you're an Aussie? You don't look like a convict, or sound like one," he said with a touch of superiority.

She bristled with irritation. She'd grown to hate that cliché, hate the reference. It was old, well past its use-by date and now irrelevant. Her eyes narrowed threateningly. "Wow, you're so original, I've never heard that one before," she said coldly, immediately turning her back on him to engage Paige and Harry in conversation. "Three strikes and you're out," she said under her breath.

"Ouch!" said James.

Teddy didn't respond and Aurora couldn't see his reaction.

"Mate, she just sorted you," said Winnie, and the others laughed. She knew she'd snapped, but she was pissed off, tired and sick of socialising and being *nice*. She had been trying hard to fit in all week and it was the proverbial last straw. The truth was also that he'd thrown her a bit.

Harry, lean and lanky, his frame perched on one end of the chesterfield next to Paige, was grinning broadly. He looked like he had enjoyed the altercation.

"That sounded like it went well?" Paige offered sarcastically.

"I know I was sharp, but I'm so sick of that convict-criminal connotation. I've been getting it for the last two years, ever since I moved here, which is odd because I've never come across it before, not in Manila, not even in Singapore."

"Not so odd," Harry said. As a history student he was happy to pass on his view. "Australia was a British colony and you're in Britain. The rest of the world doesn't care about that stuff, but we don't like to let you guys forget it was our empire and we are the motherland. It's irrelevant today as you said, but old habits die hard here. Don't worry about Teddy, he can take it. He's actually a good guy, we all share a block together, and we have way too much fun."

"Yes, I know, I've studied colonisation, but God the joke is so old now, I'm done."

"It must get annoying after a while," Paige sympathised, patting Aurora's arm.

They all continued chatting in the lounge until it was late enough to venture into town and the clubs. They called the drinking before going out "pre's" and basically the aim was to drink enough, cheaply enough to be well intoxicated before going into the expensive clubs. Aurora had learnt to pace herself, she didn't want to be too hungover tomorrow. She had her first proper lecture the next day, and the first shooting afternoon, followed by the shooting social in the evening. Having never hit a target in her life, she figured it was going to be hard enough without a thumping head. The exhaustion she would just have to deal with like everyone else.

As they began to file out of the lounge and down the drive to catch the buses into the city, the girls naturally found themselves walking with the boys they'd just met. Winnie fell in step with Aurora and continued to chat. He had an engaging personality and was warm and friendly without any awkwardness so many boys her age had. She found she was enjoying his company in spite of herself, and warmed to him instantly. With some people it just happened like that, she had discovered. You just trust them and intuitively know they are okay, and so it was with Winnie.

"Winnie, where do you live? I know you're probably sick of answering these questions too," she apologised.

"No, it's fine," he said, "I've got it down pat now. Our home is in Somerset and I went to Harrow. I'm the youngest of three kids, two older sisters."

"Is that far away from here?" Aurora asked, referring to his home.

"No, less than two hours away."

"Did you always want to come to Bristol?"

"Well, no, I hoped to get into Oxford, but to be

honest my love of a good red and a party definitely got in the way. I didn't want it that bad, obviously. My parents probably did, but they're cool now. Being the youngest, you get away with way more."

"I'm the oldest of four and you get away with very little and have to pave the way for the others in every respect. In fact you're a guinea pig as your parents try and work out how it's done," she reflected.

"Huh, mine are relaxed now, they have virtually given up with me. Anyway, I'm the only boy, so Mum dotes on me. Dad has great expectations, but Mum softens him up, keeps him realistic." He grinned at her while he spoke and they crossed the road to the bus stop together.

He was a clever boy, she was sure, you wouldn't have aspirations of Oxford and not be relatively smart. His face was open and friendly, with a smattering of freckles that went with his light red hair and pale skin. His straight hair was longer than a lot of the guys, almost so he had curtains, but not quite. Tall, at least reaching six feet, he was handsome with a cavalier attitude to life, and she imagined he wasn't easily ruffled. They continued to chat all the way into town amidst all the noise and the drunken rabble on the bus. He was easy company and their conversation flowed.

"So what music are you into?" he asked.

She had a feeling this was an important question to him.

"Oh God, I listen to everything to be honest, some old stuff, some new. I love everything from Amy Winehouse and Lana Del Rey to Radiohead."

She hit the jackpot with Radiohead. "I'm a huge Radiohead fan, what's your favourite song?"

"Oh, 'Let Down' on *Ok Computer*."

He was fully engaged, nodding enthusiastically. "Yeah great song, but I think 'Spectre' is mine."

"Wow, none of my friends are fans, it's bizarre you like them," she said, surprised.

"Well, I can be the first that does."

Honest and unassuming, his conversation was relaxed without any agenda other than to get to know her. The newly discovered mutual love of Radiohead sealed their friendship.

At the club, it was thumping bass and strobe lights. She looked around the space in the flashes of light. In the dim light she could see the tall, athletic frame of the boy she had crossed swords with earlier. He was now draped over the girl he'd been talking to all night, and was entwined with her in a corner of the club. Mission successful, she thought to herself. Winnie interrupted her study of the couple.

"Teddy strikes again," he shouted over the music following her gaze. "He doesn't have any trouble with girls."

"I can see that. He's been working on her all night."

"I think she's been more than happy to be the object of his attention."

"Eh, I just can't help but think of a spider wrapping its victim up before dragging it back to its lair. Like Shelob, you know?"

"The giant spider from *Lord of the Rings*?" She nodded and he laughed. "I'll be sure to tell him that in the morning."

"Only dull people are brilliant at breakfast."
— Oscar Wilde

Aurora woke with a start as the alarm went off. This morning was her first lecture for History of Art. She'd chosen the course because of her love of art, but fashion was her real goal. From the age of three she insisted on choosing her own outfits and would have screaming fits if she didn't like what her mother wanted to dress her in, such was the weight of her opinion even at that age. At ten she would style her own dress-up costumes for Halloween and Easter, but the fashion industry was notoriously difficult to survive in and she wanted a respectable degree to fall back on should she need it.

She yawned and stretched out on the old mattress

with its creaking springs and rolled onto her side to check her phone. There were a couple of messages from Paige and Sophie, who had stayed out a little longer. Sophie wrote, "Hey hun , where are you, you didn't say goodbye?" with a sad emoji. Sophie had been rather occupied with another young man and didn't look like she would appreciate being interrupted by Aurora just to say goodbye, so she had slipped away with Annabel and left Paige to say goodbye. Paige had written at 3 a.m., "Soz babe I won't be up for breakfast, no way I'll be out of bed before lunch. How hot is that Teddy? Too bad I have a boyfriend, but you don't?"

Aurora was regretting telling her she didn't have a boyfriend. She had been seeing a guy off and on during her gap year, but that was well over now. There had been a holiday romance, and a brief relationship in high school with the "it boy" of another school that had wounded her. Still, she didn't want Paige to try and fix any of that, or play matchmaker.

"Yes thank you for reminding me, but arrogant schmucks aren't my type, besides he looked taken," she typed. "I'll see you later, at shooting, right?"

It would be hours before she got a response. She hoped Sophie or Annabel were at breakfast. God, what would she do if they weren't? She'd have to walk into the dining room alone in front of everyone. She hated the eyes on her. Everyone checked everyone else out as they came in. Being alone would be excruciating, but she hardly felt like talking with a hangover, so at least that would be a consolation. Early on in the school year everyone was self-conscious and carefully trying to cultivate their social standing, nobody wanted to look like they had no mates and were a loser.

She threw on an oversized tracksuit and trainers

and ran a brush through her hair. She would get ready for class after. She left her block and made her way into the main part of the building and upstairs to the dining hall. She could hear the low rumble of conversation emanating from the cavernous room. All the common areas were large spaces to cope with the numbers of students and in Tudor they all had a sense of grandeur.

She cautiously made her way in. Breakfast was already well underway as she always set her alarm as late as possible. There were long rows of tables down the vast room, with benches on either side. On one side of the room the breakfast dishes were set out in bain-maries to keep them warm for the two hours of breakfast. Then there was the continental section of cereals, bread for toasting and condiments to go on top. Aurora favoured this for breakfast. There were pots of tea and coffee that the kitchen ladies attempted to keep refilled as the students quaffed cup after cup to wake themselves up for their morning lectures and recover from their hangovers. Freshers was over now and all the partying would slow down, she was assured. It had better, or she wasn't going to be able to get a degree, which was the whole point of being here.

She looked around the room and couldn't see Annabel or Sophie, they must have decided to sleep late and miss breakfast too. She felt the panic rising inside her and remembered the technique she'd been taught from a school counsellor in high school: just breathe.

She turned to go and get her cereal and juice when she heard a voice call out, "Hey, Aurora, come and join us." The boys from last night were at the far end of the room, down one end of a bench. It was Winnie's voice and even with sleep deprivation he had a ready smile on his face. His strawberry blonde hair was a mess and his face was a little paler than she remembered it from the night before, but then again the lounge had given everyone a golden hue from the hot fire.

With a sigh of relief she waved and said, "I'll just get some cereal." She filled her bowl with granola and returned to their end of the hall. There were six of them in a group and she didn't recognise them all. Winnie shooed them down the bench on one side so she could sit next to him and she could see that Teddy was going to be directly opposite her.

"This is Jasper and Thomas, who are also in our block," Winnie explained. "This is Aurora."

"Yeah hi nice to meet you," she said. They nodded and said hi but both looked worse for wear and not up for much conversation.

"You met everyone else last night, didn't you?"

"Yeah I did," she responded, casting a glance in the direction of Teddy, who was busy eating and said nothing. The others were also scoffing down bacon and eggs in spite of the alcohol fuelled night before.

"So how are the Southern Lights this morning?" Winnie asked.

"Very tired, and not ready to concentrate. Hopefully all that's required is for me to show up."

"Well, we were just discussing last night when you walked in and I was explaining your analogy for Teddy, so perfect timing," he said cheekily. Clearly he was a bit of a devil who liked to amuse himself at another's expense.

"I'd had quite a bit to drink, so had you, Winnie. I'm surprised you can even remember what I said," she answered.

"Oh I remember," he said knowingly.

"So, Shelob for me then, is it?" interjected Teddy,

lifting his head with eyebrows raised, hair still wet from the shower.

She looked across the table at him. Even in the morning light he was pretty. He had a warm tone to his skin, those blue eyes set nicely apart, and his sandy brown hair was slightly curly, much longer at the front. His features were strong and well defined, but his voice was probably his most distinctive characteristic. It was relatively deep with a beautiful timbre and that accent which was designed to make girls swoon. She was embarrassed about her own. She knew her native Australian twang was softened with a slight American rolling of the "R's", but it was still harsh, while his accent drew you in. She wanted him to talk just to listen to it.

"You've seen *Lord of the Rings* then?" she asked.

"I've read the trilogy." He was still staring, an unwavering look, waiting for an explanation, daring her to spell it out.

"Well, you were wrapping that girl up pretty tight from the beginning of the night, so I thought of a spider," she said reluctantly.

"Shelob is female, you know?"

"I do, it's just a loose metaphor."

"Shelob does more than just wrap Frodo up, though?" His tone was challenging.

"That's true," Aurora said, meeting his gaze.

"Right, so how far does this analogy go?" he asked archly. He was sitting back in his chair suggestively daring her to go there, to admit what she was implying.

"I don't know, did you stab her?" she shot back in a dry, deadpan tone. His arrogance was really beginning to piss her off. The other guys at the table erupted into fits of laughter. He didn't look particularly pleased. She continued, "Look, you did the crime, you can take the heat. I'm sure you'll cope and wear it like a crown."

"You seem to have a bit of a chip on your shoulder there?" he responded.

"We've barely spoken to each other but you can say I have a chip on my shoulder?" she countered, staring him down.

"Well you don't know me and you're making some judgements." He was leaning forward now, elbows on the table.

"It was an observation."

"Were there three of us? I have to admit I can't remember that much," he sniggered. The other guys at the table were watching the match like it was tennis, transfixed as the shots went back and forth.

She was irritated but decided it had gone far enough. "You were hardly opaque." She softened her tone, lowering her weapon.

Now he looked bemused, untroubled by the exchange. He bent down to collect his bag. "Well." He stood up to go. "I'll have to come up with a name of my own for you. You can't have it all one way." He narrowed his eyes which had a mischievous glint in them as he said it.

So he hadn't taken offence? She was surprised.

"I'm off to my first lecture for law and now I'm nicely warmed up, ready to take on anyone and argue anything," he announced to the table. "Lads, I'll see you all later at the range. Aurora, it has been stimulating," he said as he began to swagger out of the dining room.

"Unfortunately I'll be there too, and my aim is going to be woeful," Aurora said after him.

She noticed girls' heads turning from the other tables as they followed his progress through the dining hall and out the door.

"So you're going shooting too?" Harry asked.

"I got talked into signing up because I was with Paige and Sophie and they're going. I've never been clay pigeon shooting and have no intention of ever shooting anything alive. Can you guys shoot?"

She looked around the table at the faces and Winnie, Harry and James all nodded.

"Another big night," Harry said, shaking his head and changing the subject.

"Teddy manages to score every night. How does he do it?" pondered James enviously. He was an attractive boy, blonde with lovely blue eyes, in fact they were all really nice looking, she thought. Some of them seemed really quite boyish, but they were friendly and she appreciated that.

"Beats me, I barely get a look in," said Thomas.

Aurora chose not to contribute to the conversation and let them muse about the night before and their sexual prowess or lack thereof.

"The spider reference was a fair call, Aurora," Winnie said, grinning, validating her judgement.

"Well, that's what sprang to mind. I need to get ready for class, but I'll see most of you later."

She walked out of the dining hall to get ready, the boys watching her as she went.

"That was hot," said James.

"That was great." Winnie was laughing again. " She's nice, we had a good chat last night."

"Nice is boring, she's a flamethrower," Harry observed.

"I don't want to be at the mercy of my emotions. I want to use them, to enjoy them, and to dominate them."
— Oscar Wilde, The Picture of Dorian Gray

That afternoon Aurora hurried out of the lecture hall, rushing to the clubhouse to meet George and the others to drive to the range that was apparently nearly an hour away. She wouldn't be able to change, so she hoped what she was wearing would be fine: just jeans, a shirt and a light coat with trainers. What on earth does *one* wear clay pigeon shooting anyway, she wondered? No doubt there was a uniform. There was always a uniform here in England, there was an outfit to go with every pastime. No big deal, she told herself, it will be fine.

She found George at the clubhouse, looking much

the same as he did at the Freshers Fair, decked out head to toe in tweed with a flat cap and she clocked it, ahh so that's the uniform, it's not a fashion statement.

"Good afternoon, gorgeous," he said, giving her a big smile. "You're in my car with Winnie and Emma, hope that's okay."

"Yes, that's fine, thanks for driving. I already know Winnie, we met the other night."

"Ah good, well we'll just wait for everyone to show up and give the stragglers ten minutes before we head out. There's about thirty of us today."

"My car is over there," he said pointing to a black BMW with Winnie and the girl Emma already inside.

Aurora walked towards them. She was a bit late and obviously the other girls had already gone in other cars. She got in the back with Winnie.

"Hi, how was your day?" he asked.

"Okay, interesting first lecture. I think I'll like my course, but I'm just so tired," she said, looking at Emma. "Hi, I'm Aurora. You must be Emma?"

"Yes, hi. Is this your first time out to the range here then?" Emma said, smiling brightly.

"Yes, I'm a rank beginner, never held a gun, let alone hit something," Aurora confessed.

"It's fun shooting at the targets, most people enjoy it, and the countryside is lovely out there if you like that sort of thing. I do, I'm not really one for the city," Emma replied, turning herself around the front seat to look directly at Aurora and engage further in conversation.

"Nature is good. I live on a working farm that I'm sure I'll miss living in Bristol. Are you a first or second year?"

"I'm in second year, so I know what sort of week

you must have had. What halls are you in?"

"She's in Tudor with me," chipped in Winnie, "and she's been causing trouble already, upsetting my mates." He laughed. "Calling a spade a spade."

"What's the accent I can hear?" Emma asked.

"I'm Australian, but I've lived in Asia since I was ten."

"Well, Australians are known for being straight. Your mates had best take cover."

She immediately put Aurora at ease. Friendly, relaxed and comfortable in her own skin, with straight brown hair down to her shoulders, which was falling out from under the obligatory flat cap.

George came striding up to the car. "No one else will be coming now," he said, "and I need to be there to sort things out the other end, so let's go. Did I just hear you're a convict, Miss Aurora?"

Aurora shook her head. There was no way of escaping it.

"Careful, you'll lose your head," Winnie warned George.

"Are you a bit touchy about that then?" George asked, looking over his shoulder at her in the back seat.

"I don't think I'm touchy. Well, maybe just a little. I'm just sick of the reference, let's face it, it's not a compliment is it?" she asked.

"It's just something we Brits use in our banter with Aussies," said George, softening his tone.

"Yeah, you beat us in cricket too often, so we have to put you down, it's only fair," Winnie offered.

"It's because they don't know how to have a proper conversation yet, they haven't honed those skills," Emma chimed in. "They're still back in their boarding house taking pot shots at the other boys."

"Whoa, whoa, whoa, Emma I don't think you're striking the right tone. Just remember whose car you're in. You could get left out in the fields an hour from Bristol," George warned her. They obviously knew each other quite well.

Aurora had noticed that they all seemed to give each other a hard time, it was the banter they referred to, and it was mostly good humoured and expected. It was just not something she was used to. They weren't being mean, it was all in jest. Still, the convict thing had the effect of making her feel a bit like a second-class citizen.

Eventually they turned off the main road and arrived at the Barbury Shooting School. They were surrounded by undulating countryside, beautifully green and manicured lawns where she could see other people making their way to various targets, much like a golf course. They pulled into the car park and she spied the girls chatting to Teddy, James and Harry. Sophie was practically doing a dance around Teddy, and Paige kept putting her hand on his arm and laughing. Girls are so transparent, Aurora mused to herself. She took a deep breath and got out of the car, wondering how she got talked into this.

"Okay everyone, listen up!" shouted George. "If you are an experienced shot you can go into the clubhouse here and choose your gun and head straight out onto the course, just let them know you are with Bristol Uni and pay the fee. If you are a novice please come with me and I'll get you kitted out, and then you'll be given some tuition down on the practice range. You have to be up to a certain standard before we let you loose."

"Well, I'm sticking right with you then, George," Aurora said.

"Don't you worry, darling, I'm happy to hold your hand for as long as you need," he quipped.

"Of course you are, George," Emma chided him. She whispered to Aurora, "Just watch him, he's a huge flirt."

"Thank you for the warning." Aurora smiled. She was beginning to really like this girl. "Right, well, I'm off, have a good time and I'll see you after." Aurora followed George inside, paid for the experience and was handed a gun. This is surreal, she thought. She felt like she was in a BBC television series or period drama. It wasn't really what she had expected to be doing at university when she set off. Oh well, what the hell, she was here now, she had better just get on with it.

As they walked over to the range, she fell in with the girls and caught up on their day.

"Guess what I found out today from Mummy? She went to school with Teddy's mother," Paige said excitedly, turning to Aurora. She paused for effect before continuing, waiting until she had Aurora's full attention. Aurora raised one eyebrow quizzically.

"Teddy is the Earl of Trentbridge's son!" she announced triumphantly.

There was a brief silence before Aurora responded. "You're saying it like it's supposed to mean something?"

"It does mean something. Teddy is their only child."

Again Aurora looked blank and unimpressed. "Yes okay, so he's rich and the sole heir, I get that, but the weight you are giving it implies it's very important," she stated.

"It is," Paige said firmly. "Well, it means he's titled, that's why it's important. He's going to be Lord Trentbridge one day," she fangirled. "Fantastic," Aurora said dryly. "That'll make him a great catch and a great guy as he makes his way through the staff and his mate's wives."

"You're so harsh, Aurora." Paige was a bit taken aback by the force of her response.

"Sorry, all I can see is a player, isn't it more about who you are as a human being?"

They continued following George down towards the practice range.

"Yes, obviously, but still it does make him a catch." Paige was talking a little too loudly for Aurora's comfort, clearly so excited by the news.

"Okay, I'll file that away and put him on my to-do list," Aurora said facetiously.

Teddy was just ahead with Winnie and turned around, looking back at the girls from time to time. She hoped he hadn't heard Paige, whose high- pitched voice had a tendency to travel. The group then splintered further and the rank beginners had their own teacher who took them through a safety briefing, and then the step-by-step process from loading to pulling the trigger. The others were just getting their eye in before they went out on the full course.

Aurora waited for her turn to step up with the instructor and fire at the target. Casting her eyes along the row of shooters practising on her left, her eyes fell on Teddy. Sophie was next to him and appeared to be spending more time attempting to distract him than aiming at the target. Winnie was the other side of him and appeared to be a reasonable shot from what her untrained eye could see, and Teddy was clearly a crack shot even with distractions. Paige didn't look like someone whose family had a grouse moor. Apparently her entrepreneurial father had purchased the trophy asset in Scotland a few years ago. She wasn't a robust, outdoorsy sort of girl, more like England's answer to Elle Woods, but she managed to hit the target, although not with any consistency. Annabel was doing the best from what Aurora could make out, quiet and not as flashy as the other girls, she was more than capable.

Aurora's reverie was interrupted by the instructor motioning for her to step forward. She had listened to the earlier directions and attempted to concentrate; easier said than done with guns going off all around.

"Okay, just take a breath and relax, if you tense up it won't help your aim," the young instructor, Todd, told her. "Finger lightly on the trigger ready. Now look along the barrel of the gun to take aim and when you're ready shout pull, okay?"

"Yep, I can see, but am I supposed to be able to find the skeet or clay bird thingy as it's moving?" It sounded impossible to her.

"You will, don't worry. I know it seems like you'll never be able to connect it all together, but it will come and it won't take long, depending on your hand-eye coordination, maybe even today."

"No, no, let's not place any unrealistic expectations on this activity just yet. Let me keep my expectations where they are, at a very low level," she said soberly.

Todd laughed. "This is supposed to be fun you know?"

"I know I just hate learning anything new and feeling useless," she responded.

"It's okay, no one is going to laugh at you if you miss, they've all been here before," Todd said reassuringly.

"Well, that's true," came a familiar deep voice from behind her, "and most people won't, but I will."

Aurora turned her head around to see the back of

Teddy, gun slung over his shoulder, as he walked out towards the course accompanied by Winnie laughing. She felt the heat in her face as she flushed, and had to steel herself to focus once again on the task at hand. She needed to block everything out or this was never going to work, she knew that much.

"Ignore those idiots. I assume you know them?"

"Unfortunately I do."

"Right, let's crank one off, it'll be easier once you've pulled the trigger a few times."

He could say that again, of that she had no doubt. She had a carton of bullets, a double-barrelled shotgun and a temper. A wicked, unholy trio. She was determined to hit the target.

*"I think God, in creating man, somewhat
overestimated his
ability."*
— Oscar Wilde

Later that night all of the members of the Shooting Society met up at the Kings Arms pub at the top of Whiteladies, the last drinking hole before you reached the Downs. It stood high on the road with imposing arched windows which looked down onto the street. It was Sports Night, a weekly party/mixer preceded by one's chosen sport, and the Shooting Society had taken over the bar area, which was full of leather sofas and tables, now littered with young students drinking pints of cider and beer. As the alcohol took effect they all relaxed and new friendships were formed as they huddled in groups, talking about the afternoon's shooting. Aurora went to the bar to buy herself and her girlfriends a drink as it was her turn to buy a round. She was enjoying the atmosphere and the chat about the new sport she had tried, although calling it a "sport" seemed like a bit of a stretch to her.

"And how did you enjoy your afternoon at Barbury?" inquired George from over her shoulder.

"You know in the end I didn't mind it at all," Aurora said breezily. "I was a bit intimidated at first to be honest, but then I actually managed to hit a couple of targets. I believe he said it was called a 'bolting rabbit'."

"Well, it sounds as though you've made a solid start. I could tell you would be a natural from the moment I saw you," he crooned.

"Will you leave this poor girl alone," cut in Emma, who was waiting for the barman to serve her. She had quietly walked up on Aurora's left and had been listening in.

George laughed and winked at them both before sauntering off to work the room.

"He's a nice guy," Aurora commented.

"He's a flirt."

"No, he's just playing his role, welcoming the new troops and all as president."

"And here I think he's flirting his head off. I'm just a cynic at heart."

"Are you seeing anyone at the moment?" Aurora gingerly enquired of her new acquaintance.

"No, I recently broke up with someone, so I'm happily having a break from all that. We were together for two years but couldn't keep it going, being at different universities. It ended well, so it's all good."

She seemed completely at ease with her single status. "What about you?" she asked in a no-nonsense fashion.

"Me... No, I rarely get asked out and when I do it's never by the boy I want," Aurora said emphatically, rolling her eyes. "I think I repel them, or they end up my mates."

"Really? No, I think it's for a totally different reason," said Emma, smiling cryptically.

The barman returned with her drinks and Emma began ordering hers. She felt self-centred asking Emma to explain the comment, so she gathered up the four drinks using both hands and endeavoured to move across the room without spilling anything.

She wondered what Emma could be inferring as she approached her friends who were huddled together on sofas and chairs around a coffee table. *Does she think I come across cold or standoffish? Am I too blunt or unpolished?* Next to all these refined British girls she felt gauche and awkward. *Maybe*, she thought, *that's why the boys see me as one of them?* She mentally resolved to ask her another time as she carefully placed the drinks down, deep in thought about how she came across to people. Why was she so self-obsessed? It drove her mad at times. Her new friends were actually providing lots of opportunities for her to practise self-forgetting these days, and as she rejoined them Paige was busy recounting the latest drama in her relationship with Cameron. Since they had arrived at Bristol he had cancelled on Paige more often than not, and never with much of a valid excuse.

"I'm going to give him one more chance, I mean our relationship deserves that, doesn't it?"

"Of course it does," Sophie consoled.

"I have always understood that football comes first

and that 'Saturdays are for the boys', but this is just too much. He never has time for me at all? I was going to see him later on tonight, but again he said he can't make it. I said, 'I don't mind what time it is, whenever you finish with the boys, come over,' but he said, 'No, I'll see you tomorrow sometime,' and then tomorrow something else will come up."

"Here, have an Aperol," Aurora said, handing Paige her drink. "It's early days here, Paige, everyone is making new friends and he's probably trying to get to know all the football boys, and they have that 'initiation thing' coming up, don't they? That sounds horrific!"

"Oh yeah they are all freaked out about what it will be this year," Paige confirmed.

"Last year the rugby initiates had to cook naked for the older rugby guys and then sit down to eat naked too," said Annabel.

"That doesn't sound too tough?" said Sophie. "It wouldn't bother me being naked at all."

"No, I'm sure it wouldn't," Annabel said dryly, "but it might bother the rest of us."

"Does my walking around the floor naked bother you then?" Sophie asked.

"Well, since you're asking, yes it does!" Annabel responded.

"Someone apparently got salmonella poisoning," Paige added.

"The salmonella poisoning doesn't sound so great to me either," interjected Annabel.

"My brother told me about one rugby initiation where they had to bob for a carrot in a bucket of sick," Aurora said, screwing up her face in distaste.

"Aaaaaaahhhhhhhhh!" the girls squealed.

"Well, I'm concerned that Cam isn't working for our

relationship any more. We've been here a week and a half and he hasn't stayed over at all. What's that about?" Paige said, looking around at the girls for feedback.

"I just think he's busy doing his thing settling in, and he knows you're doing yours," Aurora ventured.

Paige pursed her rosebud lips into a pout, looking unconvinced and miffed.

"Hey Roars, where's my drink?" Winnie said, coming up behind Aurora, winking mischievously.

"There you are lurking behind me again," she said.

"That's Roars as in the noise a lion makes," he said, qualifying the nickname.

She ignored the comment, refusing to take the bait.

Paige took it for her. "Oh you shortened her name, but shouldn't it be Rors, R O R S?" she said, spelling out the letters.

"No, she *roars* with indignation," Winnie qualified.

The girls nodded in agreement and laughed at her expense.

"I am standing right here, thank you," Aurora said.

"You roar with outrage at the merest prod, Aurora, ergo Roars. It's Teddy's name for you," he continued.

Annabel raised her eyebrows and looked at the other girls.

"Well, I'd be just thrilled if Teddy spent time thinking about a suitable name for me," drawled Sophie with her hands on her hips, sipping her drink. "You tell him, Winnie, he can label me anytime he likes."

"You are incorrigible, Sophie," Aurora chastised.

"He is currently otherwise engaged with a second year, but I will be sure and pass on that information when I have an opportunity," he assured her.

"My God, he's busy again?" Aurora asked, wide

eyed.

"Yeah, yeah, he has a target for the evening," Winnie confirmed. "How did you guys enjoy the shooting today?" he asked, changing the subject.

The girls started chatting about the afternoon with Winnie, and slowly some of the other boys joined them and the discussion moved on to JCR elections and campaigning. Aurora had temporarily forgotten she had to write and submit a manifesto which all the students were able to read before the voting. She had time, and she wasn't terribly concerned whether she was successful or not. Paige on the other hand was already planning her strategy, and had just discovered from James that she would be running against another girl who was currently seated across the room. Paige, already not in the best of moods, was casting daggers in the poor girl's direction, sizing up her competition. Sophie was running for Social Secretary against another girl Winnie had described as "gorgeous" and "lovely". Both girls were not happy to hear either piece of news.

"Oh my God, boys, are you voting for me? You have to vote for me," Paige said, as she grabbed James' arm, looking at them all with intent. "Look at her, she doesn't look like committee material to me. I haven't seen her talking to anyone else. Have you seen her talking to anyone else?" she demanded in a clipped tone.

Before they could answer Sophie cut in. "So this Diana girl who's running against me. Doesn't she do Maths and Economics?" she said coldly.

"Yeah that's right," James responded. "You've got the right girl, she's South African, but lives in Europe somewhere. She's a rocket," he added appreciatively.

"Well, I'm not sure about that," Sophie said, looking miffed, "but I do know that I'm far more qualified because my degree is a social science. I'll have to work that into my manifesto. You know, Paige, we should put up flyers to canvas for votes."

"Wow, I've never heard anyone flex about doing social sciences before. You really do meet all kinds at uni," Winnie interjected wryly as he took a swig of his beer. Aurora allowed herself a smile at Sophie's expense, while Sophie stuck out her tongue at him and pulled an unimpressed face.

Paige ignored it all. "Oooh yes we have to! We have to start campaigning hard. I don't expect to be beaten out by that insipid-looking thing over there!" she said, shooting daggers in the direction of her competition.

It was all too intense for Aurora, who quietly stepped to the side and out of the ring of fire. The girls were fun, and she was effectively living with them, but she saw an intensity sometimes that scared her. She felt like she was walking a tightrope at times.

She headed off to the ladies, which was at the other end of the room beyond the bar itself, jam-packed with people waiting to buy drinks, and their friends who were waiting to be handed one. She weaved through the crowd, brushing past people, excusing herself as she went, occasionally bumping into someone by accident, when she felt a hand grab her by the wrist and hold on. She swung around, wondering who had the presumption for such familiarity, half expecting it to be George, only to discover the culprit was Teddy staring down at her with the full force of his denim- blue eyes. Why did time stand still when he looked at her? She moved backwards subtly, having no desire to be the paperclip driven to attach itself to his magnetic field, and in doing so she was jostled from behind and pushed even closer to him. She involuntarily breathed in; his aftershave was perfect, a blend of woody tones, dark and aromatic. Whatever it was, she knew it must have cost a bomb. He was wearing a navy, three-quarter zip, knitted cotton jumper with some nice jeans. She couldn't help but notice the clothing.

"Where are you stumbling off to?" he enquired with a smile playing on his face as he stared down at her.

"Just to the bathroom. Are you waiting in line?" she asked, a little taken aback, scrambling for something to say.

"Yeah, I'm just getting some drinks, last round before heading on somewhere else. Where are you girls going next?"

"No idea, I'll just follow the crowd."

"So, how did you enjoy one of the privileged class's favourite pastimes?" he said, referring to the shooting and mocking himself in the process.

"You know, I found it strangely satisfying, akin to a boxing class, a good way to let off steam."

"So you box? Why am I not surprised? Do you often need to let off steam?" he asked.

"You know, it seems I do of late."

"Well, I find there are much better ways to let off steam than shooting at clay discs," he said suggestively.

"I'm sure you do," she said sarcastically.

"Are you a bit of a hot head then?" He smirked.

"So I'm told. It's just the Māori in me."

"You have Māori blood in you as well?" he asked, obviously surprised.

"I do."

"You warrior, how far back in the family tree?"

"A couple of generations ago," she said carefully,

distrusting his interest.

"Oh so you're a convict *and* a savage?" he said, grinning, sending a flying barb in her direction.

"And you're obviously a racist fuckwit," she said, turning on her heel and continuing her path to the ladies. She couldn't give two shits that he was some lord's only son. What a dick, the other girls could all have him.

He looked shellshocked and more than a little disturbed. It was a joke at the end of the day, he didn't mean it literally. It was just stupid shit to say, but this girl didn't take prisoners, she didn't let it slide. The force of her retaliation had properly dispatched him and he felt it. He knew it wasn't politically correct, knew he shouldn't have said it, but such banter he normally got away with.

She returned to her crowd without another encounter and discovered that the boys were all heading on to another nightclub. The girls, however, were accompanying Paige, who had managed to pin down Cameron and was hellbent on joining him and his mates. He was apparently going on from drinks to the nightclub Gravity, described as grimy, dark and industrial.

"Come on, Aurora, you have to come with us, I need you," Paige implored.

"It just doesn't sound that inviting, Paige, and everyone we've met is going onto the Lizard Lounge. I was just starting to get to know Emma over there and she seems so nice ..."

"Sophie and Annabel are coming and Cameron made a special request that I bring you. Apparently Flynn was lusting after you at the Freshers Fair and he's been asking Cam if we can all get together sometime."

"Did Cam suggest you meet up tonight then?"

"Well, no, not exactly, but I saw on Snapmaps that he was there and so I messaged him and said, like, I was coming with my girls." Paige liked to have a posse around her at all times, she liked to be the centre of attention. "He then told me Flynn was excited to hear that because he thought you were so pretty," she said, buttering Aurora up.

"Oh my God, no, he seemed nice but I really don't want to be set up like this. If I'm going to a nightclub where you can't hear anything, I really just want to spend the night on the dance floor," she said, looking around imploringly at the other girls.

"Well, I don't know that he wants to talk all that much," Sophie said suggestively.

"Don't be so mean, Aurora. I would be there for you, you know. As girls we have to have each other's back," said Paige, laying the guilt on thick.

"Oh alright," Aurora said, buckling under the pressure, "but now I just feel a bit awkward. Like I'm some sort of offering."

"Aren't you flattered?" asked Annabel.

"I guess, but I feel a bit self-conscious to be honest."

"Have another drink," said Sophie. "You need to lose your inhibitions. Paige, go and buy a round of shots, make it two, then we head. Tonight's mission is to loosen up Roars."

"I don't want to end up completely undone."

"Are you going on to the Lizard Lounge?" Winnie called out to her from a nearby sofa, oblivious to the conversation the girls had just had. He was chatting with Emma and George and some others a couple of metres away. Aurora could see Teddy walking up to them, his hands cradling four drinks, long athletic strides easily covering the ground. He looked at her and she returned his gaze with a cold stare. He had what must have been the second-year girl trailing after him.

"Ahh unfortunately I'm not. Definitely next time, but tonight I'm needed elsewhere," she said, rolling her eyes.

"Aah well, you'll be missed," Winnie lamented.

She smiled at him and noticed Teddy was staring at her still, barely listening to the girl who was looking up at him, chattering away.

Emma was looking at the girl and Teddy, and as she followed his gaze, in turn Aurora.

*"Education is an admirable thing, but it is well to
remember from time to time that nothing that is worth
knowing can be taught."*
— Oscar Wilde

The weeks began to settle into some sort of routine, as classes and coursework imposed themselves on the students' schedule and it became less about the party, clubs and meeting people, and more about study. Aurora found that she managed to secure some time for herself, which took the form of going to the gym or studying in the library. She realised university was going to be a lot of work for her if she wanted to do reasonably well.

She was grateful to have the girls bubbling around her, but the lack of privacy was at times a strain. She was an introvert and needed time alone to recharge her batteries. Some people get their energy from being around others, and some need time out to reboot.

Paige was fanning Flynn's interest in her and Aurora wasn't sure how keen she was. He was good looking, yes and she could talk to him easily enough, but there didn't seem to be much more of a connection than that. Looks were never an important factor in the end. She got the feeling that he was trying really hard to impress her, hiding his real self, and on his best behaviour when she was around him.

He was a lad, like Cameron, reasonably confident and obsessed with his hair, which was black, thick and curly. His hands were constantly running through it as he stood leaning over her in the pub, his hand cradling never-ending pints. He'd moved to England from County Clare at the age of twelve and his Irish accent was still strong; she was a sucker for an accent. His jeans and T-shirts were super tight, all labels and flashy, he looked slick. Still, none of that was a crime, and he was very attentive. That night at Gravity, he had made it very clear he was keen, dancing with her all night, buying her drinks and constantly telling her how pretty she was. He had insisted on taking her home, saying it wasn't safe to walk over the Downs after dark, and she had let him kiss her before he left for his halls, stopping him before it went on for too long. They'd hung out in the pub as a group a few times since then. He had "good chat" her friends all said, which made Aurora nervous. She wasn't sure what he was really after, a quick fling or a relationship.

Sophie kept telling her she could have any boy she wanted, but that was *sooo* not how she felt. The boys seemed to flock to Sophie, like bees to honey, she had no trouble pulling them in. They didn't stick, though, and Sophie wasn't interested in holding on to them. Aurora didn't want her lifestyle, but she would have liked more boys to have approached her.

Winnie and his mates, apart from Teddy, were friends. She really enjoyed their company and she wouldn't want anything to complicate that. She hadn't really talked to Teddy since his "savage" remark. He just pissed her off every time he opened his mouth, but he was part of this group of friends that was forming between the girls in Aurora's block and the boys they had met in Tudor, with Winnie at its epicentre.

Winnie, James and Teddy had gate-crashed one of her frisbee games on a Sunday afternoon. Walking back from a trip to the supermarket they had stumbled upon the tournament and spied her. Bored and looking for amusement, they stayed, cracking open bottles of red wine from their shopping, sledging from their position camped out on the sideline in the afternoon sun. Aurora, already grappling with learning a new sport, had to juggle their commentary as well.

"Aurora, what's the force?" asked a teammate midpoint in a heated game. She had forgotten to call it, and as she was marking the player with the disc, it was her duty to force them to throw one way.

"Roars, use the force," came the jeer from Winnie.

"Find it within yourself," mocked Teddy.

They worked out that if someone got a block, it was called "good D". "Roars give him that good D!" James called out.

If a player dived for the disc, leaving the ground and flying through the air, it was called laying out.

"Roars, lay out, lay out," was all she heard anytime she was near the disc.

The entire sport appeared to amuse them no end as virtually everything became a sexual joke. Drunk and disorderly by the end of it, they had completely destroyed her concentration and pissed off her teammates.

Winnie was the glue, the effervescent socialite who brought people together. He was warm and engaging and obviously a people person who loved a good time. His sunny face was always smiling; upbeat and mischievous, he was always looking for fun. Aurora often found herself wandering down to the bar to meet him for a drink while James worked the bar.

James had managed to score the job of barman in the Tudor bar, and there could not have been a more well-suited person for the role. He was the blond surfer boy in the group. He'd dropped out of shooting in favour of the surfing society, going on trips with them down to Cornwall to brave freezing Atlantic waters. Aurora wondered what surf there was to be had on this side of the world, and how enjoyable it would be as they headed into a northern hemisphere winter? Tall, with blonde locks that he was growing ever longer to suit the surfer scene, he was boyish and jovial on the surface, but pretty serious about his future underneath. He wanted to go places, like his dad, a self-made man. He was just going to have as much fun as possible getting there.

The boys often played pool in another room across the hall and they trod a well-worn path back and forth to get their drinks. Tonight she had come down to the bar with the express purpose of writing her manifesto for the JCR election and hopefully getting some input from Winnie. The deadline was tonight and she had left it to the very last minute. She had no idea if anyone else was running against her, but it couldn't hurt to put herself out there and throw her hat into the ring.

"What are you writing?" Winnie asked, popping his head over her shoulder as he brought empty glasses back from the pool room to the bar to be refilled.

"I'm just trying to pen my manifesto for the International Student Rep."

"Do you need any help?" Winnie offered. "I'm not qualified in any way to be an International Rep, but I'm good at playing the game. I did it all the way through school. You just got to bullshit this stuff and make it entertaining, that will win you votes."

"Yeah," said James, who proceeded to pour more beer for his mates, "make it a laugh if you want people to read it. Wait, are we expected to read all of them?" he asked, suddenly looking worried. "Do you want a drink, Roars?" Teddy's thoughtful shortening of her name had stuck.

"Yeah, an Aperol please. Don't look so worried, they aren't supposed to be long-winded things, just a punchy few lines about why you would be good in the role, what you stand for, etc. I suppose some people will go over the top, but I'm not writing much." She looked at her screen and began to type.

"What do you stand for then?" asked Winnie. "Fiery, feminist, foreigner, determined to fight her corner and yours."

"No, Winnie, that's unlikely to be the catchphrase I adopt," she said, looking up at him and smirking. "I think I have empathy. I know what it's like and how it feels to be an international student, and because I've been living here in the UK a couple of years I feel like it's my home, but I'm still an outsider. If you were just arriving in Bristol fresh off the boat, I don't think you'd really want to put your hand up for it. It would all just be too new, so I feel uniquely placed for the position. I am a third-culture kid after all."

"A third-culture what?" Winnie questioned, looking confused. "What does that mean?" said James, equally lost.

She pulled up the poem on her laptop that she had fallen in love with when she was living in Manila. At the International School there, she had discovered that she was what they now popularly called a "third-culture kid" or TCK. "This poem really describes it better than I can."

"Colors" by Whitni Thomas, MK (1991)

I grew up in a Yellow country
But my parents are Blue.
I'm Blue.
Or at least, that is what they told me.
But I play with the Yellows.
I went to school with the Yellows.
I spoke the Yellow language.
I even dressed and appeared to be Yellow.
Then I moved to the Blue land.
Now I go to school with the Blues.
I speak the Blue language.
I even dress and look Blue.
But deep down inside me, something's Yellow.
I love the Blue country.
But my ways are tinted with Yellow.
When I am in the Blue land,
I want to be Yellow.
When I am in the Yellow land,
I want to be Blue.
Why can't I be both?
A place where I can be me.
A place where I can be green.
I just want to be green.

She didn't belong to her parents' country of origin any more, she wasn't Asian or English either. She didn't really belong in one place. But she loved all the countries she had lived in for one reason or another and England was no exception. Her upbringing had forced her to see the world and the people in it differently, had forced her to adapt, and along the way she had honed some other skills. She had matured quite fast and had an overdeveloped sense of responsibility; of course, being an oldest child had helped with that too. She felt she would be able to look out for the other foreign students.

"It means I don't totally relate to my country of origin, in my case Australia, and I'm not English, but I've been changed by your culture here in England too. I don't identify with any one place perfectly because I've been tinged by all of them. I need my own third culture 'I just want to be green'."

"Wait, I'm still lost?" said James.

"Imagine the love child of Ed Sheeran and Kamala Harris. Where on Earth is that baby from?" Winnie asked.

"Is it ginger?"

"Not relevant," Winnie said dismissively.

"Right, sorry, I'm with you now. Identity is multifaceted and shit," said James, handing her the Aperol spritz.

"But do you really feel like that? It's kind of sad?" asked Winnie.

"Like a fish out of water? Yeah, pretty much. I don't completely fit in, but it's not debilitating. It's okay, there's nothing anyone can do about it. It just is what it is, but if I'm with other expat kids, we just understand how that feels."

"Okay, so we have to help you sell that, just not so serious. Let's keep it light, you know, and make it sexy," said James.

"It doesn't have to be sexy, it's for International Student Rep, James, how sexy can it be?" she said with an incredulous look on her face. "Half of the votes are girls, you know that, right?"

"Correction, sex sells everything and you are selling yourself, so it has to be sexy," James affirmed. "You've got it, use it. I would if I were a girl in your position."

Aurora shook her head, ignoring him, and wrote a few paragraphs. It wasn't hard in the end and she inwardly chastised herself for putting it off when it flowed naturally once she got going. She had to upload a picture of herself to finish off and the other boys from the pool room wandered in at this moment, looking for their beer, wondering where Winnie had gotten too.

"Roars, are you holding up my drink?" Harry said, coming into the room and assessing the situation, running his hands through his soft curls, which were greased back off his face. He was becoming another of her favourites with his easy charm, engaging manner and intelligent conversation. Lanky, without being overly tall, and always neatly turned out, he had an artsy, stylish flair. His thick, square–framed glasses were coupled with expensive pieces and fantastic charity shopping taste that gave him a charismatic, almost nerdy look. If he could wear a blazer to class without being ribbed, he would have.

"Sorry, yes." She instinctively pulled the laptop towards herself protectively.

Teddy trailed in after Harry and went to grab his beer off the bar. "What are you engrossed in there?"

Teddy asked all of them generally, almost reluctant to engage Aurora, not looking at her directly as he took a swig of his beer.

"I'm just about to upload my manifesto for the JCR elections. I'm running for International Rep. Are any of you running for anything?" she asked, looking around at them all.

"No, I have no desire to be in charge of anything here. I'm happy just to be a foot soldier," Teddy said, finally looking her in the eye. His tone was softer tonight, more genuine. It was a different Teddy to the one she had experienced every time they had met previously.

"It sounded like too much effort to me," said Winnie.

"What photo are you going to use? Let's see your options," said Harry, the undisputed artist of the group, moving himself to her right side. The boys all crowded around her screen as she looked through some of her photos, uncomfortably aware that she didn't want them to see too much of her life, to dissect it and hold it up to the light.

Paige and Sophie entered the room as this was going on, surveying the scene of Aurora seated at the bar in front of the laptop with five boys around her. James was busy serving people further along the bar, it was relatively busy tonight. The bar was the largest communal area in Tudor after the dining hall, but it still managed to be a warm space with an open fire and big armchairs and sofas similar to the ones in the lounge. The bar itself was about five metres long, made of rich brown wood with a few bar stools dotted along it. Old black-and-white photos of past students and classes of various years dotted the walls, which were panelled to waist height and then painted a dark, sombre grey. They seemed to match Paige's mood as she approached the group.

The boys were laughing and pointing at Aurora's screen, directing her to enlarge various photos and asking questions relating to her family, etc. They all agreed she should use the photo of herself sitting on the staircase at home. She was dressed in a deep V-necked white shirt, which hinted at cleavage, with Ajax's huge head coming over one shoulder.

"Classy and sexy," Harry assured her, "and you'll get the dog vote, he's a big, black beast."

Paige entered the conversation. "What's going on here then?" Her manner: prickly and uptight.

"I have finally finished my manifesto, so I'm just choosing the photo to go with it." Aurora was pleased with herself and feeling a sense of completion. "Hey, what's the matter, are you okay?" She could see Paige wasn't her usual self.

"I'm okay, I just need a few stiff drinks. James, line them up, I'll start with a shot or two."

"No problem, Alvin!"

"Alvin?" said Paige, raising her eyebrows.

"Why Alvin?" asked Sophie and Aurora in unison.

The boys were giggling like naughty school boys who were all in cahoots.

"What, do you all sit around making up nicknames for us in your spare time?" Aurora demanded.

"Yeah, I think that pretty much sums it up," conceded Teddy, nodding and looking around at them all. "There's usually quite a few drinks involved."

"Why Alvin?" Paige demanded, pretending to be annoyed but secretly happy with the attention.

"You have a little chipmunk face," said James. "Oh

and you're orange most of the time."

Paige was more of an English rose, with her aquiline nose and widow's peak, than a small marsupial. Unsurprisingly, the boys had chosen to highlight her large, round eyes, pointed chin and the small gap in her teeth rather than her classic looks.

It seemed to be lifting Paige's spirits as she smiled at them, while trying to look outraged at the same time. "I'll have you know a gap in the teeth is one of the seven signs of beauty," she retorted.

"It's also one of the signs of being a chipmunk," said James.

"I came up with it," Winnie openly acknowledged, congratulating himself. Teddy just raised his glass to him.

"What's mine?" demanded Sophie. "I want one!"

"Give us time," Harry said. "We can't be rushed, it's a spontaneous thing."

Sophie pronounced herself left out and overlooked, as Aurora was Roars, and now Paige was Alvin. Paige was busy downing not one, but two shots. Something was not right in her world tonight, of that Aurora was sure.

Teddy ventured to get a stool and positioned it next to Aurora, who immediately felt crowded. She made protestations, which he ignored in his high-handed way as he took the laptop off her and placed it on his lap, looking at pictures, occasionally smiling and asking questions about the ages of her siblings. His jeans had rips in them, she noticed as he sat next to her. He looked very casual tonight with a simple cream sweatshirt. A small bronze-looking circle hung from a long piece of leather tied around his neck. She'd noticed him wearing it before. He was a clothes horse, she mused, he could probably wear anything and make it look good.

"Do you have any brothers or sisters?" she asked, although she knew from Paige he was an only child.

"No," he said. "It's just my parents and I, and it's pretty boring when I'm home. They want me to go home soon for the weekend, but I'm not that keen to leave here just yet."

She got the feeling he was enjoying his freedom. "Being an only child must be intense?"

"It is. There's a lot riding on the one egg," he said ruefully, turning to look directly at her for only the second time in weeks. He was close again too, too close for her comfort, she felt unnerved just sitting next to him. It was a feeling she didn't like, not with his reputation.

"The pendant you're wearing, does it mean anything?"

"I found it in the garden when I was a kid, was told it's Celtic, but I just like it. It's heavy," he said, taking it off and handing it to her.

"Wow, it's cool. I love the weight of it." She examined it in the palm of her hand. It was a dull, green and brown, worn with age obviously, which gave the bronze a lovely patina.

"My dad's friend works in the antiquities department of Christie's and he said it was a Celtic ring. It might fit on your finger, put it on." He gestured to her.

Aurora gingerly placed the ring on her right-hand ring finger and it slipped on perfectly, even with the leather still attached to it. "It's beautiful. There's something about it," she said quietly, looking down at the ring.

"I know, you can feel it too?"

Aurora nodded in agreement as she took it off and handed the necklace back. "Maybe it's because it's so old."

"Maybe. Who knows who it belonged to? I used to imagine it fell off a druid's hand or something," he said jokingly as he put it back around his neck.

She made a move to take her laptop back off him but he just used his long arms to move it further out of her reach, playfully refusing to hand it over.

"I'm not done yet," he said.

Aurora caught their reflection in the glass behind the bar. She looked small beside him, perched side by side on the pair of bar stools.

She also noticed Paige, who now had a gin and tonic to go with her shots, staring at them in the mirror. Paige then manoeuvred herself around their circle of friends to stand next to Teddy. She began to show an interest in the photos too.

"Flynn would die if he saw this photo of you!" she casually dropped. "I was just talking to Cam and apparently Flynn can't wait to see you again. He just keeps bringing you up in conversation every chance he gets. It's so cute."

Aurora squirmed, she wasn't happy to discuss Flynn out in the open yet. She liked to keep things quiet, especially as they hadn't even been out on a date, or spent any time alone except for that one walk home after being out that first night. She wasn't even sure she wanted to go out with him, or that he wanted to go with her.

"Bloody hell, quick work, Roars, didn't take you long," Teddy said, raising his brows as he stood up and handed Aurora her laptop.

"I don't have a boy," she asserted, trying to clarify the situation as he walked away. She was no longer the object of his attention, which had briefly made her feel like a chick under a brooder lamp, and she was aware she had enjoyed it. *God, don't get suckered in, you've seen him in action*, she mentally checked herself. She also felt irritated with Paige for bringing Flynn up at all. She chose not to mention it however, preferring to let it pass.

Aurora put her laptop on the bar and picked up her drink turning to Paige, "Are you okay? You didn't seem right when you came in."

"No, I've just been talking to Cam. He's just always busy and seems to have better things to do than spend time with me?" she said in a maudlin tone. "I'm worried he's interested in that girl in his flat," she confided, looking disturbed. "I've seen her checking him out. Oh, that girl running against me for vice president has been campaigning too, which is very annoying. I've just been asking everyone I meet to vote for me on top of my flyers and Facebook group. I don't know what else I can do? If I don't win, I'll be devastated."

"Do you have any reason to think he's cheated?" asked Aurora, deciding to ignore the campaigning drama.

"No, other than the fact that he's not interested in hanging out with me if you know what I mean," she said mournfully. "You and Teddy looked cosy, I didn't put my foot in it did I?" As she spoke her eyes were wide pools of innocence.

"God no, not with Teddy in particular, I just don't think Flynn and I are anything yet, so I'm not really ready to start talking to everyone about it." She wondered why she was having to explain the obvious.

"Okay, well, I'm just sooo excited, it would be so much fun if you were going out with Flynn and I was with Cam. We could have such a good time hanging out together."

"Okay, okay, just don't get carried away, I'm not sure if anything is actually going to manifest. I get the feeling he's a bit of a lad and wants to play the field, and I'm so not interested in that," she stated flatly.

"Why would you say that, he's lovely. I'm sure he fancies you."

Aurora had her doubts, but she kept them to herself. She had nothing to lose at this point.

"I don't say we all ought to misbehave. But we ought to look as if we could."
— Oscar Wilde

"Darling, come on, we'll be late to the ball," Paige said in an anxious tone as she swept into Aurora's room. "I don't want to be late, I'm so nervous about tonight I can't stand still. I need champagne!"

"Babe, you need to calm down," Aurora responded. "It just doesn't matter that much, why do you feel like so much is riding on this?"

"I don't know, I just want to win, it's important to me," she said, wringing her hands.

"Relax, you've done all you can do now, so let it go."

"Don't you care if you get your position at all?"

"Honestly, a little bit, but I won't mind if I don't. I'm not someone who likes to be in charge or run the show, really I'm the opposite. I just thought I could be sympathetic to the international students' plight because I am one." Paige looked confused, like she had no idea what Aurora was really going on about. "I'm nearly ready, let me just get my shoes and bag sorted and I'll come."

"Wow, you look really good, that's a nice outfit," said Paige, looking her up and down.

Aurora was wearing a gold, two-piece ensemble: a V-necked, spaghetti- strapped top in satin fabric that fell loosely to the waist with a matching skintight fitted skirt that finished just below the knee. Both the top and skirt had diagonal seams, which added interest and structure to the outfit. She had fine ankle-strap stilettos in a dull gold, with a vintage evening bag, and the three gold necklaces she always wore around her neck finished it off. With her dark skin and smoky makeup on green eyes, she looked every inch the striking beauty.

"Thank you, I got it on the sales rack in Selfridges at the end of summer. It was a bargain. You look very glamorous yourself," she responded, smiling at Paige, who had her hair up in a French twist with big earrings and a short black dress, "and I love your heels." Paige was in killer three- inch stilettos. It was classic, simple and business-like, and Paige certainly meant business tonight.

"I'm a shoe addict, and the higher the better when the occasion is right. I need to be tall tonight."

They collected Sophie and Annabel on their way downstairs and headed towards the dining hall, which was the venue for the night. It had been transformed into a stately ballroom for the evening with a dance floor and stage down the front. The tables were set out in three long rows with a head table that was centred perpendicular to the other three. It looked like the dining hall in Hogwarts with floor-to-ceiling dark panelled walls lined with the painted portraits of previous Tudor Hall wardens, hanging one after the other, like aristocratic ancestors in a grand house. Large candelabras hung from the ceiling and were dimmed tonight. The bar was set up off to one side. All the students had to wear black graduation-style robes over the top of their formal clothes, which met with much criticism from the female attendees.

"What is the point of wearing a nice dress if you have to cover it up with this disgusting black robe?" complained Sophie, ruby-red lips pouting. She had gone all out in a figure-hugging leopard-print dress to the knee.

They were virtually the first to arrive much to Aurora's discomfort, she hated being early anywhere, a legacy of growing up in a family where they struggled to be on time. It was always the awkward part of the evening and she preferred to avoid it altogether. Paige rushed to the bar and ordered drinks as they stood around in their small circle.

"Oh look, see that girl over there, just walking in?" Sophie said, tossing her blonde curls in the girl's direction. "That's the girl Diana who's running against me for Social Secretary. That is an awful dress by the way."

"Yes, we know, Sophie, you've pointed her out before," Aurora stated flatly, "and for the record I don't mind her dress at all, it really suits her. I've spoken to her a few times now, she's really nice."

"Whose side are you on, Aurora?" said Sophie, looking daggers at her.

"The girl is a nice person, just because she's running against you doesn't mean I can't like her, Sophie."

"Well, you know what she means!" chipped in Paige. "She doesn't look anywhere near as good as you do." She patted Sophie's arm to soothe her pride.

Drinks were scheduled for half an hour until 7.30 p.m., after which there was to be the announcement of the new JCR committee performed by the outgoing president. The new committee would then take their place at the head table. Paige was practically hyperventilating now. Aurora was a little nervous too: she did want to get the post now that the moment had arrived, it would be fun to be a part of it all. There were about ten positions from the looks of the top table and the opportunity to make some new friends working together was appealing.

The room was filling up quickly as the students flooded in. There was a bit of a commotion at the entrance to the dining room as Teddy, Winnie and all the boys from their block entered in a large pack. They had clearly been "pre-ing" in their rooms beforehand and were loud and disruptive already; laughing and joking with each other. Dressed in their dinner jackets, they reminded Aurora of the golden age of Hollywood, young Cary Grants.

They swaggered in looking older, sophisticated and handsome. Winnie saw Aurora, nodded and smiled in her direction as he strode into the room saying hi to various people, ever the extrovert, engaging with as many others as possible.

They went directly to the bar like everyone else and made their way over to Aurora and the girls. Teddy was last to get his drink, detained by a girl who had approached him and placed her hand on his arm, laughing and tossing her hair as she chatted to him. He looked like a gorgeous, young Leonardo DiCaprio walking into the ballroom of the *Titanic*. He appeared mildly amused but excused himself and made his way directly over to join his friends. His eyes met Aurora's as he walked towards the group, catching her out. Again he boldly and openly stared at her. She felt he was looking straight through to her core, intense and disarming.

Winnie stood alongside her and broke the spell. "You look gorgeous this evening," he said, nodding approvingly.

"Thank you, but you beat me to it, you guys all look so great tonight."

"We do our best. I have to say we are well primed for the forthcoming festivities and appointments, and as not one of us has volunteered for anything, we'll be at liberty to amuse ourselves."

"I love your trousers, Harry, they look amazing with your dinner jacket!" Aurora was stroking his arm, feeling the velvet, navy dinner jacket while admiring his tartan trousers.

"It's the Sinclair family tartan, Roars." His attention was then drawn to Paige and her theatrics. "Jeez, Paige, what's wrong with you? You look stressed."

"Don't talk to me, I feel like I'm going to be sick," she answered while fanning herself.

"Well, perhaps I had better take that drink off you," said Teddy, attempting to lift it out of her hand, "we don't want you to be sick at the start of the night."

"No, I need it!" she said, clutching on tightly, pushing him away. "This will all be over soon one way or the other."

Winnie rolled his eyes and Aurora stifled a giggle. "You don't look so worried, Roars?" Winnie asked.

"No, not really, but now it's here I guess I'd like to get it."

"You're a sure thing, the other two running don't stand a chance, don't worry," he whispered confidently.

"You're sweet but I don't think I am. I don't know many people, no one from previous schools or connections like so many other people here do. Paige and Sophie campaigned hard, introducing themselves to everyone, and I just couldn't do that."

"We told everyone we know to vote for you, so it's in the bag."

"Okay, Winnie, thanks," she said, unconvinced.

Their conversation finished as the outgoing president stepped up to the mic and the DJ killed the music. The chattering gradually stopped as people realised the formalities were about to begin. The former president made his opening remarks about the responsibilities of the committee, how much he enjoyed his particular position and what the experience had taught all those who had taken part in the JCR. He began announcing the new appointments starting with his replacement:

"In the position of president we have Reuben Fox." Much clapping followed as the new president shook hands with his predecessor before making his way to his seat in the middle of the top table. Next it was Paige's turn and she held her breath, her body braced for the announcement. "His vice president will be Paige Palmer." Paige let out a very audible sigh and tottered quickly out to the front in her stilettos, smiling broadly with relief. "Your Treasurer will be Eleanor Hartley."

Then he got to the role Sophie had canvassed hard for and she gripped Annabel's arm tightly, staring down at the ground. "Your Social Secretary will be Diana van der Byl." And the pretty blonde Sophie had pointed out earlier walked to the front to take her place at the table, smiling shyly. Sophie looked close to tears and stony faced, but held it together, just. International Student Representative was next and, as Winnie had predicted, "Aurora Bond" was the name read out. The boys around her nodded their approval knowingly as Aurora took her place, which as fate would have it seated her next to Diana van der Byl.

With the formalities over, everyone was asked to take their seats and dinner began.

"Hi, congratulations," said Diana, smiling as they sat down together at the table. "Wow, I'm glad that's over, how about you?"

"Congratulations to you too. I didn't think I really cared, but you know once you put yourself out there, you sort of can't help but want it."

"I know, I totally agree. How will your friend Sophie take it?" asked Diana.

"I'm sure she'll recover, probably in an hour or two, but if I was you I wouldn't approach her. It will be a little raw right now."

"Okay, I won't. I've been getting vibes off her and the other girl Paige all week," said Diana.

"I'm sorry, they were both really hyped for this," said Aurora, attempting to excuse their hostility. "I love your dress, you look like Hailey Bieber at the Met Gala."

"Thanks so much, I was totally going for that look!" she said, beaming. From what Aurora could make out, Diana had all the boys half in love with her. James regularly brought her name up in conversation and openly lusted after her. With her long blonde, wavy hair, brown eyes and full red lips, she was considered very attractive by everyone. Softly spoken and obviously a gentle soul, she appeared kind and considerate, with a touch of vulnerability. "You look amazing too in all gold, not everyone could pull that off. You look so sexy," Diana said to her admiringly.

"Thanks. I love clothes, it's a hobby, although I'd love to end up working in fashion one day."

"You should, I always notice what you put together, you're obviously really talented," she said in her lilting South African accent. "What star sign is that around your neck?"

"Oh, I'm a Virgo," Aurora said a little sheepishly, feeling it immediately revealed her perfectionism. Her hand immediately went to the symbol.

"I'm a Cancer, we're supposed to get on really well," Diana said happily.

They chatted off and on through dinner in between meeting some of the other committee members. Reuben, the new president, was very much a statesman in the making as he introduced himself and then proceeded to make sure everyone on the committee knew one another or were introduced. He continued to work the room all evening and was clearly going to enjoy his role. London-born from Nigerian parents, he told them he was studying law, hoping to work in corporate law eventually. Outgoing with smiling eyes, he appeared to be a good choice and the girls both agreed he would be fun to work with.

The wine was flowing and, as it was included in their ball ticket, they all drank as much of it as they could. It was raucous by the time dinner was finished and everyone could mingle. The music was turned up and the lights turned down. Sophie was well on her way to getting smashed, drowning her sorrows, now boring the pants off some poor girl she knew. Aurora was glad it was a female friend, and not another guy. Paige was party central on the dancefloor, flying high and celebrating her victory with a crowd around her just as the new vice president should. Aurora and Diana were joined by James and before too long he dragged Diana onto the dancefloor.

Aurora found herself alone and realised that, for perhaps the first time since she had arrived at Bristol, she felt at ease, she wasn't anxious, happy to just watch everyone as she sipped her white wine. Perhaps she was beginning to feel a part of it all now? Her reverie was short-lived as Reuben came along and coaxed her onto the dancefloor.

"You can't stand there watching, it's not allowed tonight," he said, taking both her hands and pulling her onto the floor. He spun her around quickly, and pulled her in close, placing his hand in the centre of her back.

"Wow, you can dance?" He had caught her off guard.

"Yes," he said with a smile.

"You are one of the only guys who can actually dance," she marvelled with her eyes widening.

"I know, it's great, girls love it. My parents ballroom dance and taught me some basic moves."

"Well, you're very good. Girls can follow, but the guy has to know how to lead." He moved beautifully in time with the music, fluid and rhythmic.

Together on the dancefloor they were mesmerising to watch, gliding across the floor, with Reuben regularly sending her away and whipping her back, a lone mirrored disco ball periodically illuminating them in strobes of light.

As she was dancing, Aurora noticed Teddy talking to the same girl she had seen him with at the beginning of the night. She kept touching him and laughing, flicking her hair around, and Aurora could guess how their evening would end up. He wasn't particularly attentive, though, was really only half paying attention to the girl, but she was clearly oblivious, either that or she didn't care. His eyes were scanning the room, flicking left then right like he was searching for something. A moment later his eyes settled on Aurora. She had taken off the black gown that was covering her outfit to dance. In the darkened room the gold satin fabric shone slightly in the gloom as she was whirled around by Reuben. Teddy stood still staring at them.

The ball finished and many would go out in town to the clubs. As they were ushered out of the dining room, Aurora found Winnie and some of the boys and migrated into the bar with them. The fire was lit and Winnie was straight to the bar to order for them all. They slumped into the sofas by the fire. Paige was one of those girls who appeared impervious to the pain of high heels. Aurora was not and she buckled, taking off her shoes, which were killing her after dancing. White wine all night could be dangerous and the state Sophie was in bore witness to that. She was cosying up next to Harry, playfully pulling off his glasses, and he was politely declining her advances, reminding her they were mates, that she was plastered and needed to sober up. She ended up passed out on his shoulder as the group of them sat around talking in semi-darkness by the fire.

Winnie came back with not one but two bottles of Prosecco. "We're going to toast the ladies' success tonight, lads," he said as they filled glasses and passed them around. "Girls, don't take this the wrong way, but good luck and may you all be friends at the end of it."

"What a thing to say, why wouldn't we all be friends?" asked Paige.

"Because committees are full of egos and people who love to be in charge. It can get ugly, get your armour on and form alliances," he said jovially.

"Don't," said Aurora, covering her ears, "or I'll be resigning before I even start."

"You'd better grow another skin, Roars," said Winnie.

"I'm going to enjoy every bit of it," said Paige defiantly. "I love running things and I'm good at it."

"Case in point," Harry said mockingly as he pointed at Paige.

"No, it will be great on your resume, Aurora, don't listen to him," said Paige. "Where's Teddy gone, he hasn't come in?"

"Yeah, well, he may be tied up," said James, smirking.

"Literally," Winnie agreed, raising his eyebrows suggestively.

They sat by the fire talking for an hour before Teddy strolled in with his bow tie now hanging loose around his neck, two buttons on his shirt undone, hair dishevelled. He looked untogether compared to how he had started the evening.

"Here are my comrades," he said, striding into the room, arms wide, looking relaxed and happy. "What are we drinking? I'm ready for another, it's been at least twenty minutes."

"Prosecco in honour of our female companions' success tonight," answered Winnie.

"No, sorry, that's not champagne. I'm getting a

bottle of Dom," he asserted.

"Even better if you're paying," said Winnie, unphased.

"That's excessive, isn't it?" asked Aurora.

"Are you not worth it?" Teddy turned to look directly at her as he posed the question.

My God, she thought, he's just been with another girl, cast her off and now he's flirting with me, flashing his cash. She didn't answer and just looked at him, a little surprised and uncomfortable.

"Yes, Teddy, buy me a bottle of Dom, I'm definitely worth it," said Paige, batting her lashes, leaning back against the sofa.

"How's your boyfriend doing, Paige?" asked Harry. She threw him a dirty look.

Teddy returned with Dom and insisted the girls drink that. He seated himself in the only available seat on the sofa next to the sleeping Sophie. Aurora was in a single armchair by the fire next to him. The conversation turned to the events of the evening. In the bar the crowd dwindled but the group of eight lingered in the sofas by the fire, content to talk, drink champagne and reflect on the night. The music being played was softer now, more Khalid and Charlie Puth, less drum and bass.

Teddy had begun to open up after drinking solidly all evening. "My parents are desperate for me to go home for the weekend. I've been avoiding it, to be honest."

"That's so sweet," said Paige. "My parents are too busy with business and travel to come for a weekend, but I might meet Mummy for some shopping in London soon."

"Well, one of the perks of being an only child is

doting parents. They say they are too busy to come down here but they want me to go home soon. Why don't you all come with me? That would make it way more entertaining," he dropped casually.

"Oooh sounds like so much fun," Paige said excitedly. "And Cam would be so jealous too."

"Well, so glad we can be of service, Paige," said Winnie sarcastically.

"Yeah, I'm trying hard not to feel used and abused," Teddy commented.

"Or insulted," Harry added.

"Well, it's about time the female student body got some payback," interjected Aurora, unable to resist the opportunity.

"Yes, you're always taking advantage of some poor girl," chastised Annabel.

"You girls are obviously misinformed. You assume I'm the abuser, when in fact it's the opposite. I had to extricate myself from the clutches of a persistent girl tonight. I'm the victim," he said, smiling, enjoying the banter.

"How will your parents feel about you bringing what, like, seven people home for the weekend?" Aurora asked incredulously.

"My mum loves having guests and they are dying to meet my friends. We've got lots of room and we can just hang out, play tennis, or do whatever we want."

Paige and Annabel were nodding enthusiastically.

"Sure, I'll go," said Harry.

"How old is the scotch in the decanter?" asked James.

"Older than you are, and you're not getting your hands on it," Teddy shot back.

"So, I don't really do public transport," Winnie

announced, looking around expectantly.

"I've got my Defender," said Teddy, rolling his eyes, "but it will only take five of us."

Sophie had by this time woken up, looking groggy and still drunk, but had managed to comprehend the plan enough to slur, "I've got a car."

"Fantastic!" said Paige. "The girls can go with Sophie and the boys with Teddy."

"I don't know, I'll have to see how much work I have," hedged Aurora. "How far away is it?" She thought it would be fun, but questioned whether she would feel comfortable staying with a lord and lady. Here at university, she tried to ignore the class divide, telling herself it didn't matter, because she truly believed it didn't, but she was aware of it all the same. All of this group had gone to expensive boarding schools, had country piles and escaped to beach houses around the world. A few of her classmates and friends in Asia were from very wealthy families; extreme wealth was one thing, but English aristocracy was something else again. She didn't want to feel out of her depth.

"Your estate is in Gloucestershire, isn't it, Teddy?" It felt like Paige had made a point of saying "estate". "I can't wait to see it, I've heard so much about it from Mummy."

Teddy ignored Paige, answering Aurora's question. "It's about an hour away, not far. It will be pretty relaxed and we'll be allowed to do our own thing. There may be a shoot on I think because it's that time of the year, but we don't have to participate."

"Oh I'd love to shoot!" continued Paige.

"Me too," said Sophie.

"Sure, whatever," said Teddy as he turned back to

face Aurora again, blue eyes dark and intense. "Will you come?"

"To define is to limit."
— Oscar Wilde, The Picture of Dorian Gray

Late on a Friday afternoon, deep into autumn, they piled into the two cars. The boys were in Teddy's Defender, old and rusty, music on loud, and in high spirits they hit the road. The car looked like a bit of a wreck from the outside, but inside he had installed a top-class audio system and it was blaring. The girls followed behind in Sophie's little hatchback, Paige riding shotgun, Annabel and Aurora in the back. The days were getting shorter and shorter now, classes had just finished for the week and it was dark already as they set off.

When it came to boys, Sophie came across as a racy

little red Corvette; however, she drove like an old woman, nervous and unsure, so cautious she was dangerous: crunching the gears, slow to react and seemingly unable to change lanes. Aurora thought she would die of frustration.

After twenty minutes Winnie rang. "Right, so what's wrong?" came his voice over the Bluetooth audio.

"Nothing, what do you mean?" answered Sophie, baffled.

"With your car?" he said bluntly.

"No, it's all fine, no problem," she answered, still puzzled by the question.

"So, it's you then? Look you're driving too slow, so we're going to leave you behind. Google Esslemont, Gloucestershire and you'll find it. Give us a call when you get close." With that he abruptly hung up and the girls watched the Defender disappear down the road ahead of them.

"Well, that was rude!" said Sophie.

"Soph, darling, you're a terrible driver, I love you and all, but you can't drive for shit," Paige criticised as she changed the music.

"Yeah, it's true, Sophie, you drive like an old woman," echoed Aurora. "I'm surprised the guys stayed with us as long as they did."

"Really? What do you mean?"

"We've almost died about three times," added Annabel.

"Well, I've only had my licence for a year," Sophie grumbled defensively.

"A year too long," Aurora mumbled under her breath.

An hour's drive turned into more like two, but they got there in the end. They called Teddy on approach and he directed them in. "As you come along Bath Road, there will be a pair of large gateposts on your right that form part of an arch. There's no obvious sign, the name is carved into one of the stone gateposts, but there's a lantern lighting it up. Go through the archway and follow the drive along; this will take about five minutes, you'll cross the river as you go over the stone bridge and then the road bears left and up and you'll see the house."

Esslemont sat high on the hill. Thoughts of Jane Austen's Pemberley sprang to Aurora's mind. She gazed transfixed through the window of the little blue car as it put-putted up the hill along the drive towards the colossal house, which loomed ahead lit up in the darkness like St Paul's Cathedral. Large trees lined the drive as it curved upwards to the house. In the evening light, Aurora could just make out some horses in the fields.

The name Esslemont had Welsh origins, meaning "low hill", and it had been the Talbot family seat for many generations. A classic Georgian pile, grand, beautifully proportioned, and simply elegant. Large rectangular windows, perfectly symmetrical, spread out either side of the main entrance and rose up in three rows.

Aurora felt her nerve go, suddenly feeling sick and anxious. She wasn't from this world, and although it was fascinating, she was losing confidence as they slowly climbed upwards. The other girls twittered animatedly, impressed but unphased. They were all very well off themselves, and had discussed little else on the drive up tonight. Who had the money at Bristol, who their family connections were and of course Teddy's title and family. Aurora had contributed little to the conversation, having nothing to add. In the expat world, people didn't attempt to categorise or define each other by their economic bracket, you all needed to get on and make friends. It was a small, transient pond and everyone was in the same boat. It simply didn't matter. She didn't want to be judged, or judge anybody else by their net worth.

Teddy, surrounded by dogs, was outside to greet them as they drove up. A pair of mastiffs, a pair of English pointers, and three French bulldogs. He directed them where to park and helped them unload while the dogs swirled around them all. Paige was clearly terrified by the mastiffs: she froze, looking concerned as one of them put her through his security check, sniffing with great care and diligence.

"Don't worry, they're friendly," Teddy assured her. Aurora was stroking the other one and found their presence soothing. Big dogs would be a welcome distraction. Teddy showed them the way inside and Aurora took a deep breath and followed him.

The grand entrance hall welcomed them, the floor lined with black-and- white marble tiles, doors leading off on both sides to other rooms. Large box hedge topiary pots were both outside and in. Aurora wondered whether a butler would be appearing. A beautiful staircase rose up to the floor above, beckoning all who entered to ascend. The family ancestors looked down from the walls above.

"Just drop your bags here, we'll get them when we go up, but come into the drawing room and get a drink first."

They went through double doors off to the side of the entrance hall and found the rest of the guys engaged in conversation with Teddy's parents and another couple. As they walked into the large lounge room, Aurora was happy to linger at the back, taking in the beautiful interiors; ever the aesthete, she drank it all in. The room was long and rectangular, a fireplace centred on one wall with sofas and armchairs arranged for conversation around it. It was painted Georgian grey, all the sofas and chairs were covered with white loose covers, scattered with cushions. The floors were stained a dark, walnut brown and were covered in sisal rugs. Accents of black and silver were dotted around in the form of picture frames, lamps, amid the antique furniture. It was extremely chic and stylish and wouldn't have been out of place in a Ralph Lauren catalogue.

His parents were older than Aurora expected: they looked like they were in their late fifties or early sixties, both greying and dignified. The fire was on as they sat drinking cocktails. As Teddy made the introductions, they stood and shook hands with the girls. The other couple were called the Macfarlanes, friends of Teddy's parents here for the weekend of shooting, having arrived from London earlier in the day.

"We're so glad to meet you," enthused Teddy's mother. "We can't wait to get to know all of you," she said warmly. "We've just been getting acquainted with the young men here. Paige, you look just like your mother. How are your parents? I haven't seen them for a good few years?"

"They're fine, thank you, they send their regards. They said to wish you good luck for the weekend, Lady Trentbridge. I think they meant in regard to having to deal with all of us, not with the shoot," said Paige.

She laughed. "Please just call us Constance and Tom."

"They have plenty of birds of their own in Scotland, don't they?" enquired Teddy's father.

"Oh yes, they have a couple of shoots each season, I'll go up for some of them," Paige confirmed, smiling broadly, basking in the attention.

"And how are you all finding Bristol, are you happy there?" Tom continued as the attentive host.

Paige and Sophie chatted away about life in Bristol, giving them all the details on their courses, the JCR and their social life as they stood talking.

Teddy took the opportunity to motion to Aurora and Annabel to take a seat and join the boys and their family friends, Bill and Maggie, on the sofas near the fire. He then poured them a drink before coming to sit next to Aurora. He handed her a hefty gin and tonic and sat down, quietly turning to ask her how the drive was with raised eyebrows, obviously amused.

"Her driving is a nightmare!" Aurora whispered, exasperated. "I was so surprised, she lives in the fast lane but drives like Grandma."

He laughed. "Well, come home with us on the way back. We had a great time."

His parents joined them then on the sofas and there was more general discussion about uni life, the joys, and the pitfalls. Winnie, Harry and James, clearly in their element, told stories from Bristol and filled Teddy's parents in on his life there. Teddy looked like he would rather they didn't give too much away. They at least had the wherewithal not to mention his conquests.

Aurora felt Teddy's mother's gaze upon her from time to time. She looked like a force to be reckoned with, tall and slim with angular, Germanic features and a perfectly styled curled bob, à la Lauren Bacall. Clearly she had been a beautiful, young woman and now she was an elegant, older one. Aurora imagined she would not have been amused to hear how her son was breaking hearts at Bristol; then again, perhaps she would be proud of his prowess with the girls. Aurora could see where Teddy had gotten his height and physique. She was dressed in a cable-knit sweater over the top of a shirt, with tailored trousers and a pair of Tod's. Constrained, conservative and classic.

His father, Tom, the Earl, was a tall man also, but rounder and softer in the middle of his large frame. He had on round tortoiseshell glasses and his grey hair was combed from the side but kept falling in his face, which suited his jovial manner. He wasn't severe or formal at all, so not what Aurora was expecting from a lord. Having never encountered one before she had imagined someone quite stiff and reserved. He was clearly a clever conversationalist and exceedingly charming as she watched him engaging the boys. Stereotypes – sometimes they were spot on, and sometimes they were way off.

Aurora was still making her observations when she was brought back to the conversation at hand by Teddy's mother asking, "Aurora, are you British or are you an international student?"

"I'm a British student, but I'm originally from Australia."

"Named for the Southern Lights," Teddy added. Aurora cocked an eye at him, surprised he would refer to the term from their first meeting.

Constance continued to inquire after Aurora's upbringing. As she told her story, she was aware that no one else was being quizzed in the same way. She figured it was because she obviously didn't look British.

She must just be curious, fair enough, she thought.

"Ah so you're well travelled then. What area of business are your parents in?"

"My father works in the city." If she was guarded, it was because she had the feeling that she was ever so slightly being interrogated. "My mum is a psychologist by trade."

"Do you have any East Asian heritage, Aurora?" Constance asked. "You said you lived there too?"

The question immediately made her feel uneasy. "No, well ... yes," she stuttered. "No Asian heritage, it's Polynesian, I have Polynesian grandparents." Aurora heard her voice drop a couple of octaves.

"Well, you conduct yourself well," Constance praised, allowing herself a smile. Aurora recoiled from the back-handed compliment and her eyes darted in Teddy's direction in time to catch his mortification. His brows were furrowed, his expression tense. Constance appeared oblivious to her son's reaction and to the insult she had just delivered.

He smiled an apology on his mother's behalf, his eyes kind and concerned. She could feel her self-esteem and confidence draining out of her body and pooling on the floor. She wished her physical form could follow them.

His mother appeared to be satisfied, but she was interrupted by her husband, who announced that they needed to get away for dinner or they would be late for their reservation down in the village.

"What are you young ones going to do tonight?" he said, addressing Teddy as he placed his scotch down.

"I thought we'd just go down to the pub and grab dinner, we'll just walk home after, don't worry about us, we'll sort ourselves out."

"I wasn't worried in the slightest, son, you know me, I leave that to your mother." Constance looked mildly irritated. "Tomorrow morning, if any of you are interested, you are welcome to join us on the shoot. We will be heading out at 10 a.m. sharp."

"Breakfast will be laid out from 8.30 a.m. in the orangery off the kitchen, so just come down whenever you wake up," Constance told them, standing up.

The kids said thank you as the adults departed. Aurora relaxed a bit; at least meeting the parents was over, they weren't nearly as intimidating as she thought they might be. She kept reminding herself they were all just people after all.

"I don't want to go to heaven. None of my friends are there."
— Oscar Wilde

The pub in the village was named The Wild Rabbit. A traditional local pub originally, now post-makeover it had been upgraded, both in decor and in the gastro sense. A fine dining restaurant out the back was full on a Friday night, but the bar at the front served food as well. It was more relaxed and as they entered it was clear it was popular too, bustling and busy with locals and visitors.

"It's busy because of the shoot, wait here, I'll just be a sec," said Teddy.

He went to the bar and heads turned to him as

people acknowledged his presence. It was obvious he was well known, but Aurora detected a touch of deference as well. He spoke quietly to the publican, who had gone straight over to see him, shaking his hand warmly over the bar.

He returned. "Right, we're over here by the fire at that corner table," he said pointing to a round table.

Right, best table in the house, thought Aurora, *no flies on him.* He certainly was acting the consummate host. He'd given them a quick tour of the family home before dinner and showed them to their rooms. Charming and humble, he matter-of-factly showed off the house, which was nothing short of breathtaking. His room was at the top of the elegant staircase, to the right along a landing; his parent's room was on the opposite side of the landing, which formed the other half of the gallery and surveyed the central entrance hall below. There were two wings off this central part of the old building, the girls' rooms, which were to be found down one wing, the same side as Teddy's parents' room, and the other wing would house the boys, closest to Teddy's room. Each of them had their own room, which stunned Aurora. She couldn't help but ask in awe, "How many bedrooms are there?"

"I don't know – more than ten, less than twenty. It used to be used for large country parties, and my parents still host large gatherings from time to time, but not often now. Mum does like to see them filled and appreciated, though."

"It's just beautiful," she said simply. He looked pleased and smiled as he showed her into her room last. It was the first room down the wing and had a view to the front and side of the house. The same tall, graceful Georgian windows provided the light, the bed faced the windows, with the fireplace along the right wall. It was simple, but stunning. Sisal carpet on the floor with a sheepskin rug, neutral soft furnishings in cool tones, against pale grey walls, and plants, lots and lots of greenery everywhere. Furnished in what were obviously antiques with black-and-white photographs of horses covering the walls.

"My mother likes plants, she insists they provide lots of oxygen in the day, and the ivy, valerian and jasmine help you sleep. She virtually hires a team to take care of them."

"I'll bet. Well, I'll be comatosed in that case. Does she collect old horse photographs?"

"No, those are our family's horses over the years." The history was everywhere throughout the house. You couldn't help but be impressed, it was special.

"Okay, people, I'm heading to the bar. What are we drinking?" Teddy said, rising from the table.

"Wine and lots of it," Winnie commanded, banging the table.

They ate and sat drinking and talking about nothing and everything for a couple of hours. Glasses were filled and emptied, refilled and re-emptied, before conversation began to quiet down.

"What's everyone doing for Guy Fawkes?" asked Paige, looking around the table. If she was hoping for a sensible reply, she would be disappointed.

"Getting drunk and lighting shit on fire," Winnie said unashamedly.

"Same here," said James, pinging his wine glass.

"Aren't we all," agreed Teddy, his hair flopping into his eyes. "Fire is fun."

"I'm going back home, I think," said Annabel, who was from Jersey.

"What are your plans, Roars?" Winnie asked.

"Nothing. We don't celebrate it. I didn't even know who Guy Fawkes was until I moved here. We had Cracker night in Australia, well, that was until fireworks were banned."

"You didn't know about Guy Fawkes?" asked a shocked James, who looked at her like she didn't know who Santa Claus was.

"It's British History. I didn't learn it." Aurora was used to these sorts of reactions when she admitted she didn't understand or share the same customs.

"Didn't you watch *Horrible Histories* as a kid? I'm sure there was an episode on him," said Harry helpfully.

"No, never heard of that either," she responded, hopelessly lost.

Sophie's eyes lit up. "You know, like the 'Monarchs' Song'," she said joyfully. All the girls except for Aurora began singing the song from the TV show with glee: "William, William, Henry, Stephen..." Teddy sat in the corner across the table just watching Aurora thoughtfully. The girls insisted on singing the song for way too long, until Winnie started winding them up with a bored expression. Aurora sat uncomfortably through the performance, wondering how singing the song was going to enlighten her, and why everyone always thought it would.

"How could you not have seen it?" asked Paige.

"The same way you guys have never seen *Blinky Bill*," she answered. She made her point effectively as they all looked at her with blank expressions.

"What about *Raven*?" asked Annabel.

"Great TV show, that was my childhood," said Harry.

"Nope."

"*Horrid Henry*?" asked Winnie.

"Still no."

These conversations always made her feel like she lacked a proper education or childhood, when she merely had a different one to theirs; the curse of the third-culture kid. It left her feeling apart. She noticed Teddy studying her closely and when she met his gaze he looked away quickly.

"Did you guys get DreamWorks in Australia? You know, *Shrek* and *Ice Age*?" asked James tauntingly.

"Yes, obviously we got *Ice Age*, James," said Aurora, now annoyed. Alcohol had relaxed her to the point that her facial expressions were giving her thoughts away and James decided to shut up. Feeling stupid and three steps behind everyone else always triggered her anxiety and made her bristle with irritation.

"Oh my God, PTSD!" Sophie cut in theatrically, bringing her palm up to make a stop sign and interrupt the conversation.

"From *Ice Age*?" Winnie asked, bemused.

Sophie began to regale them with the tale, her tongue loosened by red wine. "Okay, so there was this one guy I met in the first week of Freshers. He wasn't really good looking, but I thought like, good enough," she said, shrugging. "He seemed nice anyway and we went back to his room. I noticed he did have a rainbow light-up keyboard and two monitors, which I raised an eyebrow at, but I thought he was just a bit of a geek, so all fine." She paused for a moment to take another sip of her drink before continuing. "Then we shagged." She motioned to indicate that it was nothing special. "I must have passed straight out because I can't remember anything else, and then the next thing I know I open my eyes and *boom*, the squirrel from *Ice*

Age is on the TV. I look over, and this guy is sitting up in bed watching intently," she said slowly and dramatically. There was a collective intake of breath from the table. "It was the single weirdest experience of my life," she said breathlessly. "I got straight out of there, like fast. Like what was wrong with him, right? What kind of psycho watches *Ice Age* after shagging?" They all exhaled into peels of laughter.

"Maybe he was trying to get rid of you?" Winnie managed to explain, while practically wetting himself.

"It worked," said Teddy in hysterics, losing it.

"I'm not telling you who it was, it's just too embarrassing, but let's just say never again," she said with conviction, waving her finger side to side drunkenly.

"It was Jasper, wasn't it?" suggested Harry facetiously.

"Honestly, Soph, you have to cool it, you'll take home a serial killer if you're not careful," warned Annabel.

"Your nickname from now on is Scrat," said James, giggling at his ingenuity. "You wanted one, you got it, Scrat."

"Oh yeah, that'll do." Winnie was doubled over, holding his stomach.

"Why Scrat?" Sophie and Paige asked in unison.

"Because it's the squirrel's name," said James.

"God, what is it? Is it a squirrel or a prehistoric mammal?" Teddy mused as he stared at the ceiling, trying to remember the creature from *Ice Age*. "You do share, shall we say, certain characteristics," he said with a sardonic grin.

"The weird ass thing that chases the acorn, dies often, but always rises again," added Harry.

"Is just obsessed!" James spat out the words laughing.

"You're all awful, mean boys. I don't want that to be my nickname." Sophie looked most put out.

"Soph, you don't get to choose," James corrected, "we make up the name and you get given it," he explained like she was a three-year-old. "There's no choice involved."

"Hun, you're the ditzy squirrel thing, just go with it. I'm a chipmunk, it's no big deal," said Paige.

At closing time they all tumbled out of the pub and walked haphazardly back along the road from the village, the low wall girding the estate guided them back to the gates of Esslemont. Joking and laughing, they were well past tipsy. The alcohol combined with the cold autumn air hit them like a wave as they came outside. James and Sophie bounced off one another as they weaved unsteadily along the footpath. He'd been harassing her about being Scrat, now he was sharing some of his stories with her, making her feel better. He wrapped his arm around her as they slowly progressed forward. Pairs naturally formed: Annabel was talking with Paige, Winnie and Harry close behind were interjecting and interrupting their conversation. Teddy fell in beside Aurora. It felt like he was taking every opportunity to be with her, or was she imagining it? They ended up a little way behind the others. They had never talked just the two of them alone, she had avoided him after their first couple of run-ins and he'd also kept his distance, sensing he'd gone too far. She was struggling as the alcohol took control, but even in an intoxicated state she knew she had to keep her guard up around him.

She slipped up as she heard the words, "You smell

nice," come out of her mouth. "What is it?"

"Tom Ford," he answered, smiling softly down at her.

"What? What are you smiling at?"

"Wow the wine has hit you, hasn't it?" She nodded in response. "So, I could ask you anything right now and you might actually answer me truthfully?"

In her foggy brain warning bells were going off, sensing danger. *God, don't ask me if I find you attractive?*

"Maybe."

"You didn't seem keen to come away this weekend. Are you pleased you did?"

Happy to answer that, she smiled up at him, a sleepy, dreamy smile. "Yes." She staggered a little as she answered him and he steadied her, holding onto her arm, looking amused.

He had left the car by the front gates so he could drive them all up to the house for the last mile. James and Sophie, up ahead, were now getting cosy.

"You two knock it off," Harry called out, "you'll regret it in the morning."

Teddy opened the cab at the back and threw James and Sophie in, shutting the door behind them. "Those two are a mess." He walked back to the driver's side. "We'll put three across the front seats. Roars up here," he said, patting the seat. He crossed to where she stood, scooped her up in his arms like he was about to cross a threshold with a new bride, her arms naturally wrapping themselves around his neck, and placed her on the middle seat before climbing up next to her. It happened so fast she didn't have time to protest, she was struggling to keep up with what was going on. She didn't think she'd drunk that much, but she was gone.

She wanted to lean all over Teddy, wanted to just fall asleep on his shoulder, she was suddenly so tired, and he smelt so good.

The last thing she clearly remembered was saying, "You've been so nice today, so different."

Winnie jumped in the front, the other side of her. Paige, Annabel and Harry were all giggling in the back. Teddy sped up the drive and around the back of the house.

"We'll have to go in through the back. I'm not having you lot anywhere near my parents' room," he said, shouting over his shoulder to them in the car.

"Roars is completely gone," observed Winnie. She was slumped against Teddy in the front seat. He and Winnie appeared to be the only two not totally slaughtered. Winnie of course was, but he had such a tolerance he never appeared to be. Teddy had felt somewhat responsible to remain cognitive so hadn't gotten smashed.

"I know she is, I'll carry her upstairs."

"Will you now?" said Winnie, raising his eyebrow at Teddy.

"Don't be stupid. I'll open the back doors, but help me get the others in quietly, and for God's sake separate the two idiots in the back," he instructed.

The others all piled out of the car, staggering and giggling into the house, through the kitchen where the dogs slept, and up the backstairs. The air was still with fine particles of mist floating and revealing themselves in the outdoor lights. Teddy waited until they'd all gone inside before picking Aurora up again. The movement woke her, she was semi-conscious now, eyes half open. The male mastiff Zeus had come outside, checking all was well.

"I love your dogs, I have a dog too. I love my dog," she said, leaning against his shoulder, arms around his neck again.

"Do you now?" He laughed walking in the house, carefully angling sideways so they both fit through the doorway.

"I love animals, all animals." She paused, looking intently into his face. "Do you love animals?"

"I do," he answered soberly, "that's why I don't go out on the shoots. I don't like to see the birds die."

"Huh, I really love otters. Mated otters hold hands when they sleep so they don't float away from each other. Did you know that?" she asked, head still resting on his shoulder as he began climbing the stairs.

"I did not know that, but I'm glad you told me." She could feel his arms wrapped around her as she clung on, breathing in his aroma.

"You're strong. Am I heavy?" She looked up at him with one eye open, head still resting on his chest.

"No, definitely not, you're light as a feather, but I need a rest here," he said halfway up the stairs. He put her down gently and she lay slumped on the stairs leaning on one elbow studying him.

"You're bad, but you're being nice to me. I know what you're doing," she slurred.

"Yep, you are all over it," he said. "You come to my house as a guest, get completely hammered and force me to carry you up to bed," he said, mocking her. "I'm terrible." He hoisted her up again. "You just need to go to bed."

"Yes I do." Her eyes shut. "Alone," she added a second later, still with eyes closed.

"Yes, absolutely," he agreed. He got to her room, breathing heavily, placed her onto the far side of the bed, took her shoes and coat off, pulled back the covers, rolled her back over and covered her. Her eyes were already closed again. He paused for a moment, watching her sleep in the dark, the only light provided by the dimmed hall lights. Her chest rose and fell gently with her breath, lips slightly apart, dark hair falling across the pillow. Smiling softly, he closed the door.

"I have the simplest tastes. I am always satisfied with the best."
— Oscar Wilde

The headache woke her, forcing its way through her subconscious to the surface. She listened for any sound. There wasn't any noise coming from the surrounding rooms or hallway, all was quiet. *Oh God, I'm in my clothes still, did someone have to put me to bed?* she thought with dread. She began to get flashes and snippets of the evening before. It was foggy, and she wasn't sure all of it had happened. She realised that Teddy may have been involved, he was driving and she was sitting next to him; correction, lying on him. *Oh God, what did I say?* She checked her phone: messages from Flynn, her family, the girls and last of all from Teddy. *"We'll be in the orangery downstairs when you wake, Sleeping Beauty."* She needed a shower.

When she found her way into the orangery at the back of the house, there was only Teddy, James and Winnie left. She got lost on the way there, so many corridors and rooms to navigate.

"Ahh here she is. You were hammered! Well, for you that is!" Winnie looked very amused. "Don't think I've ever seen you like that." He grinned from his place at the large dining table. The rich, warm smell of coffee pervaded the air and their empty plates were still in front of them.

"Yes, thank you, Winnie, I have pretty much figured that out. I don't know what happened, we got outside and it just hit me."

"Yes, it did," Teddy chimed in, "like a friggin' freight train."

"Okay, well that is pretty much how it feels right now," she said, wincing.

"Winnie you're in charge of recovery, work your magic on Roars so we can get down to the stables."

"I'm on it," Winnie said, jumping up and heading to the kitchen.

"Winnie said you've ridden, so we're going out, will clear our heads, and I really want to see my horses." Aurora looked at him with misgiving.

They sat in the gorgeous glass-walled and roofed room that they referred to as the orangery. It flowed off the kitchen and ran across the back of the house and connected various rooms up. It was here the dogs slept, in multiple beds by a wood-burning stove. It must have been difficult to keep warm, but it felt cosy and snug as they sat at a huge farmhouse-style dining table. At one end the wood burner was blazing by the large cloud sofas, again covered in white slipcovers. Pillows were scattered randomly across them. Blinds made out of striped ticking were partly pulled across the clear ceiling and some of the windows, and softened the feel of the cold glass. Again plants were everywhere, this time it was ferns. Aurora inwardly admired the room and in particular a collection of antique botanical prints that covered the only solid wall available. The space was relaxed and informal and it looked like the family spent most of their time here.

The dogs came and said good morning, crowding around her, competing for attention. Winnie re-entered with coffee and a glass of orange-flavoured Berocca to wash down the Panadol.

"Did the others all go on the shoot?" she asked.

"Well, Scrat and Alvin were keen to show off to Teddy's parents, and Harry loves it," said James.

"And Annabel?" asked Aurora.

"Oh yeah I forgot about Annabel, she's there too," added James.

Teddy was looking at her from across the table. "Breakfast has just been cleared by Elsa, but it will be warming in the Aga. Can I get you anything?"

She shook her head. "I don't know if it's a good idea." The big mastiff had come to her side and was awaiting attention. She obliged and tickled him behind the ears.

"Toast?"

"Okay, maybe one piece, thank you." She watched Teddy leave the room then put her head in both hands.

"Rough night huh?" said Winnie. "Not as bad as his." He gestured at James. "It seems as though he and Scrat wrestled for the acorn last night."

"God, James, why?" She looked up at James in disbelief.

"I didn't mean for it to happen, it's not like I had control, this shit just happens."

"No it doesn't, James, it's a choice, at some level you make a choice." She wasn't about to let him off that easily.

"Yeah, but she offered, it's not like I was going to say no. She made a choice too," he said defensively. He looked like a naughty schoolboy trying to plead his case.

"She always makes that choice!" Aurora said, raising her voice, exasperated. "You like Diana, though, I know you do?"

"Yeah, okay, that doesn't even come into it. It was just a shag, don't stress, Roars, it's not a problem."

"Fabulous, you're restoring my faith in men," she said derisively.

"Why have you lost faith?" Winnie asked. "I'm sure Teddy was a gentleman as he put you to bed." He was grinning broadly.

"I'm not Alice and this isn't Wonderland, so you can just lose the smile, Winnie." He continued to smirk, enjoying her discomfort. "I couldn't even really be sure someone had, but I had these flashes come back to me, so I figured," she said, cringing. She went back to stroking the dog as Teddy returned with buttered toast and a jug of water that he placed in front of her. Warm buttered toast smelt good to her now it was here.

"Yeah it was me." He smiled smugly. "You were very chatty."

"Was I? About what?" she said, alarmed.

"Your likes and dislikes, your passions, you know, otters came up." James and Winnie exchanged looks, but said nothing. She shuddered internally, she might as well have been stripped bare. She shook her head, closing her eyes. She guessed she must have been raving.

"Okay, you know what, on second thoughts I don't want to know." She didn't want details, ignorance was better. She felt vulnerable and exposed and now she was expected to go out riding with just the lads.

"How much have you guys ridden?" She directed her question to Winnie and James.

"Well, we used to hunt quite a bit as a family," Winnie offered, "although not that much these days. I kind of grew out of it, but my sisters still have horses."

"And you, James?"

"Pony club for years."

Aurora looked despondent. She had ridden a lot when she was younger, having lessons in Singapore and Manila at the Polo Club, but in the last few years, not much. She would be very rusty and riding out with boys born in the saddle, just great. To top it off she was decidedly outnumbered.

"I didn't bring any clothes to ride in," she said thinking of an out, "no jodhpurs or boots? I can just watch you guys."

"Don't worry, we've got loads of spares at the stables. One of the girls will sort you out," he said, dismissing her excuse.

"They'll have all of it?" She looked at him, hoping they wouldn't have boots or something.

"Yes, they will have all of it. If you can ride, you're coming out," he insisted, refusing to let her off the hook.

They arrived at the yard after midday, a beautiful complex matching the house. The entrance was through an archway, boxes were arranged in a square around a central courtyard. At the far end was another arch that led out to two arenas, one fully enclosed for wet weather and one outdoors. Beyond that were paddocks that opened up to 2000 hectares of the glorious Gloucestershire property.

"Right, okay, so this is Lucy, one of the grooms," Teddy said, introducing a girl, "she'll be able to kit you out, Aurora." He disappeared and Aurora followed the young woman to the tack room. She must only have been seventeen.

"I've got some joddies here that should fit, and what size shoe are you?"

"I'm a UK five."

"That's easy enough, just tell me if these are comfortable or not." She handed Aurora a pair of long black riding boots. "You'll all need helmets too."

"Sure will. I haven't ridden much in the last few years, so I'll be rusty," Aurora said gingerly as she slipped the boots on.

"Okay, well, I'm sure Teddy will take you out in the arena first, just to be sure you'll get on okay with Dorian." *Okay, so let's hope my horse isn't named after the Oscar Wilde character*, she thought, feeling more than a touch nervous. "Just change in here," Lucy said after she fitted Aurora's hat. She went off to give the boys theirs. The jodhpurs were classic cream and rather tight. She had worn a long-sleeved base layer with a gilet vest over the top in navy blue with brown leather trim. With boots to the knee she felt dressed for Hickstead. She had to stifle a giggle when she first saw the guys kitted out to ride today. It was odd to see them dressed in riding clothes, breeches and boots, they looked so different. She hadn't known many guys who rode, and after a minute she decided it was a look she could get behind.

When Aurora came outside, Winnie and James were holding their horses, a large grey gelding and chestnut mare.

"So, who are you two riding?" she asked as she put the helmet on.

"Winnie's on Nugget," said James pointing at the dapple grey, "and apparently this is Afterglow." The chestnut mare gleamed in the sunlight and swished her tail impatiently.

"Stop, that's a joke, did Teddy tell you that?"

"He did," said Winnie, now cackling.

Teddy came out leading a very pretty black gelding with a white star. "Roars, this is Dorian. Please be gentle with him, none of your usual treatment, he's my old horse." Dorian was about sixteen hands, not too big, and nuzzled her hand looking for anything she might have to offer.

She took hold of the reins. "So you've given me a beautiful boy with a corrupted soul? I trust that he bears no resemblance to his namesake?"

"You're referring to Oscar Wilde's Dorian, and no he doesn't. He's an Anglo-Arab, an old schoolmaster, he'll look after you." He had a kind eye and Aurora patted his neck as she stood alongside him.

"Okay, thank you. Now what is James' horse really called?" she asked with a smile.

"Piper, and he has to pay one today for his misdeeds last night," Teddy said, smirking at James as he took his horse from Lucy, who led out a stunning dark bay, his espresso brown body nearly black like his mane and tail. The horse was massive, probably seventeen hands she guessed, with a lot of presence. The horses were obviously all finely bred animals, but Teddy's was the most striking as he danced around, moving from one foot to the other, already keyed up." Okay people, let's just see how you all get on with them in the arena before we go out."

They followed him out of the yard to a mounting block. James and Winnie were on first and went into the arena to warm up. Aurora's headache had gone and the adrenalin was in her system now as she pulled the stirrup irons down the leathers and prepared to mount.

"I just need to check your seat," said Teddy, smiling and watching her from behind. "It looks fine, but I need to see it on horseback."

"Excuse me?" she said, swinging her head around to check him. He looked good in his kit, very much at home in grey coloured jodhpurs, long black boots and a black gilet over a long, fitted, black base layer.

"In the name of safety, I need to check you have three correct paces, out you go," he flirted as she swung her leg over. He smacked the rump of her horse, sending her off into the arena. He went and leant over the fence, amusing himself at their expense.

"Roars, your stirrups look too long, how do they feel?"

"Yeah, like I'm reaching for them, really."

"Come here and I'll adjust them," he said, walking into the centre to get to her.

"It's okay, I can do it," she said, beginning to fumble around and pull on the leather. He ignored her completely, moving her leg aside to adjust them. His touch in broad daylight made her quiver and the horse, feeling the tension, moved under her. Teddy moved to the other side and did the same again, this time all the while looking up at her and holding her gaze as he expertly changed the stirrup hole. It sent shivers up her spine and her stomach lurched.

She moved off afterwards and put Dorian into trot, then five minutes later asked for canter and he went like a dream, beautifully responsive but sensible. He carried his tail high, a result of the Arab blood in him, as they moved gracefully around the arena.

"Are you all happy? I don't want anyone to break their neck." Teddy clearly felt responsible, which was good because she was more than a little concerned herself. She would have to take it easy. At least the horse seemed very obliging.

"Nugget and I have an understanding, I think," said Winnie.

"I'm good with Piper," confirmed James. "Let's go." He was clearly enjoying himself.

"Yeah I reckon I'm okay. I'm rusty, but it's coming back to me," Aurora said positively.

"I'm confident you'll get into rhythm with him quickly," Teddy said, swinging himself easily into the saddle of the big bay, and then leading them out.

"Are you enjoying yourself then?" she asked archly, pulling alongside him.

"I'm having a great time," he said, looking behind him to see how close his mates were. Winnie and James were happily chatting a few metres away. "You're finally talking to me."

"You so asked for everything I dished out."

"Yeah, I did, I get it. I'm sorry, I didn't mean to offend you, really I didn't. You are savage, and I don't mean in the native sense," he said quickly, holding up his hands, letting the reins drop.

"I'm my mother's daughter."

"Your mum is fiery then?"

"Yes."

"My mum's pretty tough too," he said. "She's nice and all, but she's formidable. She used to practise law, she was ruthless."

"She is a little intimidating. Well, more so than your dad, who seemed like a bit of a joker."

"Yes, she is. I can see how you would get there."

"So, where are we going then?"

"I'm going to give you a tour of the property and throw in a challenge or two for fun," he answered cryptically.

"Oh God, no challenges today, just a nice gentle hack sounds good."

"So how much riding have you done?"

"I loved it growing up, but I haven't ridden much in England, too busy with school. You look like you're pretty into it?"

"Yeah, I am. I event as much as possible on Bear here," he said, patting his horse. "It's been a big part of my life until uni. I'll do more in summer, and I play polo too."

"Of course you do," she said dryly, unsurprised to hear he was part of *that* set.

"Yeah, I play for the uni," he admitted a little reluctantly. They had a rep, much like the Shooting Society.

"So, are you an Oscar Wilde fan, naming your horse Dorian and all?"

"We didn't breed him, he came to us as Dorian."

"Okay, well, I'm a fan," she said, patting the horse.

"I'm pleased to have paired you up then. I haven't read any of his novels, I'm more into historical fiction or fantasy myself."

"So, you watched *Horrible Histories* too then?"

"Not often." He gave her a considered look as he

weighed up whether to say what was on his mind.

"What?... Just say it?" She wondered what could make him suddenly look serious.

"You wrote in your manifesto for student rep that you know what it feels like to be in a strange land where nothing is familiar and you're the foreigner wherever you live, the odd one, that you know what it's like to be other." He looked at her sincerely.

"Yes." She paused momentarily before adding with surprise: "You actually read it?"

"I did and I didn't really understand what *other* meant until last night during that conversation. I got it then." He paused for a bit before adding thoughtfully, "Does that happen a lot?"

"All the time," she said flatly.

"It must make you feel left out, leave you feeling a little empty?"

Aurora just stared at him, touched that he of all people should understand.

"It does."

"It's pretty basic stuff. It's human nature to want to be part of the tribe."

"If it's basic stuff, why does no one ever get it?" she asked earnestly.

"Because they're just having some bloody fun, enjoying their memories, talking shit, too busy worrying about themselves to think about anyone else. To understand, they'd have to put themselves in your shoes, and most people don't like to do that. Most people are only thinking about themselves, that's human nature too."

"I try not to react, but I had too many drinks last night." She looked guiltily down at his horse's hooves as Bear pranced along the bridleway.

Teddy, sensing her mood change, decided to change the subject. "You must have read *Lord of the Rings*?" he guessed. She giggled shyly, remembering their breakfast scrap and looked across at him. He had a grin on his face. "The Shelob reference gave that away."

"Yeah, I'm sort of into fantasy too," she admitted. "So, are you a *Game of Thrones* fan?" she asked, fishing for common ground.

"Of course. How far down the rabbit hole can we go?"

"All the way," she said confidently.

They discussed their favourite scenes, season eight, and debated how the show should have ended, then moved on to Marvel and *Star Wars*.

"So, tell me more about otters." He was playful and jovial today, gone was the caustic humour from their earlier meetings.

"How much did I reveal?" She looked away, out over the rolling green fields, noticing how they gently undulated in this part of the country on the edge of the Cotswolds. The view was spectacular.

"You said that they hold hands when they're sleeping so they don't lose each other, which is something I didn't know and I watch a lot of *Animal Planet*."

"I know, isn't that amazing?" She turned back to make eye contact. "They are just the cutest animals, I have to admit they make me melt. Mother otters also tie their babies up in the kelp while they look for food. They just do it for me."

He was smiling at her. "I can see that."

They were quiet for a moment. Teddy was looking back to see how far behind the guys were.

"Do you want to give them a run up this rise?" he

said, looking ahead. "Yes, I'd love to." She had forgotten how much she enjoyed riding, especially on a well schooled horse. The hill before them had a long, slow gradient and Teddy now urged Bear into a canter and she followed suit on Dorian.

They continued to ride for about an hour through the extensive farmland of the estate, eventually reaching a river where they turned left, continuing along its banks and following it as it meandered through the rolling green countryside. The autumn leaves were falling, and swirled in drifts around the base of the trees. It was out of a book and off a movie screen. The wide river flowed slowly and patiently through the greenery. In her short life Aurora didn't think she'd ever experienced so much beauty in one place as she had during the last twenty-four hours at Esslemont.

Conversation was easy, the boys' harassment of each other funny, duly tempered in her presence, and Teddy was nothing short of charming and gracious. She felt herself relax with him as she spent most of the afternoon laughing while they rode through the estate with the sun on them. They naturally found themselves next to each other over and over again, talking about the horses and riding, or the farmland and what they usually reared or farmed on it.

The sun was weakening and clouds were approaching as they headed further into the afternoon, and as they entered a more woody section of the property it became darker still. After fifteen minutes they came out of the woods and found themselves on a manicured rolling lawn.

"Okay, so now we are on a section of the cross-country course, it's designed by Captain Mark Phillips, so it's a proper challenge. We can jump some, but take it easy. Eventers and amateurs pay to bring their horses here and put them round the course," Teddy informed them.

"Okay, I'm in," said James. "Pip and I are up for taking a few." He put the rangy mare into a canter and disappeared up the rise towards the course.

"If he does anything to that horse, I'll kill him," Teddy said, thinking out loud, watching carefully, "she's one of my mum's favourites."

"Shit, who loves Nugget here?" Winnie panicked, stroking the big grey's neck.

Teddy just smiled before spurring his horse off in pursuit of James, who was taking his first jump. Teddy collected the big bay in, approaching the fence as one unit, driving him forward and soaring over it. He wheeled the big horse around and cantered back towards them. Aurora watched him mesmerised, feeling like she was in a trance and having an out-of-body experience. She had to concede she was impressed. The best things in life come out of the blue, she mused, when we don't contrive or orchestrate, they just happen naturally.

"Come on, the next one is more forgiving than this fence," he shouted down to them, his handsome face lit up. Winnie and Aurora cantered up after him and so it began. The horses felt the excitement and responded in kind, on their toes and pulling, keen. The wind had whipped up now, and it didn't help to settle them down, dark clouds were brewing from the west.

As she reached Teddy, he quizzed her: "Have you done much jumping?" He was looking up at the rising front and then back at her, concerned.

"A bit but always in an arena, never anything like

this."

"He's a pro, you don't have to drive him over, just let him take control, he loves it, but don't push it if you don't want to. Err on the side of caution, you don't need to jump anything."

The boys took off one at a time, putting the horses at the odd fence, missing out some, except for Teddy, who was guiding Bear through the course. The young horse had a lot of scope but was pulling hard and wanted to be in charge, he was a handful. At first Aurora was intimidated and fear settled in her gut as she looked at the solid fences, so she just cantered along beside them all, but then she felt like she was really missing out. "Come on, come on don't wuss out," she said, chiding herself.

The next fence was a sizable but simple log and she set Dorian at it. "Come on boy we can do this, take me over," she said to the horse, sitting in on approach, letting him decide how he wanted to take it. His ears went forward and he cantered up to it, gathering himself and effortlessly clearing it. She took the odd fence thereafter, growing in confidence, mindful that she didn't want to be too stupid, but also not a coward. It was exhilarating and the adrenaline rush after each fence was sensational. They all had a ball and as they climbed the last rise, she let Dorian have his head. She rocked forward in the saddle; the horse responded, stretching out and flattening, his powerful black haunches propelling them both up the hill, his tail held high like a banner fanning out behind him. He felt like a race car hitting top gear. The wind tore at her face and tears streamed down in response as they glided past the others. As she pulled up she wiped them from her eyes, her face glowing and animated. "That was so much fun, he was amazing!" she gushed to Teddy, unable to contain her joy and pleasure.

"That's the thoroughbred in him, he can move."

"You were flying, Roars," said Winnie, arriving. "Nugget here isn't built for speed."

"No, he's built more for comfort," said Teddy.

They headed for the stable complex, now in view ahead through the paddocks. The wind continued to build, gusting at times, wild and tempestuous, which only added to their exhilaration.

"You ride well," said Teddy admiringly as they rode four abreast.

"Not like you guys, but thank you. At least I didn't fall off. I was being a bit of a sook and didn't go over the first, like, three fences, but Dorian here gave me confidence."

The boys looked at her strangely. "What did you just say? Sook?" asked Teddy, confused. "What's a sook?"

"You know, sook."

"No, we don't," said James, "is that some sort of weird Australianism?"

"I thought it was universal, it's a wimp, someone with no backbone," she explained.

"Oh you mean like a wuss?" said Winnie.

"Yes, or as you often like to say, wet," she answered.

"I don't actually think that describes you." Teddy said, shaking his head. She felt herself glow from the compliment.

She was pleased she had come out, pleased she had pushed herself. The weekend was turning out to be full of surprises.

"I can resist anything except temptation."
– Oscar Wilde, Lady Windermere's Fan

Dinner was in the grand dining hall. Tonight they were all attired more formally. It had been a day of changing. Breakfast clothes, shooting and riding clothes, changing again for afternoon tea, and now dinner. There was correct attire for every activity. For dinner the girls had all elected to wear dresses. Aurora had brought along a demure ankle-length silk satin dress with puffy bishop sleeves. It was in a rust colour with tiny shank buttons covered in the same fabric all the way down the front to knee height, before it fell into a split. Chaste and elegant, but interesting. The girls chatted away about the day while getting dressed, doing hair and makeup in and out of each other's rooms.

"Aurora, can you help me style this?" came Sophie's voice from down the hall.

"Sure, coming." The girls were constantly asking for her advice when it came to choosing an outfit or styling and she was flattered. She considered Sophie's outfit for a second. "You need more jewellery. What do you have?" Sophie pointed to a small bag on the bed.

"So, you and Teddy looked cosy at afternoon tea?" Sophie prodded as she stared in the mirror.

"Did we?" Aurora looked mystified as she combed through her jewellery. "I'm really only just on speaking terms with him."

"Oh okay, well, he seemed flirty to me."

"You think everybody's flirting all the time, Sophie." Amused, Aurora smiled at her as she handed her a long chain with a pendant.

Sophie laughed, more like a guffaw. "I love boys, I just do, can't help it."

"I know, you're just you."

The boys opted for chinos and shirts, unlike Tom and Bill, who were both wearing sports jackets with pocket squares. Teddy's chinos, though, were fitted with side pockets and cuffed at the ankle, just above his chocolate brown loafers, and showed off his athletic frame well. Aurora loved his sense of style; like he needed that on top of the rest of his attributes. Harry could also really dress and he looked gorgeous in black trousers and a black cotton shirt, simple but striking with his black framed glasses.

As they entered the formal dining room, Aurora was dwarfed by its grandeur. From the chandelier hanging majestically metres in the air above the enormous, ebony regency dining table, to the padded high-back chairs covered in classic Bowood chintz, it was opulent and elegant. Large family portraits of immense scale lined the walls again, capped off by an exquisite French trumeau mirror that hung above the marble fireplace. The room was simply painted in a stone white to allow the portraits on the wall to be the main feature. Thick textured curtains in a taupe covered the windows.

"The house is absolutely beautiful," Aurora said to Constance over drinks. Constance looked pleased in her wide-legged trousers and silk shirt, her outfit a reflection of their stylish home. Aurora thought to herself *how strange life is. Less than a month ago I was calling her son a racist fuckwit and now I'm here making polite conversation.*

They took their seats and Aurora found herself seated between Bill and Winnie, down the same end of the table as Constance, who was at the head. Teddy was sitting on his mother's right, nearly opposite Aurora, and at the other end of the table at the head was Teddy's dad, Tom. It all was extremely formal and Aurora again felt wobbly and cripplingly self-conscious. She mentally thanked her parents for being so pedantic about table manners. Caterers had been brought in for the night and dinner was served by their staff. They started with a wild mushroom soup and homemade sourdough, the mushrooms having been foraged for in their woods, followed by roasted partridge shot on the estate.

"Teddy, what interests are you pursuing outside of law?" Bill inquired.

"I'm playing polo and rugby and I've joined the Shooting Society with all of these guys," he said, gesturing to all of his friends at that table.

"Rugby, yes, you used to be very good at it as I recall."

"I'm just not built for it. I need to put on some serious bulk, and it's just not happening," Teddy explained.

"You look like you've filled right out to me."

"Yes, I'm in the gym a lot now, but I'm still the lightest guy on the field by far."

"I'm glad you've continued playing, Teddy, you loved it during your time at Radley," said his mother. "Have you signed up for any associations?"

"Ahh no, Mum, I'm happy just doing sport."

Constance didn't look thrilled with his response and began to talk about the virtues of being engaged with committees and causes. Aurora was sitting next to Bill, who then turned his attention to her, including her in conversation.

"Aurora, do you play any sport?"

"Apart from the clay pigeon shooting, which I've never done before, I've taken up ultimate frisbee." *Here it comes*, she thought, knowing he wouldn't have heard of the sport, it would not have featured at Harrow and Eton.

"Ultimate frisbee?" Bill pondered, trying to recall if he had ever come across it before. "What are the rules involved?"

"It's played on a football field with end zones, and you score by catching the disc inside the end zone. You can't run with it, it must be passed from player to player, like netball."

"It's a sport for virgins," Winnie whispered teasingly.

"The Shooting Society is considered the ultimate

posh twat sport, you know?" she whispered back.

"What made you want to join that?" interrupted Teddy, watching them, and leaving the conversation with his mother.

"My parents both played, they represented Australia, but it's just an amateur sport," she answered shyly.

"That's cool." Teddy nodded appreciatively.

"Wow that's impressive," said Bill. He was probably only being polite, but Aurora had already decided he was a pleasure to be seated next to.

"How unusual. Do they actually run that as a sport at Bristol?" asked Constance, who was forced to abandon her hopes of coercing Teddy to join the Conservative Association. Her tone suggested the idea was outrageous.

"Ahhh yes they do." Aurora wasn't sure if she was interested or trying to make a point. "It's a proper sport, recognised by the International Olympic Committee, they're hoping to be included in the Olympics soon," she muttered, attempting to defend the activity.

"Well, I'll look out for it, I've never come across it before," Constance declared.

Aurora thought she was warming up, but obviously the woman was hard to read. She took a deep breath and tried to settle herself down. She could feel Teddy's eyes on her and looked up to meet them; they were kind and seemed to be saying *don't worry about my mum.*

They moved on to the main course and she struggled with the partridge. Although it was supposedly similar to chicken, she had never eaten a game bird before and wasn't coping with the strong flavour. She was starving, having eaten little during the day, and decided to load her plate with the roasted celeriac, parsnips and potatoes, hoping the hostess didn't notice. All the vegetables were homegrown on the estate, Constance had proudly informed them earlier.

Bill was an ex London banker. He amused them all during dinner with his conversation, stories of his travels and interesting snippets of life. To say he was charming would be correct, but it was the ease with which he delivered a story, relaxed and effortless, his manner devoid of arrogance, indisputably comfortable in his own skin. Aurora was envious, she wanted to feel that way as she sat at the table, amused by the dialogue, but feeling somewhat in awe. She knew she wasn't a lesser being, she was just as worthy as anyone else sitting there, but this was a different world, one she hadn't ever touched before, and all she could do was attempt to keep up and contribute where possible, try to keep her head above water.

The conversation turned to art trading and Aurora found that she could participate more as Bill talked about the art he bought and sold as a hobby. She felt like she was in the hands of a seasoned pro when it came to dinner conversation. Together they discussed new and up-and-coming artists, what mediums he was interested in and various movements. Teddy was being grilled by his mother again. Tonight was probably her only opportunity as she saw it to get in his ear. They had differing views, as he was content to cruise, play sport and party hard this first year.

Annabel, who was sitting next to him, politely looked the other way and watched Winnie tease James and Sophie while Bill and Aurora talked. Winnie was holding court at the centre of the table, subtly stirring the pot. With James sitting opposite, next to Sophie, it was just too tempting. "How was the shooting today, Scrat?" he prodded. "Did you bag anything so far this weekend? Grouse, pheasant, cockerel?" he baited.

"Winnie," she said, looking daggers. This would only serve to spur him on.

"Come on, you rarely miss your mark once you've acquired a target," he said, enjoying his wine, grinning wickedly.

James looked reasonably unruffled, fully expecting the ribbing to go on all night, as he made his way through the dessert of baked stone fruit with mascarpone cream. Paige, sitting next to Winnie, was laughing and drinking her wine, but kept looking down the other end of the table towards Teddy, trying to assess the conversation there. She clearly wasn't remotely interested in the discussion Harry was having with Tom and Maggie about sustainable farming.

At the conclusion of dinner, Teddy pulled out the chair for his mother and they all thanked her as they rose from the table. The younger generation was now free to do as they pleased and they settled around the wood burner with the dogs.

"Winnie, go and get your guitar," Teddy demanded. Winnie disappeared upstairs, returning with it to the orangery, apparently ready to play for them.

"How come I've never heard you play?" Aurora quizzed, narrowing her eyes and looking put out.

"What? Was I going to just start performing in halls? Who wants to be that guy?" He pulled a face that said he certainly didn't.

"We would have loved it," Aurora reprimanded.

"Well, I shall play for you now. What would you like

to hear?" he said with mock formality. He took his shoes off and sat in the corner on top of the U-shaped sofa. His audience sprawled below in comfort.

Teddy went to retrieve more wine, which Aurora refused, determined not to repeat last night's performance. She sat down on the floor next to the mastiffs' bed in front of the fire. Ever since the first night, the big male, Zeus, had been following her around every chance he got. His partner, Hera, was also a big softy. Tonight they were stretched out like a pair of lions. The two pointers lay in their beds, exhausted after a day in the field.

"Can you sing?" asked Annabel in surprise.

"Oh yeah, he can sing. He's good," said Harry, nodding in appreciation while he stroked a French bulldog on his lap.

"'Castle on the Hill'," Teddy called out, returning with two bottles of wine and a bottle of Baileys.

Winnie began to play, clearly at home with the instrument, his voice mellow, smooth and strong. The girls' mouths fell open, rapidly followed by squeals of delight. Winnie smiled at the adulation. Aurora listened beaming. She reflected that having someone surprise you is rare and one of the great joys in life. Some people are in a rush to show you all of themselves, lay out their achievements, their assets, monetary or physical. Others have the confidence and humility to slowly reveal themselves to those worthy, to those who get close enough.

That set the scene for the next few hours: provided red wine kept coming, he would play. They requested songs and his repertoire was wide and varied and they sang along with him. Teddy offered Aurora a Baileys; he had been a most attentive host again, she thought.

She felt he'd been trying to engage with her all day. Was it because he was the host? Was it expected of him by his parents? Was she receiving extra special attention? He handed her the drink and sat down on the rug beside her and the dogs. The mood had calmed now. Aurora could feel Paige's eyes on them and she squirmed in the glare. She had sensed her scrutiny ever since she had returned from the shoot, soaking wet and in poor humour. The heavens had opened just after the riders had returned and the shooters had been caught in it. Aurora tried to ignore Paige's attention now; nothing was happening, nothing would happen. She could resist Teddy's charm and bad weather was not her fault.

"Goo Goo Dolls," Teddy requested.

Winnie took a swig of his drink, thirsty from singing. "Yes, excellent taste as always, mate, which one are you after?"

"'Iris'," he said, leaning back against the end of the sofa staring into the fire, his face turned away from the others, leaving it visible only to Aurora while he slowly stroked a dog.

Winnie began to sing and at some point in the song, Teddy turned his head to look directly at her, drawing her gaze to him. She resisted; it would be inviting him in and she wasn't willingly going there, she continued staring straight ahead. She'd been stealing glances at him all night, listening to his conversation, watching him handle himself in company, and admiring his form. She knew she was guilty of that, and he'd caught her a few times. Perhaps she had encouraged him. Winnie's honeyed voice, combined with the chords on the guitar, were an emotive combination. Perhaps it was the alcohol, the warmth of the fire and dogs, or the words of the song, but Aurora was moved. Unable to stop herself, she looked up at Teddy, whose gaze was relentless. He was the only guy she'd ever known who seemed to devour you with his eyes, a whole conversation with just a look. In semi-darkness the fire gently smouldered.

At the end of the song he leant over to her and quietly asked: "Would you help me take the dogs out before bed?" She didn't feel she could refuse and with every passing moment she was feeling more and more drawn to him. They slipped out to the boot room and put on wellies. She borrowed his mother's Barbour, putting it on over her silk dress to protect her from the cold.

The dogs were reluctant but compliant, they knew the routine was not negotiable. They dispersed into the garden once outside and Aurora breathed in the damp, fresh air, re-invigorated from the earlier storm, earthy and pungent, full of life. She caught Teddy's unmistakable scent too as he approached her, standing close. The garden was laid mainly to lawn, enclosed entirely by thick hedges, and an old walled kitchen garden lay off to the left through the mist the rain had left behind.

"I'm sorry about my mum. I think she means it as a compliment, you can never be sure with her."

"I can see it runs in the family," she said sarcastically, swinging around to smile lightly so he knew she was joking.

"Well, bigotry aside, I hope you've had a good time so far?" he asked, moving closer, looking at her reaction.

"Well, the parts I can remember have been very good." She grinned, looking at him behind her. He smiled at her reference to the night before. "You've been the perfect host," she said lightly.

"So, are you seeing someone at the moment?" he asked cautiously without looking directly at her.

A little taken aback, she answered slowly and carefully: "I'm talking to someone, a friend of Paige's boyfriend." She didn't look at him either, continuing to watch the dogs as they made their way around the garden.

"That guy Paige was talking about. But you're not with him per se?"

"No, I'm not *with* him, I've been out with them in a group a couple of times, but that's all. There's not much to say at the moment, he just keeps messaging me and he did ask me to go out this weekend, but I chose to come here." She took another couple of steps. She felt a bit like she was being stalked by a big cat, but then he was so very charming about it, so charming that it was pleasant to be hunted. She continued to walk further into the garden, towards the walled area, keeping him on the move.

"Great, so I can enter the fray then?" he asked, smiling cheekily.

"You can, but the only person you'll be sparring with is me." If he got too close it would be dangerous, she could feel it, and although he'd appeared to be nothing short of lovely and genuine this weekend, she was still skittish.

"I thought we'd moved past that?"

"Maybe we have, but it all depends on your behaviour," teasing him now.

"I've been trying to figure out how to get you alone, away from everyone else," he said sincerely, moving around to stand in front of her, forcing her to look at him. He was very much entering her personal space now, and she had vague recollections of intimacy from last night. She was aware that she wanted to fall into him again. She raised her eyes and he just held her gaze, not moving any closer, hands in his chino pockets, waiting for her response.

"Hey, what are you guys doing out here?" came a voice from behind them. Aurora jumped. Paige had followed them outside and now stood ten metres away, arms wrapped around herself, shivering in the mist; a ghostly apparition.

"Just putting the dogs out before bed," Teddy answered calmly, looking over at her. "You need a coat," he said, redirecting his gaze back to Aurora and holding it, "it's quite cold."

"I'm okay, I just wanted some fresh air. Winnie has stopped playing," she said, staring at them, assessing the situation and taking it all in.

"Fair enough, he must have just about strained his voice by now," Aurora murmured, looking away.

"We're coming," Teddy said gruffly, whistling up the dogs then turning to look at Aurora again, but the moment had passed.

They moved back inside and Aurora sat down beside Winnie, feeling flushed. "Winnie, you've been holding out on me, you're amazing." He was sitting back on the sofa having a well earned rest, worn out now from a long day and night.

"Thank you, I've got a little band together at uni, a couple of guys I've known for a while and we're practising each week."

"Well, I think you've found your calling. It's really cool. I had no idea.

Do you write your own songs too?"

"I do, but they aren't ready for anyone to hear yet."

Paige interjected, "You're so good you could play at one of the balls or parties. You know I could get you a gig? The next big event is the Valentine's Day Ball and the theme is Classic Movie Couples," she proudly announced.

"Great theme," said Harry.

"You guys gave me the idea," said Aurora, unwilling to let Paige have the credit. "The way you all walked into the last ball, like you were part of young Hollywood," she mocked.

"Obviously we sold it," said James confidently.

"So, you all have to get partnered up and choose a pair to go as. Aurora, you could ask Flynn to go?" Paige said suggestively.

"I could, but I'm so tired right now I'm not thinking about it," she said, refusing to entertain the conversation. "I think I'm just going to head to bed. Where's Annabel?"

"She's gone already," said James.

"Take Soph with you, girls, we don't want her roaming the halls after dark," said Teddy, who was locking the back door.

"I resent that, I'm not a child to be minded," she piped up, "and it wasn't just me!"

"Babe, come on," Paige said to Sophie. "On past form you cannot be trusted, up to bed."

"Tomorrow, let's just sleep in and play tennis before heading back," Teddy suggested, looking to catch Aurora's eye, but she was already moving towards the door. They all agreed a relaxing start to the day sounded good.

Aurora lay in bed, thoughts whirling happily through her mind, unable to sleep from the interaction with Teddy as she thought about the day's events. It was impossible not to feel flattered with the attention.

Half an hour later, as she was just drifting off to sleep, she heard whimpering and scratching at her door. She opened it to find Zeus, who had managed to get out of the orangery and was roaming the house freely, finding his way to her room. "What are you doing up here, you naughty boy. You're not supposed to be here, come back downstairs."

She took him by the collar and down the main staircase; she didn't dare try to find the back stairs, the house was so enormous that she wasn't confident navigating it. The hall lights on the main landing were left dimmed all night and in the gloomy light she found her way to the kitchen and deposited the big mastiff there. "Good boy, I'll see you in the morning for a cuddle."

On the return trip she paused at the bottom of the main staircase, in the dim light above she could see there was movement on the landing. A small figure was moving stealthily along. Aurora saw a flash of blonde hair and immediately assumed Sophie was making her way to James. However, at the top of the staircase, Paige came briefly into view before turning right and going straight into Teddy's bedroom. She didn't knock, she didn't hesitate, and she disappeared inside.

Aurora heard the sharp intake of breath, only to realise it was her own. Her stomach dropped, her mind was reeling. It suddenly hit her that they could have something going on. Paige was territorial around Teddy, she had worked hard to impress his parents all weekend, and it would explain the constant scrutiny. The realisation hit her hard in the solar plexus. She was shocked. Her thoughts turned to Teddy. It was so naive to think he'd done an about face within 48 hours. Her hands went to her face as she realised too late that she'd let her defences down, she had let him in. Aurora climbed the stairs in a daze, staggering back down the hall to bed.

So it's all a game? He's been playing me. What about Paige? What about her boyfriend?

She felt like a gullible fool, mixing in these circles, trying to convince herself people were just people, that the class issue didn't exist today, kidding herself that she could ever fit in. Suddenly she felt so ridiculous. She lay in bed listening to the rain pouring down, contemplating it all.

Eventually she drifted off to sleep, confused and full of crippling self-doubt.

12

Aurora woke and immediately remembered the scene from the night before. She sat up in bed, looking around the beautiful room she was sleeping in. The girls had said she had the nicest room last night when they were all getting ready together. She opened the curtains and looked out at the view: green manicured lawn stretching down to paddocks filled with horses. It sure was pretty, even on a grey morning. The sun would be lucky to break through today. As she thought about what she had seen the night before, she felt the anger start to rise inside her. Last night before she went to sleep, a part of her brain had tried to tell her that she had gotten it all wrong, that he hadn't been flirting with her all day. However, in the sober morning light, he so obviously had. Perhaps there was a reasonable explanation for Paige's nighttime visit? Aurora just couldn't think what could be so pressing. She couldn't find a reasonable explanation, because there wasn't one, she rationalised.

Breakfast was a quiet affair as one by one they made it to the orangery. Harry was making pancakes with Annabel in the enormous, professional- looking kitchen. His artistry seemed to know no bounds, and he was a dab hand in the kitchen as well. Teddy was dressed in his riding clothes and had obviously already been out. Aurora, subdued after her nighttime discovery, sat next to James and Winnie, avoiding chat with Teddy, amusing herself playing with the dogs. Paige was the last to come down, as the clock approached midday, looking somewhat contrite. She didn't look at Teddy as she took a seat and poured herself a coffee and took a pancake.

"You slept late, Alvin, big night with the chipmunks?" questioned James. She gave him a sour look and took a sip of her coffee. She was not a morning person at the best of times.

After breakfast, it was time for the promised game of tennis, a round- robin competition of Harry and Winnie's conception. Aurora wore a pleated tennis skirt, white polo and her younger brother's V-neck cricket jumper to keep warm. They headed out to the court that lay at the far end of the back garden, through a gate in the hedge. There they found a hard court and a weatherboard pavilion with comfy chairs and a table.

"Okay, this will be a round-robin competition, every

pair will play each other, best of three sets, and the partnership with the most sets won in total wins. The Viscount here has agreed to keep the refreshments flowing all afternoon."

Teddy looked bemused and gestured for Winnie to move it along. "Get to the important bit, who's playing with who?"

"Well," said Harry, "we decided that, as we have four girls and four boys, obviously mixed doubles had to be the way to go, so we selected teams randomly out of a hat, seemed the only fair way not knowing anyone's ability." Aurora felt herself mentally requesting she be spared Teddy as a partner. "So, we have Annabel and James, Teddy and Scrat, Alvin and myself, and Winnie and Roars."

There was a rumbling of reactions to the announcement. Teddy was looking less than thrilled. Winnie came over and high-fived Aurora. "Can you play?" he asked quietly.

"Yeah I can play," she said with some grit.

"Good, we've got this," he whispered to her. He knew that if she openly acknowledged she could play, then she could really play.

First up was Annabel and James versus Teddy and Sophie, and the games began. The two teams were relatively evenly matched. James and Teddy, clearly very athletic boys, were both carrying their partners. In the end Teddy and Sophie prevailed over James and Annabel but it was an even match. Harry and Paige were the weakest combination, and they were up against Winnie and Aurora next, both very capable players who put them to the sword quickly. Winnie had great technique, but not as much power or athleticism as Teddy and James. Aurora was on fire: angry and competitive, she let loose. Sport was important in her family and tennis was a game they played well. Her mother told stories of her grandfather diving across the tennis court to get to a ball in a family game of tennis.

As she stepped onto the court to play Teddy and Sophie, Aurora looked at him properly for the first time that day. She couldn't restrain herself as she stood still opposite him on the court, a cold stare boring into his soul. She saw he was perplexed, not really understanding the reason for her change in humour.

The game began with Winnie's serve, which he held comfortably. Teddy was next and his powerful serve saw him win that game, but not before there was some wicked net play, with Sophie taking blows until he took control and told her to move back and leave most of the shots to him.

During Sophie's serve, Teddy tried to start mid-court and move back to help her at the baseline, but Aurora, seeing this, wound up her forehand, aiming directly at his body every time the ball was served to her. "Whoa, that was savage!" said Winnie, laughing as Teddy took a blow just under his ribs. With Sophie's serve being on the weaker side, it was easy to manipulate. There was no mistaking it was "game on" and the spectators were amused, watching the match play out with interest.

"Wow, Roars is playing with fire in the belly," said James.

"She seems to have Teddy firmly in her sights," commented Harry.

"Poor Sophie looks a bit shellshocked out there!" observed Annabel.

By the time Aurora's serve came around, there was no mistaking who had a target on their back. Winnie was enjoying himself on the net: "Don't let Soph and I get in the way at all, Roars, get stuck in." Any mistake by Sophie or Teddy and he pounced on it at the net, backing up his team mate. They duelled back and forth, a power struggle was taking place. Teddy looked somewhat baffled, and he kept trying to catch her eye. He was playing his shots too, but it was obvious she wanted to bury him.

As they changed ends he deliberately went to her side and tried to reach her: "Aurora what's going on today?" but she refused to respond. Defeat to Teddy and Sophie came after two straight sets. At the conclusion of all the matches it was obvious Winnie and Aurora had been dominant, even before adding up the number of sets each team had won.

"We are the champions my friends ..." sang Winnie, as he poured himself a drink from a jug of water.

"Remind me never to get on your bad side," James directed at Aurora, who stood off to the side away from the crowd around the drinks table.

"I'm just competitive, I guess," she said as lightly as she could muster, and began walking away.

She couldn't wait to get back to Bristol now and made her way directly to the house. Smashing the ball at him hadn't really quelled the disappointment. She realised that disappointment seemed to be the overriding feeling she was experiencing. She was disappointed in herself for letting someone like him in.

"Aurora, what's wrong?" said Teddy, chasing her down, well ahead of the others. "I thought we had a moment last night?"

"We did, Teddy, but then you reverted to type!" she said as scathingly as she possibly could.

"I did what?" he stammered, looking completely

lost.

"I know Paige went to your room last night, and I can't think of a reasonable explanation as for why?" she said, eyes full of condemnation. She saw the look of realisation cross his face as it dawned on him she knew, and that was all she needed. She strode back to the house ahead of him, tennis skirt swishing side to side from her vigorous strides.

"No, no, no," was all she heard from behind her.

She went to her room and packed, flinging things into her bag carelessly. The girls were in and out of her room, chatting as they all packed.

"Hun, you were fierce out there today, you okay?" asked Paige, looking concerned.

"I'm fine, I'm just too competitive when it comes to tennis, you know." Aurora was going to fan this competitive spirit thing like her life depended on it.

"I thought you were angry with Teddy," said the ever-observant Annabel.

"No, why would I be angry with him, he's been a superb host," she lied.

"He has," agreed Annabel.

"It's been so good, I don't want to go back to halls," wailed Sophie. "I like it here, who wouldn't want to live here?" she asked them all plaintively.

"Yes, well, most of the population don't live this way, Sophie, so I'm sure you'll cope," Aurora snapped. The other girls looked at each other and Annabel raised her eyebrows. Aurora stayed silent then. The girls continued chattering away without including her. She pretended all was normal, anything else was too difficult and she didn't want a scene or any drama, she just wanted to get away.

As they said their goodbyes and thank yous to their

hosts and the Macfarlane's, it was a genuine exchange of gratitude. Bill approached Aurora and kissed her goodbye warmly. "I wish you all the best with your studies, Aurora. Thank you for your company at dinner last night, Maggie and I were saying this morning how much we have enjoyed spending time with you all."

"Thank you, it has been lovely to meet you both," she said warmly. He moved on to speak to Annabel, and Aurora knelt down to Zeus and said goodbye to the noble dog.

"He took a fancy to you, didn't he?" said Constance approaching her.

"I took a fancy to him really," said Aurora. "He's an absolute beauty, so enormous and dignified."

"Well, that is what they are known for." Constance looked tenderly at Zeus and smiled softly at Aurora.

"I miss my dog, but not long until Christmas and term finishes. I can't wait," Aurora confided.

"Teddy tells me you come from a large family, that must be lovely?"

What was Teddy doing talking about my family life with his mother? She was a little surprised.

"We have a lot of fun, but it comes with noise and chaos," Aurora admitted. She thought about her home and family and how different the atmosphere was, then added: "We are quite a rambunctious group all together."

"Yes, well, I suppose so. There are pluses and minuses for every situation in life. We find it very quiet here for Teddy, unless we have guests or family. The family are mostly older, so not very exciting for him. It was lovely of you all to spend the weekend," she said with actual warmth. Aurora was surprised by the change in her demeanour. *Maybe she doesn't think I'm beneath them all.*

"Thank you so much for having us. I had an amazing time riding yesterday."

"Yes, Teddy said you were all out on the course too?" Her tone was encouraging but there was still a starchness about her that made all thoughts of a hug goodbye out of the question, not that Aurora felt the inclination at all.

"Well, that was the highlight of the weekend for me."

"Horses are an important part of our life here. Teddy spends all of his time at the stables when he's home. Come and visit us again," she said with a nod.

"Well, thank you again for having us." Aurora smiled. She couldn't very well say I'd love to come back right now, she was hardly feeling it, but she was surprised by her kindness and Teddy's dedication to his horses. She hadn't expected that from him, not from the boy she saw at university.

As they drove away back down the long drive, Teddy's parents stood out front, waving them off. Aurora had chosen death by a thousand cuts and was travelling with Sophie and the girls rather than ride back in the same car as Teddy.

"*The truth is rarely pure and never simple.*"
– Oscar Wilde, The Importance of Being Earnest

Christmas came around quickly after their weekend away. Aurora had her first big essay due just before the end of term so she was busy, spending long hours in the library researching and writing, often bailing on lunch dates and coffee. Then there were the JCR meetings, as the committee was busy planning out the rest of the year's events. They were also in the midst of organising the Classic Movie Couple Ball on Valentine's Day.

The Christmas break was going to take them through to the end of January, so they didn't have a lot of time. She attended meeting after meeting as they worked through the calendar. It was a more enjoyable experience than Winnie had predicted and through it she was becoming friends with Diana as they spent more time together. Paige still wasn't a fan of Diana, but Aurora couldn't understand why, she seemed to have such a sweet disposition. Then again, Paige wasn't a huge fan of Winnie and everyone loved him. Aurora suspected it was because Winnie enjoyed making fun of her.

The ski trip bookings opened up as well and there was a mad scramble as everyone tried to get onto it. The holder of the largest annual student ski trip in Britain was an honour that went to Bristol University. It was an event not to be missed, they had all been told at the Freshers Fair. This year it was to be held at Val d'Isère and competition to get online and booked in was stiff. Aurora, Paige, Sophie and Annabel were all successfully registered and paid for, greatly relieved as it was announced the trip was fully booked within forty-eight hours.

When Aurora's mother came to collect her at the end of term, she rushed down the steps of halls to meet her in the car park, delighted and relieved to be going home. It had been a long term and she longed to be home. Navigating this next stage of her life without parental guidance on hand had been an adjustment.

As they drove back along the M4 she talked about the weekend at Teddy's. She hadn't confided in anyone about her mixed feelings for Teddy. "He was so genuine I was really sucked in, even in spite of what I knew, you know? And I was just disappointed in the end, like really disappointed."

"Yes, I do know. Guys like that who have it all going for them are hard to resist, but throw in charm and that is nigh on impossible to hold out against," her mother agreed. Samantha Bond was often mistakenly thought to be Filipino, short in stature with rounded soft features. Her skin was a shade darker than Aurora's and her eyes were very dark brown.

"I know, we had such a good time out riding, we seemed to really connect and then all the time he's carrying on with Paige. I just couldn't believe it, I was so angry." Aurora's face was still etched with disappointment and confusion.

"Did you talk to her about it?" asked her mum, trying to figure the situation out as she drove just above the speed limit, periodically looking down at the speedometer. She figured you could always get away with travelling ten kilometres above the limit, but she tended to have a lead foot and a poor track record with the police. She couldn't afford to be caught speeding again.

"Well, no, she has a boyfriend and she hasn't said anything about Teddy, I just didn't feel it was my place. Also, she doesn't have to answer to me, I wasn't in a relationship with him, as far as she knew we weren't even good friends, so I had no right to be jealous."

"Yes, but she must have seen him paying you attention all weekend?" her mother pointed out. She was beginning to smell a rat.

"Oh yes, she definitely noticed, there were looks, but that's all." Aurora was reluctant to think her friend had been at fault; the blame she had laid at Teddy's door.

"Well, I knew a boy like that once and the only solution was to stay well away from him. Give Teddy a wide berth, because he'll only reel you in again when he has the chance," her mother warned. "Find someone who's really interested in you. Don't you think you and

Paige should have talked about it, though?"

"I just couldn't bring it up. I haven't seen Teddy much, really, I've avoided him, and I usually just eat with the girls in the dining room."

"Something's not right there, it doesn't all add up." Aurora could see her mother was calculating, working through the scenario in her head, trying to figure it out.

It felt good to be able to talk to someone about the whole situation.

She'd decided not to mention what she had seen to anybody that was there that weekend. As Paige had a boyfriend she didn't want to be responsible for any trouble if it should come out she'd been unfaithful, but the knowledge had been hard to keep to herself.

As they cruised home, "Driving Home for Christmas" came on the radio and she felt happier with every mile they covered. She realised during the drive that she'd been wound up quite tightly at university. It was a relief to be having a break, to be with people who loved and knew her well. She felt alone much of the time, even surrounded by people. Often left behind as her friends talked about their TV shows and experiences at boarding school. She pronounced words differently as well, and was always being corrected. It was the whole fish out of water thing. If she called a pepper a capsicum no one knew what she was talking about. If she asked for the bathroom she was corrected and told she should ask for the loo; "There isn't a bath in there, Aurora." Even though she spoke the same language it sometimes made real communication and connection more difficult.

She wondered if it was simply the cultural divide? Without familiarity surrounding her, supporting and providing a natural scaffold, she had to do it for herself.

When she was with her family it was different, they did it for each other.

About a half hour from home she found herself reflecting on her relationship with her girlfriends. The more she got to know them, the more uncomfortable she felt. Shouldn't it be the opposite, she pondered? It always took time to bond with people but this was different, this was something else. At times she still felt anxious, uptight and ill at ease. Falling out with girls was high on her fear list, they could be so savage, so vindictive and it played on her mind as she watched her friends interact or listened to their conversation.

When they pulled up in front of the house, the door flew open and Ajax burst out, barking excitedly and running in circles around the car. Her siblings came pouring out of the house to greet her. It was good to be home. Sebastian was the first to get there, even taller and broader in the last couple of months. Lanna was next and her delight to have her big sister home was written on her sunny face. A people person, she had missed her sister's companionship and now through the holidays they would sit up late chatting, watching TV and playing with makeup. Evie, engrossed in a Netflix show on her iPad, was slow to realise Aurora had arrived home and came running out last, miffed the others had gotten the jump on her.

It was not a peaceful house, it was loud, full of arguments as the family bounced off one another and the children fought to assert themselves, but they were honest with one another and it was a house full of love when it came down to it all. They relied on one another totally, they had no other family to lean on around them and that made them a tight unit.

Aurora was with her tribe again for now, and she

sank back into the fold like she was laying down on her comfy queen bed mattress. Her father would be finishing work for the Christmas break today too, and once he returned from London they would have a celebratory dinner down at their local pub. The holiday break stretched out before her and she savoured the thought of all the festivities that lay ahead.

Christmas Day rolled around, the absolute favourite time of year for her family. They loved a cold Christmas. Although they missed extended family, it just felt right that it be cold at this time of year. Stockings could actually be hung over a lit fire, mince pies and mulled wine sated cravings for something warm and spicy and you actually felt like eating roast turkey, Christmas pudding and all the trimmings.

Nicholas Bond was the undisputed chef in the house. His wife did most of the cooking, very competently, but Aurora's father cooked for sheer pleasure and did so with aplomb, whenever he was home and had the chance. So, Christmas was his time to shine and invade the kitchen, taking over as he basted and nurtured the turkey on Christmas morning. Her parents would bicker over the state of the kitchen as they shared the space. Her father wasn't the tidiest person in the world and her mother bustled around, attempting to clean up after him, often putting away a spice, a mixing bowl or washing up something he still had plans for.

"Nicky, do you still need these?" she asked, holding up a bag of carrots. "This place looks like a bomb hit it!"

"Later I will. I've just used one for the gravy stock, but I need to cut up more to go with the meal."

"Well, I need to clean up. I can't bake in this mess, there's no room." Her mother's brows were beginning to furrow, her hands on her hips, and Aurora could see the warning signs, but her father, absorbed in his cooking, was oblivious.

His glasses were always propped on top of his head, ready for action. "Just push them aside. I'll use them later," he said absent-mindedly, pulling down his glasses to read the recipe while stirring the gravy.

Aurora and Lanna, sitting at the kitchen table, could see there was no chance this was going to fly.

"No, I'm putting them away, you can get them out later. 'A good cook is a clean cook' my grandmother used to say." She proceeded to tidy up as she saw fit, all the while looking vexed.

Their parents were the antithesis of each other when it came to looks. Nicky Bond was whiter than white, his wife's Polynesian heritage stood in stark contrast. Different in nature, looks and temperament, but together they worked.

Samantha would always do dessert, which varied from a yule log one year to steamed chocolate pudding another. A keen baker, that was her contribution to the meal, although these days she had to do battle for the task with Evie, who no longer considered herself a protégée but a fully fledged graduate of her mother's baking school. Therefore, there were at times three cooks in the kitchen and it often felt crowded. Their kitchen was the hub of the house and where they naturally congregated. The Aga was kept busy at this time of year, producing meal after meal, and the kitchen table by the tall picture window always had a child or two seated at it, as something bubbled away on the hotplates. It was always toasty warm and inviting.

Aurora resumed her long walks and enjoyed the space. She needed to recharge her batteries before returning to Bristol. With Ajax by her side, she always felt safe no matter how remote or how far she walked. She thought of Teddy with his family alone in the big house. He had tried to talk to her once after the weekend at his place, just in passing in the dining room, but she'd said she was in a hurry and couldn't chat. She wasn't interested in hearing what he had to say, it didn't matter any more.

She tried to let it go and move on. Flynn was still texting her and she enjoyed their chats. He had already suggested they get together when they were back at uni, he seemed keen, which was nice, it was easy. He wasn't exactly setting her world alight, but she was trying to keep an open mind and just see where it went. Paige kept saying she should ask him to the ball and in the end she thought, why not? He seemed like the nice guy who was interested in her.

She sat in front of the fire one afternoon with her family, drinking tea, eating shortbread and mince pies, on one of those days between Christmas and New Year when you lose track of what day it is, and began to give her outfit some thought. "Mum, who do you think I should go as to the ball? Any suggestions?"

"Gosh, I don't know, there are so many options, have you got any ideas?"

"I wanted to go as someone I look like, really, anything else is quite hard to do."

"Troy and Gabriella," Evie interjected excitedly as she sat doing a puzzle with her dad on the coffee table.

"Thanks, Evie, but they aren't really iconic."

Evie's eyes darkened into pools of obsidian in her little, round face. "They are to me," she said indignantly. She was a fireball; her Māori grandfather said she descended from Hongi Hika, the great Māori warrior.

"What about Arwen and Aragorn?" suggested her dad.

"Or Han Solo and Leia?" said Lanna.

"Yeah, not bad. I think I could do Leia," Aurora said, mulling it over.

"Ariel and Eric," said her mum, looking up from her paper.

"I love Ariel, but no, not really Hollywood and I'd need a red wig, which I don't think would suit me." As she reflected on the Disney princesses she was reminded of Pocahontas. "I'll tell you one thing, I won't be going as Pocahontas. God, I'm still pissed off about that comment."

"What comment?" her mum asked, looking up from her paper, her upturned eyes narrowed slightly.

"Teddy made a comment about me being a convict and a savage. We were talking about something, I can't even remember what now, but the fact we have Māori blood in us came up and that was his response!"

"Wow, he's sounding worse the more I hear about him. I hope you put him in his place." Her mother had "the look" on her face, the "look of thunder" her grandmother had dubbed it, but it was an indication that anyone who had provoked such a look was on thin ice.

"I did, you would have been proud."

"Well, I should think so, in this day and age, really?" She would file it away, Aurora knew it would not be forgotten overnight.

"Yes, really. He apologised while we were at his place."

"Okay, well that's something, so long as he learns," her mum said grimly.

In the end they settled on Uma Thurman and John Travolta's characters from Pulp Fiction, Mia Wallace and Vincent Vega, definitely iconic.

New Year's Eve whipped around and Aurora spent it with her best friend from high school, Chloe, a vibrant strawberry blonde with a French mother and an English father, who had been raised in France. She had moved for sixth form and connected with Aurora in a way that nobody ever had. Confident, outgoing and single minded, Chloe was a different character to Aurora, but they laughed and cried together through the stress of their final two years of high school. Of course they had other friends, but they were considered an inseparable duo who went everywhere together. For Aurora it was the first time she had ever truly had a best friend and she cherished their friendship.

Over the last few years they had developed a tradition of always spending New Year's together, whatever was going on, and this year it presented issues for Aurora.

During her gap year, Aurora dated a boy called Dylan, who was a few years older; their relationship was neither deep nor long. Aurora struggled to feign affection, and as their light went out, Chloe commenced a relationship with his best friend Ollie, and Ollie was adamant they spend New Year's Eve with him at Dylan's party.

"Aurora, come with me to Dylan's, Ollie just won't understand if I blow him off. He wants me to go to Dylan's party later. I said I was happy for him to do his own thing, that I always spend New Year's with you, but he's really upset," said Chloe, busily applying mascara in the mirror. Her tone suggested it was a minor inconvenience that needed to be overcome.

"Uggghhh I really don't want to go. I don't want to spend New Year's with my ex and his new girlfriend. Remember her from last year?" Aurora looked aghast at the memory. Chloe shrugged and shook her head, so Aurora continued, "She's never been friendly and she certainly won't be now she's dating Dylan."

"Oh putain, no I don't remember anything from their last party except the football chanting and singing. It was like we'd walked into a Tottenham game." Chloe rolled her eyes at the memory.

"Dylan won't want me there either," Aurora moaned.

"No, he's fine with it, Ollie spoke to him, please come ..."

"Oh alright, but I'm not looking forward to it."

"Merci, I will make it up to you, I promise," said Chloe, coming to stand next to Aurora and look into the mirror with her. "You look great, show him what he missed out on."

The girls ended up going to a party with old school friends in Cambridge beforehand, along with Bas, whose mates were there also. It was great catching up with everyone in the holidays now they were all scattered at uni the rest of the year. Aurora's only problem with going out with Bas was keeping her female classmates away from him.

Not long after they arrived, her fears were confirmed. "Aurora, Hannah is making a play for your brother over there. She just told me she fancies the pants off him," said Phoebe, an old classmate who found the whole situation amusing.

"Noooo, I'll kill her. She knows he's off limits!" Aurora was furious as she stood across the room, watching the girl making moves on her brother. "I've got this," said Chloe, raising both her hands before moving in the direction of the new couple to let Hannah know it was a bad idea. Chloe came in handy warning girls there would be repercussions if they carried on. It deterred most, Bas's judgement took care of the rest.

Afterwards they went and joined Ollie and his friends. *It's only a couple of hours*, Aurora told herself. It was a prospect she had not relished for good reason; however, her friendship with Chloe was more important than putting up with the discomfort of seeing an ex for a night.

Towards the end of January, Aurora had her first round of exams, so after New Year's she was on study leave and spent much of the time studying at home. The month of January slipped past as she studied hard and sat exams, which went reasonably well as a result of the work she'd been putting in. For her it was always about consistent effort. She couldn't leave it until the last minute and then cram like some people did. Her brother Bas would leave everything to the last minute and then buckle down in earnest, usually pulling it out of the bag, she on the other hand had to work.

As she said goodbye to the family again, she realised it was that bit easier now she had done it before.

"Hearts are made to be broken."
— Oscar Wilde, De Profundis

As soon as Aurora got back to Bristol, all hell broke loose.

"How was your Christmas?" Aurora asked Paige when she returned.

"Fab, Cam and I went to a party with the boys for New Year's. How was yours?"

"Christmas was lovely, so nice to be home for a while."

"What about your New Year's?"

"Well, New Year's was not the highlight. I went to a party in Cambridge with my best friend Chloe, and then to another party at my ex's house with his new girlfriend. She was predictably unpleasant."

"Sounds awful," she said, screwing up her face.

"Oh, and to top it off my brother was at the first party with his friends and I had to watch girls throwing themselves at him all night. Like I said, not the highlight of the break."

"Babes, that's terrible, but you're back now. I'm off to meet Cam for coffee, so I'll see you after," Paige said, smiling sunnily. There wasn't a ripple on her pond.

A few hours later it was a different story as Paige came storming in with a tear-stained face, black eye makeup running, distraught and upset, her face twisted in emotional pain.

"Cam just broke up with me," she sobbed, throwing herself onto the bed. "We've been together a year and just like that he broke up with me!"

"Paige, I'm so sorry, but he wasn't treating you right," Aurora said gently. "It shouldn't be that hard to get your boyfriend to spend time with you, you know. You're better off on your own, really you are!"

"But I love him, I do, I really do and I thought he really loved me."

"I'm sure it feels awful right now, but you will survive. Let me make you a cup of tea." Aurora tried to leave to put the kettle on.

"No, I need something stronger," Paige demanded.

"You know you really don't, just start with tea, you can move on to something else after," she said, attempting to placate her. "What happened?"

"Well, we met for coffee, which is weird because he never drinks coffee, he really only likes going to the pub, so I should have known something was off. He just said he didn't want to be in a relationship any more. Can you believe that? I think there's another girl, I can just feel it." Aurora thought to herself that there were probably several other girls and he wanted to just be a free agent and play the field for a change. She wondered if she should ask about Teddy now, was it inappropriate or insensitive? she pondered. She was still curious to know what had happened between them.

"If he wants to be single, let him go. You don't need him, he wasn't making you feel good about yourself, no one needs that."

Paige was beside herself and before long Aurora called in reinforcements so she could go to dinner with Diana and her friend Liv. Liv Dooley, a tall attractive girl with a sharp, auburn bob, was a sporty and athletic friend of Diana's. A real outdoorsy kind of girl that you could imagine hiking, scuba diving and one day climbing Everest. On the face of it, Diana and Liv appeared to be polar opposites, but they were friends in spite of this. They gelled and obviously had something in common. Aurora wondered what it was and was looking forward to finding out. She had organised to meet them in the dining hall and Paige didn't have an appetite, so she left her in the care of Sophie and Annabel for an hour, suggesting they didn't let her get totally pissed. She was fast becoming the mother hen of the group.

She rushed into the dining room, looking around for Diana and Liv, locating them at the far table, and commenced to load up her plate. Reuben joined the queue behind her.

"Did you get on the ski trip, Aurora?" he asked casually.

She turned around, smiling at him warmly. He was so funny, she thought, he seemed older than many of the other guys here, his manner, his dress and his intense approach to running the JCR. She could imagine him four years hence working in the city with a burgeoning career. "Hey Reuben, yes I did, I'm looking forward to it, you?"

"Yeah, it should be fun and a welcome break by then too. I know I've been working you all hard this term, so we deserve to let loose on the ski trip." He was much more in favour of fine wine and good food than a game of rugby or a trip to the gym. Entertaining and a little bit extra, he always made the JCR meetings fun, otherwise they could easily have been very dry affairs.

"It's fine, I'm so looking forward to doing movie couples for the ball. That gets me excited, you know?"

"Okay, well, I'll remember that. You love a theme then?" He was laughing at her, but he was always amiable.

"I do, the decorating is my favourite thing to work on, I think." She finished serving her food and made her way to her friends.

"Hi, sorry I'm late, we've had a drama upstairs, Paige has just split from her boyfriend. It's, like, time to call in the emergency services, all of them at once."

"Oh I'm so sorry, is she okay?" Diana was always concerned and compassionate, even for someone who really hadn't shown her their best side.

"She will be. It wasn't part of her plan for this year."

"She'll get over it," said Liv bluntly, almost dismissing the notion of love.

"Are you seeing anyone, Liv?" Aurora couldn't help but ask after the comment, curious as she'd seen her with a guy at the previous ball.

"Sometimes I am, but I'm really not all that interested at the moment. I'm just so busy, it's not a priority for me."

"So, therefore she has a guy who is desperate to commit to her," Diana said ironically, raising her eyebrows. "Always the way, isn't it?"

"Mum says 'treat 'em mean, keep 'em keen'," Liv said wryly, "but indifference seems to work just fine."

"They have to work for it, don't they?" Diana looked around at the other two for confirmation.

"I think when it's right, it's right," said Liv.

"Don't ask me, I'm no authority on the subject," said Aurora, shaking her head. Her track record wasn't great with guys. She had never managed to navigate romance successfully. After being hurt in high school, she had never really let herself go. The boy had gone to a nearby private school and they met at a party. He was clearly popular and oozed boyish charm. He had pursued her relentlessly until he got what he wanted, then dropped her like a rock. It had nearly sabotaged her final results and the scar had never healed properly.

During the course of dinner, Aurora organised to go and see a band with Liv, Diana and a couple of others the following week. It would be nice to do something social with a different group of people. She got a sense that Diana and Liv were both very down-to-earth types. What you saw was what you got and she felt comfortable in their company. It was nice just spending time with them.

After dinner, as she was returning to her block, she walked past the pool room just as Teddy was coming out. She hadn't seen him since she had returned from the break, it must have been nearly two months and she felt the usual jolt go through her body as she realised who it was. He strode out, running his hands through his hair, black woollen pea coat over jeans. He always looked like he'd just stepped out of a catalogue.

"Hey, Roars, wait!" he called out, seeing her walk past.

She hesitated momentarily and was about to continue walking on, but something made her stop; probably the pea coat, if she was honest. "What, Teddy?" she said brusquely.

"Come in here," he said, dragging her into the bar area opposite, his voice low and alluring. It was relatively empty at this time of night. "Let me buy you a drink?" His eyes were pleading with her.

"Really, why? Now's not a good time, Paige is in a bad way, she's broken up with her boyfriend and we're all in damage control upstairs."

"One drink?" he said, not giving anything away and ignoring Paige's plight.

"Just one, okay," she relented, wondering why she had agreed. Curiosity she supposed.

"Okay." His tone was serious.

She took a seat by the fire, where he joined her a moment later. He took off his coat, revealing a fitted white T-shirt, his Celtic ring on leather the only accessory. He'd been busy in the gym during the break from the looks of it. She sat soaking up the heat, she was finding the dead of winter in Bristol cold and dank. It was drizzling and miserable outside as usual. She looked at him expectantly, waiting for him to start, this was his show after all. He made a bit of small talk for a while and then launched into the real reason for asking for a chat.

"I think I know what you think happened at my place that weekend," he said, looking her in the eye as he stumbled through the sentence. "I get you're angry at me and I don't know how, but you must have seen

Paige go in or out of my room, either that or she made something up and told all of you girls," he continued, "and I may be guilty of many things but I am not guilty of that."

"Right, so are you saying she didn't go into your room then?" Aurora was laying a trap for him, her expression neutral, wanting to see if he'd lie.

"No she did but ..." he said reluctantly, dropping his head momentarily.

"I know she did," Aurora cut in, unable to hold her tongue. "You were right in the first instance. I saw her go straight into your bedroom. I was at the bottom of the stairs in the dark. She didn't see me and she strode straight into your room. She was invited!" Her speech was like a volley of bullets, filled with ire.

"No, no, no, not invited. She'd messaged me and said she needed to talk, said it was important, I tried to put her off, but then she just came into my room anyway!" he said defensively, his voice rising a couple of octaves.

"Come on, who would do that?" Aurora asked incredulously.

"She would," he exploded, making a face and gesturing in the direction of Paige's room. "She wasn't invited!" he said, exasperated. "She just came in and started talking about how her relationship really wasn't working, how unhappy she was and asking me what I thought she should do. I told her to talk to you guys. She was trying it on. I had to send her packing. It was embarrassing."

"What? I find that really hard to believe, I can't imagine doing that and I can't imagine her doing that," Aurora said, shaking her head.

"No, you can't imagine doing it, but not all girls are

the same, trust me.

How did you come to be there anyway?" he asked, confused, trying to understand why she was at the bottom of the stairs.

"I wasn't joining the queue if that's what you're thinking," she said sarcastically, a little outraged by the question. "I was there because Zeus was wandering around upstairs and was scratching at my door. I put him back in the kitchen just in time to catch *that*!" she said, indicating her distaste, eyes flashing.

"Oh God, okay, that makes so much more sense. The next day you just flipped. My head was spinning. You kept looking at me like you wanted to kill me." He put his head in his hands, groaning.

"Look, it doesn't matter anyway, you don't have to explain to me, you can do what you like," she said flatly, disappointment etched on her face. "I have to go, it's fine."

"No, it's not fine, I didn't do anything and I'm not guilty."

"Okay, you're not guilty, I won't think less of you. Satisfied?"

"You don't think much of me to start with, so no, I'm not." He sensed he was losing the battle, she wasn't coming around even with the truth.

"Teddy, I don't need to trust you, I don't need to believe you, I'm not in a relationship with you. It just doesn't matter, I'm seeing this other guy, he's coming to the ball with me. Thanks for the drink," she said.

"Don't go," he said, looking at her pleadingly.

"I have to," she said sadly.

It was hard to walk away. She wanted it all to be true, but she knew he was trouble. She didn't need trouble, her mother's words came back to her, "He'll reel you back in." As she walked away she thought about the conversation, brief as it was. He seemed genuine, that was the problem, he always did. Guys like Teddy would always have girls throwing themselves at him, whether Paige did or didn't, somebody else would. Maybe she should ask Paige what had happened, but was it worth upsetting the friendship? The whole thing was making her feel confused and disturbed. She didn't have the courage to bring it up right now. *Just let it go and stay away from him*, she told herself. *He's in the "too hard" box.*

She went back to her block and to Paige's room. The girls were congregated there and Paige was now drowning her sorrows on an empty stomach, into the gin and tonics. Laura from the ground floor had come up to lend her support.

"I have been such a good girlfriend, I bought him a really nice watch for Christmas and took him with us to the Bahamas. I mean, I was devoted."

"Yes, you were," soothed Sophie, turning to look at Aurora for help. "I'm not built for this," she whispered.

Annabel took a turn. "Just forget about him and have some fun now."

"You've been miserable with him anyway," pointed out Laura.

"Yes, but this is sooo painful, I can't bear it!" she said, tearing up again.

"Who gave her gin?" Aurora whispered. "It's a depressant!"

"It's all I had left," said Sophie.

"Roars, can you put your record player on and play me some Amy. I want to hear 'Love Is a Losing Game'," Paige said in a maudlin voice.

"Babe, that is sooo not going to be helpful right

now, you know, you don't want to go down that path," Aurora warned.

"Yes, I do, I really do, it's how I feel and you're always saying you feel how you feel."

"Well, yes, I do, but there is such a thing as feeding a negative emotion too and playing that is only going to escalate the situation here," Aurora insisted.

"I want to hear it, put it on!" demanded Paige.

"Oh my God," Aurora murmured to Annabel as she left to dutifully put the record on.

It went on for some hours and close to midnight the girls went to move off to bed. "I can't sleep alone tonight, I just can't be alone," Paige begged. "Someone please sleep with me in my room?" The other girls all looked at each other.

Aurora's room was the closest. "Sure, I'll drag my mattress across the hall."

"No good deed goes unpunished."
— Oscar Wilde

Aurora slept on Paige's floor for a couple of nights and was relieved when she headed to Paris "to shop it off with Mummy." A week or so later, and Paige was in a much better space, still bruised but two pairs of Jimmy Choos had done wonders. She'd come out shooting today and although she was still up and down, she definitely seemed happier. They were having drinks afterwards, talking about the upcoming ball. Paige, Sophie and Annabel decided they were now going to go as *Mean Girls* from the classic movie.

"Oh my God I have to be Regina," declared Paige, "I loved Rachel McAdams."

"Okay, I don't mind, we'll be the other two," said Annabel, looking at Sophie.

"Oh it's such a shame you're going with Flynn, you could have been Lindsay Lohan's character," said Paige, turning to look at Aurora. Aurora was somewhat surprised by the suggestion. All through January, Paige had kept going on about the ball and how Aurora should ask Flynn, and now suddenly it was a shame she was going with him?

"Thanks, but I've made an outfit now and I'm really looking forward to it. Flynn seems happy to come as John Travolta's character anyway."

"Soph and Annabel don't mind changing their costumes and going as *Mean Girls*, do you?" she said, turning to them for confirmation.

"No, it's fine, we were only going as Samantha and Carrie," said Annabel.

"Who was who?" asked Aurora.

"That's not hard to guess, is it?" said Sophie laughing.

"No, I'm gonna go with you as Samantha, Sophie," Aurora returned smiling.

"So, Flynn is your date, is there any progress?" Sophie probed, raising her eyebrows in question.

"You know, I'm starting to like him more. He's been growing on me. That accent, I could listen to him talk all day. He asked me to go out with him and the boys over the weekend, but I had tickets to see Rudimental with Diana and Liv, so I couldn't go," Aurora shared.

"He asked you to go out with the boys?" Paige repeated, her head snapping around to look at Aurora.

"Well, yes, but I couldn't go. I had other plans, so I haven't seen him in the last week, but he said he'll message me tonight and maybe we'll meet up."

Paige's whole demeanour suddenly turned frosty and her speech stilted. "I need to speak to you alone."

"Sure, what is it?" Aurora said, perplexed. They went to a corner of the pub and sat down.

"You know, if you are going to continue to see Flynn, and by association Cam and his friends, then I think it will just be too painful for me, you know. It's like I suddenly don't exist," she said irritatedly.

"Well, I just think it's early days after the breakup and you probably need time to heal. I don't think Cam was there from what Flynn said," Aurora offered, attempting to placate her.

"It doesn't matter, suddenly you get to go out with them and I don't." Paige looked most put out.

Aurora looked at her, concerned, her brow furrowed. "Okay, but you aren't seeing one of them now," she said, trying to understand. "I guess they don't invite you because of Cam, it would of course be uncomfortable for both of you. I get it doesn't feel good, it must be really hard, but what, now you're saying I shouldn't go out with Flynn at all because you broke up with Cameron?"

"If you're going to continue seeing him, I just think it will be too painful for me. You are going to have to choose between us. Either you see him or me," she said flatly as she delivered the ultimatum.

Aurora was taken aback and stared open-mouthed at Paige as she processed her words. "Paige, you can't be serious! Let me get this straight, since you are no longer going out with Cam, you no longer want me to see Flynn?" she said slowly and concisely.

"Exactly."

"You must be joking?" Aurora said, stunned.

"No, this isn't funny for me!" said Paige, who was

almost hostile.

"You know, Paige, I have been in your shoes. I have been in exactly the same position. My best friend from high school is currently dating my ex's best friend. They got together just after we broke up, and I have to deal with that because I don't have the right to tell her she can't go out with someone. I just had to suck it up. You know I just spent New Year's Eve with them, and with Dylan's new girlfriend, and let me tell you, it wasn't great, but it's called life. We don't get to arrange it to suit ourselves."

"If you want to continue to see him, you're going to have to choose between him and me," she stated, undeterred.

"You don't have the right to tell me what to do, you do get that, right?" Aurora asked, mystified. It was like she was the supporting cast to Paige's main act and now she needed Aurora to exit stage left because the scene had changed.

"Well, you know how I feel!" Paige turned and walked back to Sophie and Annabel.

Aurora took a minute to process the situation, trying to make sense of it. She could see Sophie asking what had just happened and their reactions as Paige obviously gave them her version of events. Aurora decided not to discuss it any more now and chose to go and join Emma over by the front bar. She felt awkward and uncomfortable as she could see the girls huddled closely together, the way girls do when there is a juicy bit of gossip to dissect and pour over, and five minutes later they left the pub. Ordinarily they would never leave without her. Anxiety and fear settled into the pit of her stomach. This is what she feared, what she dreaded with groups of girls. It plagued her through high school until she met Chloe and they just got each other. It was like her worst nightmare coming true.

She looked around the pub, the guys weren't here tonight. Winnie had said something about a lock-in somewhere, so they wouldn't be turning up.

She chatted with Emma and some of the second-year students for a while.

"You okay?" Emma asked. "You seem preoccupied."

"I'm not quite right, I just had an argument with Paige."

"What over?" Aurora explained the situation and Emma looked unimpressed. "So, she's been encouraging you to date this guy, invite him to this thing Friday, and then tonight she just comes out with it's him or me?"

"Yes, basically that about sums it up. I'm a bit shocked, I think. She has just broken up with her boyfriend, like two weeks ago, so it's fresh. It's changed things for her, you see."

"It doesn't matter, you can't demand that. It's controlling, don't you think?"

"Yes, I think so."

"And she is jealous, of course."

"Jealous of Flynn?" Aurora looked confused.

"No, jealous you are being invited out with those guys. The whole 'I don't want to be forgotten' comment. Is everything usually about her?"

"Well, lately it is, of course," conceded Aurora. "Speaking of being self- obsessed, you know you once made a comment about knowing why boys didn't ask me out that often, what was that about?"

"Oh well, I think it's because you're pretty and no pushover, and most guys are too scared to ask you out, so you only get left with the overconfident schmucks, the dicks, if you know what I mean?" Emma said, smiling.

"Well, I don't feel that pretty, but thank you. I have met my fair share of dicks, though, that's true." Aurora looked despondent at the thought and found herself chewing on a fingernail before realising and pulling her hand away from her mouth. It was a nervous habit that her father always chided her over. "I think I'm going to go home now. I'm not in a partying mood any more, but thank you for listening."

"Sure, I'll catch you next week, I hope you figure it out."

The next day Paige still wasn't happy and was adamant that Aurora rescind her invitation to Flynn and join them as the Mean Girls quartet. "If you're really a true friend, you will put me ahead of a boy," she said as they all had breakfast together the next morning.

"Paige, it's not about the boy, I don't even know how much I like him, it's the principle. You were fanning this hard and now you're asking me to be rude to someone who's only been nice to me. It isn't fair!"

"He won't care if you cancel. It's just too painful for me to be around him," she repeated. Annabel and Sophie looked uncomfortable and awkward, offering no input. Paige left the table and went to another group of girls. Aurora tried not to be paranoid but she could see her talking animatedly and other girls at the table turning and looking over at her periodically. It wasn't hard to guess what they were talking about. Her stomach lurched, food was out of the question. She felt tears rising inside, and she swallowed hard, forcing them back down.

Again Paige didn't sit with them in the evening,

instead choosing to sit with other girls from her course. The same telltale looks being cast about the room in her direction. It felt like the whole dining room was talking about her. The fear inside of her flooded her nervous system as she watched Paige gathering followers behind her cause. It was like battle lines were being drawn, like she was amassing an army of followers.

Aurora cautioned herself to not blow this out of proportion, but her heart rate was rising rapidly and she hadn't been able to eat all day. Her chest seemed to ache as she struggled to hold back the emotion.

She talked to Annabel and Sophie during dinner, trying to explain her view. "I just don't think it's fair to suddenly expect me to uninvite the guy and drop everything because she's broken up with Cam?" she explained.

"You have to see it from her perspective," said Sophie. "They have just broken up."

"Yes, she's just broken up with Cam, not with Flynn," Aurora said, still baffled.

"I'd hate to see you fall out over a boy," added Annabel. "You could just uninvite him."

"It's not the boy, don't you see? It's the principle! A friend doesn't ask you to choose. On top of that, I know she's seen Flynn since she broke up with Cam, so why is it suddenly too painful to see him at the ball? It doesn't make sense."

"It just reminds her of him, I guess," said Sophie lamely.

"I'm sorry, it just doesn't seem right to me." Aurora was standing her ground. "My best friend has been dating my ex's best friend since we broke up. I introduced them, it's exactly the same situation and I have to deal with that. I honestly don't even know if I really like this guy, I've hardly seen him in person, but she wants me to halt everything because it now doesn't suit her and that's not right!"

"Well, why don't you talk to her tonight when she gets in?" suggested Annabel and they left the conversation there.

Aurora wondered why they couldn't seem to see her point. She called Chloe and they talked it through.

"I didn't have any right to stop you seeing Ollie, it didn't even occur to me," she said.

"No, I have to admit I knew it wouldn't be easy for you having broken up with Dylan, but we didn't get together to hurt you, it just happened," Chloe concluded. "This chick sounds like she just wants everyone to fall in line behind her, is she the quintessential queen bee?"

"I don't know," Aurora moaned. "I never thought about it before. We've just been friends because we virtually live on top of each other."

"Well, she sounds like an unreasonable cow to me. She thinks she's the director and you've just gone off script." Chloe was never one to beat around the bush. "It's not how the scene is supposed to play out in her mind."

Later that night Aurora could hear the girls talking in Annabel's room next door. She could clearly hear Paige talking about her, saying how awful it was that she was insisting on taking Flynn to the ball. "How could she do this to me after I've been such a good friend to her?"

On top of that she could hear Sophie and Annabel agreeing along. "She's just not seeing it from your perspective."

"I know, right. It's outrageous."

Aurora was starting to feel really nauseous now, but there was nothing in her stomach to throw up. She had bitten her nails down to the quick in a matter of days. Her brain continued to work feverishly: *Should I go in there and confront the situation? Give them all the chance to tell me to my face? Or is the best thing to just ignore it? I wasn't meant to hear it anyway. "What other people say about me is none of my business", isn't that a saying? What have I done that's so terrible?* She was filled with the sense of impending doom. She knew at her innermost core that this was not going to end well.

She decided talking about the issue again was the best course of action. She got off her bed and wandered out into the hall, but when she knocked on the door there was no answer. The hollow sound of the knock and the silence that followed echoed through her whole body and down the corridor. She waited there, staring at the blank, white door. Confused, lost and alone. She almost would have preferred them to be openly angry, at least then they would have acknowledged her existence. She wondered where to go from here.

She shuffled back to her room. She could feel her heart racing again, and decided to call for help. She picked up the phone to her mother and asked for her advice. Having a psychologist in the family had its perks when you weren't being psychoanalysed. Besides, the anxiety in the pit of her stomach was unbearable. She had always been vaguely aware that she didn't feel a hundred per cent comfortable around Paige and the others, and she had noticed certain behaviours of theirs that made her uneasy, but now the anxiety had risen so far she felt out of her depth and in danger of drowning.

"Mum, I have a situation here that I need help with." She explained what had happened and told the story of the last twenty-four hours.

"Right okay, well, I would ignore their poor behaviour and try to rise above it and do the right thing. When Paige goes back to her room alone, speak to her, if she'll open the door that is. Try to explain that it would be too rude to uninvite the boy. Tell her that you care about her and you have no desire to hurt her. I think she's probably just feeling really insecure, that's my best guess," her mother finished. "Sometimes just being kind even when you don't feel like it can heal a situation. However, it isn't right that she is asking you to make a choice between her and this boy. You have to stand up for yourself too."

Aurora sat in her room, essentially waiting for enough time to pass to try again. Filled with angst, she could do nothing else but obsess over the situation. Sick to her stomach, she waited until she thought she heard Paige go back to her own room. Then she knocked on her door. There was no answer.

"Paige, I know you're in there," she called out. This time it slowly opened for her. "Can I talk to you about all this," she asked. "I don't want to fall out, I really don't. I'm sorry you feel hurt about it."

"Okay," said Paige. She was flat and gave nothing away but went and sat on her bed, leaving the door open for Aurora to enter. Aurora gingerly took a few steps inside.

"I can't uninvite Flynn now, I've bought his ticket. I can't do that, but it's not because I don't care how you feel, it's because it would be so rude. I value your friendship and I know this is a tough time for you."

"It's fine, I'll go with the other girls. It's fine," Paige

assured her in a clipped tone as she stared out the window.

"I know how upset you've been over the breakup, but you can't expect me to just ditch Flynn the night before?"

"It's fine, I don't care any more." Paige had a vacant expression for the entirety of the exchange, refusing to engage.

"Your friendship matters to me," Aurora said, trying to reach her.

Paige nodded but offered nothing further, so Aurora left it.

"Do you want to get ready together like usual?" Aurora asked.

"Sure, it's fine," Paige said.

Aurora had grave misgivings, it was like talking to a wall. She felt this crippling loneliness, as she walked back to her room, completely isolated in her own group of friends. She was in a black hole, falling deeper and deeper, reaching out for something to hold on to, but there was nothing there. She noticed a pain in her chest that had gotten progressively worse throughout the day; tears she refused to cry.

She lay awake for a long time that night, replaying everything that had gone on between Paige and herself, trying to make sense of it all, trying to figure out what she was missing. Why was Paige so adamant? Why did Sophie and Annabel agree with her so vehemently? Paige's last words rang out in her mind coldly: "It's fine." It was not fine, it was anything but fine.

"A good friend will always stab you in the front."
— Oscar Wilde

They got ready together. Aurora helped them with their outfits, there wasn't much to do to look like the "Plastics" from the movie, but the energy between the girls was all wrong. As they walked to the taxi that would take them to the Bristol Museum, Sophie was still saying, "You know it's not too late to change your mind and come as one of us?"

Aurora was still baffled by their attitude. The unease had been gnawing at her throughout the day. She went to the library in the morning in an attempt to be productive, but found she couldn't concentrate on anything. She knew in her gut something was wrong, but there was nothing she could do about it, other than hope the evening was uneventful. It was this sense of helplessness that disturbed her. The pain in her chest continued to build as she resisted the urge to cry.

The Bristol Museum is a beautiful old sandstone building on Queens Road in the centre of Bristol. Inside, the cathedral-like space with its galleried landing rose up some ten metres high with a curved glass canopy forming the ceiling; a theatrical space. Drinks were in the first hall, Winterstoke, followed by sit-down dinner in the adjoining hall.

When they got inside, they joined the guys, which was a welcome relief. Aurora hadn't seen much of them during the week and was desperate for an influx of new energy to water down Paige and her "Plastics". Teddy and Winnie had come as Maverick and Goose, and Harry and James as Iceman and Slider, complete with Ray-Bans, flight suits and attitude.

"You guys look great and comfortable in character," Aurora said. Anxious and uptight, it came out more sarcastically than she had intended, but James was undaunted.

"What, devastatingly handsome, charismatic men?" he asked, grinning.

"Young, rambunctious idiots with huge egos was more what I was thinking, to be honest," she replied, smirking.

Teddy was smiling, staring at her again. "Who are you?" he asked. He did look devastatingly handsome behind the Ray-Bans, his hair was parted on the side and slicked down, aviator suit unzipped with a white T-shirt under, just showing off some dog tags.

"Mrs Mia Wallace." She had made the shirt just like out of the movie, paired with black cigarette trousers and ballet flats, her long hair under a black bobbed wig. Her makeup was done to accentuate her eyes in black kohl, playing up their natural almond shape so her green eyes popped, but the rest was very natural, except for red lips. It was stunningly simple but effective and he just did his thing of enveloping her in his gaze.

"And where is Vincent Vega?" he asked casually.

"Coming a bit later." Flynn had texted earlier to say he was running a bit late.

"What the hell are you guys?" Winnie asked Sophie, Annabel and Paige.

"We're the "Plastics" from *Mean Girls*," answered Paige.

"Well, if plastic is what you were going for, then you nailed it," said Teddy dryly. All three of them had caked the makeup on, thick foundation, stripes of bronzer, blinding highlighter and bright pink lips. They were dressed predominantly in pink, in short, short skirts and high heels.

"You know the theme is 'Classic Movie Couples', right?" Winnie asked Paige. "This is your gig, but you're not following your own theme?" Winnie was giggling at the absurdity of it all. Paige was not amused and glared at him before walking away.

As they took their seats at the round tables, Aurora saved a seat for Flynn and they started dinner. *Where is he?* They were half an hour into dinner when he eventually arrived. He had worn a black suit jacket over a white shirt with an amulet around his neck, just as Vincent Vega did, tucked into black jeans and shoes.

He came and said hello to Aurora and then went to greet Paige who was the other side of the large round table. Paige stood up and embraced him like long, lost friend. She then pulled him down to sit next to her.

Aurora felt herself stiffen. He looked across at Aurora but dutifully sat where Paige placed him. Paige then proceeded to devote her night to him. Her whole body was turned his direction as she appeared to hang off his every word, laughing and flirting her head off. Flynn appeared to be enjoying the attention. Paige kept putting her hand on his arm as she giggled, her crossed legs turned into him.

Aurora began to feel even more uncomfortable and anxious, *what was going on?* She felt like she was in a sadistic thriller and some shit was about to go down, she could virtually hear the tense music. One minute Paige couldn't bear to see the guy and now she was all over him?

Sophie and Annabel tried to distract her throughout the meal and plied her with wine. She couldn't eat anything. She felt herself begin to fall apart. She'd tried to sort this out and still maintain her values and morals, do what she felt was right, and now she was being humiliated in front of everyone as her date, whose ticket she had paid for, was sitting across the table with Regina George.

At the conclusion of the meal, Flynn moved off with Paige back into Winterstoke Hall, where the themed evening continued as a DJ played music from the movies. Aurora caught his eye as he left and he gave her a wan smile but made no move to detach himself from Paige's clutches. Nervously, she looked around for Diana and Liv and with relief found them still at a table, dressed as Cher and Dionne from *Clueless*.

She walked with them back into the front hall to the bar and dancefloor. She chose not to talk about what was going on with her and the girls, holding it in, not wanting to start World War III. A smiling Reuben, who was dressed as Agent J from *Men in Black*, came and joined them, nursing a stuffed toy pug as his companion, Frank. Aurora couldn't help but giggle and momentarily felt lighter. *It's okay, it's okay, stop freaking out.*

Paige and Flynn were now stationed in a corner of the bar. He seemed totally uninterested in spending time with her, content to bask in Paige's attention. She tried to talk to him but he blanked her, making it obvious he wasn't interested in engaging.

Aurora couldn't make sense of it, why had he suddenly done an about- turn? She felt belittled and embarrassed. Why was he totally ignoring her? Three days ago he was asking her to go out with him and his mates, what had changed? She hadn't seen him for anything to have changed.

"Danger Zone" from *Top Gun* came on for the boys and Winnie dragged her onto the dancefloor. It was nice to feel safe for a moment with someone who felt like a solid friend. She couldn't talk to him about any of this, though. She knew boys weren't interested in girl fights. She could see Teddy dancing with some other girl as usual. *He will have moved on by now*, Aurora thought.

A few songs later, Laura came up and said, "I've just requested the song from *Pulp Fiction* that Mia Wallace and Vincent Vega twist to. He's going to play it for you. You look so great as Uma, do you think you can get your John Travolta up to dance?"

"I'll try, but he doesn't seem keen."

As the song came on, everyone's eyes turned to Aurora as she approached Flynn again and grabbed his hand. "They've put this on for us, Flynn, will you come and dance?"

"No," he said, pulling his hand back, "I'm good

here." He stood still, refusing to move from the bar with Paige. Paige tried unsuccessfully to hide a smirk as Sophie and Annabel turned away, cringing from second- hand embarrassment. Aurora felt herself recoil from the insult. She wanted to run out of the room and leave, to flee, but instead she had to pretend all was okay, pretend she wasn't feeling hurt and betrayed, pretend it wasn't happening. It would have been so much better if he hadn't bothered to come.

She turned away, feeling like the stuffing had just been ripped out of her and stood bleeding out on the dancefloor, all eyes on her.

After a moment she saw a hand outstretched, coming towards her. "Mia Wallace is worth being thrown off a balcony for any day of the week," Winnie said, referencing the film and coming to her rescue. He held his hand out to her and she gratefully took it. They danced and their friends joined them, forming a crowd. It was a relief, but it couldn't remove the sting from the slap in the face she'd just received. Aurora could feel herself losing control, she'd had too much to drink and now was reeling. Out of the corner of her eye, she could see people watching and whispering to each other. She could see Teddy staring intensely at her with concern as the tears welled up in her eyes at the conclusion of the song.

She fled the room in a daze, running outside and down the street to the small courtyard garden outside. She tried to compose herself but the pain in her chest from suppressed emotion made it impossible, and then suddenly the dam broke. She could no longer stop them, tears poured out of her in great, heaving sobs. In desperation, she phoned her mother.

"Mum, I can't do this any more, I can't do this ..."

she said, and an emotional, garbled outpouring followed. "I've been living with this sick feeling in my stomach for a while now. I feel so anxious most of the time. I don't fit in. I don't belong." As she spoke, she cried.

"You've made friends, though?"

"It's like, I ... I ... I ... don't get it, like I don't speak the same language."

"Are you okay?" her mother said.

"I can't do it. These girls have been my closest friends since I started at uni, I feel like I just want to curl up and die. I don't understand what's going on. I don't understand what I did?" She began to cry wholeheartedly.

"What's happened?"

She tried to speak but only a sob came out. Her mother waited until she made another attempt and she finally managed to say, "I'm so humiliated."

"Aurora, I don't understand."

"These girls were my friends but it's like ... like I'm being punished, like they hate me." She was barely audible through the sobbing and the heavy intake of breath in between.

"I'm sure they don't hate you."

"I ... I... can't keep doing this, Mum. I just want out. I feel like I want to die."

Her mother understood it was a cry for help. "Honey, we'll come and get you, you sound like you're in a state. Put one of those other girls on," her mother demanded.

"Mum, I ... I ... I don't want to go back in there, I don't want to see them."

"This is about your mental health. I'm not taking any chances, put someone on the phone now."

Aurora found Sophie just inside the door, who looked worried as she handed her the phone. Tears were still rolling down Aurora's cheeks, she couldn't stop the flow now they had started.

"Sophie, I'm on my way down to collect Aurora. I don't know exactly what's gone on there, but Aurora is really upset?" Samantha Bond said in an authoritative tone.

"Oh it's over this boy," said Sophie, "but we've really been there for Aurora."

"You haven't though, Sophie, have you? You were all gossiping about this with Paige last night and Aurora could hear you through the wall.

When she knocked, you pretended you weren't in there. That's not really supportive now, is it?" There was silence down the end of the phone for a moment.

"I ... I ... It wasn't really like that ..." Sophie trailed off.

"Can you keep an eye on Aurora until I get down there, it will take us a couple of hours. I'm worried about her mental state, you understand what I'm saying?"

"Yes, yes, I'll look after her, we're here for her."

"I'm sure you are," Samantha said dryly.

Sophie handed the phone back awkwardly. Aurora hesitated for a moment, then made her decision, turning back to the door, running outside and down the stairs, away from the Museum and up the street towards halls, tears streaming down her face. She heard footsteps following from behind, which were getting louder.

"Roars ..." a deep voice called from the dark. It was tentative but warm and familiar. She assumed Winnie had followed her outside.

"Winnie, please, I just want to be alone."

She turned around to see a tall figure striding intently through the darkness, his face concealed by the shadows. It was only when he stepped out into the light, she could see it was Teddy Talbot. Aurora withdrew further, mortified.

"Are you alright?"

"What does it look like?" Aurora said, sniffling to stem her running nose.

She could feel her makeup running down her cheeks, the black ink-like droplets staining her shirt. She was a mess and the last person in the world she would want to have seen it now had a front-row seat.

He stood stoically, looking at her like she was a spooked horse that was out of control. Not knowing what to say but just wanting to help. He tentatively reached out a hand in an attempt to calm her down, but she retreated further. "I'm out," she said, holding both hands up, backing away from him.

"He's not worth it, the night's not over," he said, shaking his head emphatically.

"Mine is," she replied flatly. She couldn't bear it, she didn't want his sympathy. The night was well and truly over for her. It wasn't about Flynn, she didn't really care about him, but the humiliation Paige had deliberately inflicted hurt. They'd been friends for months now, or so she thought, and it felt like a vindictive attack. She'd slept on the girl's floor for two nights, for fuck's sake. She felt herself spiralling down in a well of grief and hurt. She turned and hailed a taxi, diving into the back. Teddy stood on the street, watching it disappear down the road.

"To love oneself is the beginning of a lifelong romance."
— Oscar Wilde, An Ideal Husband

Her parents arrived hours later. "If I see that girl, I'm not sure I'm going to be able to control myself," her mother admitted on approach. "I just want to wring her neck. Girls always have so many issues at this age!" she ranted, fuming.

"Well, in that case don't get out of the car. I'll go and get her." Nicky Bond put his hand out to physically restrain his wife and opened his car door. He disappeared around the corner and five minutes later Aurora came back outside with him looking broken, eyes red and swollen, emotionally spent. They travelled through the night getting home near dawn. Aurora slept, collapsing, exhausted, in the back.

The next morning, with her head clearer, they talked some of it through. She had an emotional hangover that would last for days. She felt bruised and battered, shaken up from the experience. Her mother broke some of it down for her after they discussed the whole situation, the ins and outs of it all. They were sitting in the farmhouse kitchen around the large table at the end of the room, drinking coffee by the warmth of the pale blue Aga, large windows framed the countryside beyond, bare at this time of year. Rain was forecast later and the sky was a dull grey outside. Her dad was out walking the dog alone, giving mother and daughter some space.

"Right, so this girl has gone to war over this, you see. You've broken rank and she is going to send you to the wall for it, punish you, teach you a lesson. However, we always have to look at our part in any situation because that's all we have control of. We can't control anyone else. You must have had a feeling that Paige wasn't all she appeared to be?" Samantha was trying to get to the nitty gritty of the drama.

"I did. I often felt anxious, but they are the girls in my block, what was I going to do? I had to get on with them," she said plaintively.

"Yes, get on with them, but not be their best buddies. Your mistake was not listening to your instinct. It was telling you repeatedly to move in another direction. You need to listen to it!" her mother urged. "Paige wasn't someone to let get too close. Look at the whole situation with Teddy now. What do you think happened there?"

"I don't know, maybe he was telling the truth," Aurora said miserably. She felt duped, ashamed that she hadn't been able to read the situation correctly, and guilty that she hadn't really given Teddy any time when he tried to tell her what had happened.

"I'll tell you what I think happened. She saw Teddy liked you. She saw this guy all the girls were chasing, a future lord, a real catch, was showing interest in you, so she tried to sabotage it."

"Mum, Teddy is a massive, excuse my French, 'fuck boy' okay, he's no angel." *That's a fact he can't be excused for.*

"Be that as it may, in this case he may not be guilty. I have heard that term before, by the way." Samantha was not about to let her insight be sidelined by modern terminology.

"Yeah maybe, I don't know, but that's not my concern right now. I got this text from Flynn at some point later in the night saying, 'You're a nice girl and all, but you just came on too strong.' I honestly don't know what the hell he is talking about. I didn't speak to the guy all night, he wouldn't dance with me, I mean, I hadn't seen him to be able to come on too strong?"

"Well, you'd had a fair bit to drink. If you're not sure, you could ask someone neutral how it looked from their perspective," her mum suggested, "but it still doesn't excuse his behaviour. I can't work that one out." She considered the problem as she rose to pour more coffee.

"It's a guy's way to get out of being a dick," chipped in Bas, who loped into the kitchen for more food. He was training for the decathlon and was impossible to fill. "It's an easy out, you were too keen, too much, so I had to back away, sounds like a crock of shit to me," he said as he lifted the glass-covered cake stand and cut himself a piece of carrot cake.

"Yes, I'm inclined to agree, but in any case he was disgustingly rude, even cruel," her mother said, her voice full of compassion. Aurora stared out the window at the undulating fields and looked up at the sky as tears filled her eyes. Her mother moved around the table and held her as she began to cry again.

"Mum, don't give me sympathy, it sets me off again," Aurora said forlornly. "Just don't."

"It's better to cry about it and let it out, always is."

Lanna had now wandered in after Bas, looking for morning tea too.

The younger kids had been lingering outside the kitchen area, aware of the drama and keen to understand, to assist. "You know, in *Mean Girls* Regina George tells the hot guy that Lindsay Lohan's character is getting with that she's obsessed with him, that she's thinking about baby names, you know like really over-the-top stuff. Maybe she did that?"

"Oh my God, no, stop," said Aurora.

"Surely she has more imagination than that?" her mother remarked cynically.

"Nope, that could fit," Sebastian said, giggling his head off. "That's so pathetic it fits. She chucked a Regina George." His big brown eyes were reduced to slits as he squeezed them shut, laughing. Aurora almost managed a smile as her brother enjoyed his own assessment of the situation. "Girls are batshit crazy," he said and laughed.

His mother cut him off. "It doesn't really matter what she said or why he did that, none of it reflects on you. That's their behaviour, they have to live with that, but you don't have to. You may find out, or you may never know."

The conversations went on and Aurora knew she

would have to return and face it all. There was no escape, she felt adrift and alone. Isolation and fear melded together and fell like a black, suffocating blanket over her soul. She felt herself spiralling down into despair, unable to pull herself out, unable to explain it fully to anyone. Winnie reached out to check on her and she gave him the background story, telling him nothing of her depression. The blackness became more oppressive and Samantha Bond could see her counselling wasn't reaching her daughter, could see she would need more support than she could provide, she was too close, too involved.

They talked about her getting a therapist or a counsellor at uni but only in vague terms as a possibility, hoping she would come out of it by herself.

As her mother drove her back to school two weeks later, they talked in the car.

"What I've observed is that girls between the ages of sixteen and twenty-one have a pretty tough time, often suffering from all kinds of issues that they eventually grow out of. I think going out into the world alone and independently for the first time is extremely daunting for young women and they often need support, so don't feel like you're alone," said Samantha.

"I don't want to go back. I feel like I have just wasted the first half of this year and I haven't made any friends, like I have to start again, and start from scratch," Aurora confided.

"You know that just isn't true, it isn't reality, Aurora? You will have other options, maybe you haven't put as much time into these other people, but they are there. What about that girl on the JCR you're friends with?"

"Diana? I just don't know her very well, and her and

Liv are like best friends," she explained, still feeling despondent.

"She can still be a friend, though, can't she?"

"Yes, and Paige doesn't like her, so we won't be bumping into each other if I hang out with her."

"Why doesn't Paige like Diana, did she ever give a reason?"

"Not a valid one, just doesn't like her vibe or something, the same as Winnie, really." Aurora stared blankly out the window at the passing view.

"Just reach out to her, don't be mute, speak up for yourself. You know Paige will be, so speak *your* truth," her mother urged. "And then there are all the boys, they're still friends, aren't they?"

"Well, yes, Mum, but they are guys and they do their own thing a lot, you know?" Aurora was mildly sarcastic, becoming irritated with helpful suggestions, she needed to find her own way through this.

"Paige sounds like the classic alpha, Sophie and Annabel are betas and you're a gamma." Her mother was right into her psychology now, but Aurora cut her off.

"Okay, Mum, I don't know that this will help," she said snappily.

"Well, it helps to understand the dynamics sometimes." Her mother ignored the tone, determined to impart as much wisdom and support as she could in the small amount of time she had left with her daughter.

"I'm dreading just bumping into her in the hall, I don't want to talk to her again."

"Well, she may surprise you, I hope she does, because you can't carry this resentment, it will only hurt you in the end."

As they drove along the country roads away from home and safety, the song "Towards the Sun" by Rihanna came on the radio and her mother swung the car off the road, turning to look at her. "This song becomes your mantra, play it every day, remember the words and just keep moving forward. When you feel yourself faltering, when you feel overwhelmed, remember those words, remember our whakataukī: *Te tiro atu to kanohi ki tairawhiti ana tera whiti te ra kite ataata ka hinga ki muri kia koe.* Turn your face to the sun and the shadows fall behind you. We're all with you, urging you on." Aurora began to cry, the emotion spilling over with her mother's words. "Paige tried to belittle and humiliate you, don't let her! Hold your head up, speak your truth and learn from it. Trust your instinct, it won't lead you astray." As she said it, tears were in her eyes as she felt her daughter's pain, she was living it too.

"Mum, I need counselling, I don't think I'm right, I feel so black."

Her mother reached out and squeezed her hand. "Well, we will get you some."

"I've already called and made an appointment with the counsellors at uni, I'll start there."

She felt ashamed of being unable to cope, ashamed that she couldn't bring herself back up to the surface, but it was also a relief to throw the towel in, a relief to admit she needed help, a relief to think that there would be some support back in Bristol. She was tired of holding herself together there, of feeling so alone.

"Be yourself; everyone else is already taken."
— Oscar Wilde

As fate would have it, Aurora bumped into Liv outside as she arrived back in halls. Unable to stop herself, the story poured out of her in a torrent. The damned-up emotions and the emotional trauma evident.

"I wondered where you disappeared to that night, suddenly you were just gone. We didn't know what had happened, but it was obvious something was going on. There were always signs that Paige was a real piece of work, though?"

"Yeah, I know, I just kept overlooking them."

"I can see for you living there in the same block it could be difficult." Liv was an excellent social navigator. She had attended boarding school throughout high school as her father worked for the UN. She appeared robust enough to have enjoyed it and flourished. "I've known a lot of girls like Paige and it's best to steer clear of them."

"Well, it's not going to be pleasant, but I have nothing to say to her. I tried to talk to her about it, she said it was fine, obviously she already had a plan in motion. I don't get Flynn, though, but I really don't care."

"Come on, what a fuckwit! Who does that to a girl, for any reason, it's just shit, isn't it?"

"Well, it felt like it, I can tell you."

"Whose room are you in for the ski trip?"

"Oh God, I had forgotten about that, theirs of course."

"Well, I would rethink that one. You can stay with Diana and I? We'll just get a triple instead of a double," Liv said matter-of-factly. She was straight to the point and Aurora had no trouble with that. You knew where you stood and she vastly preferred her frankness.

"Are you sure? I know three isn't a great number."

"Yeah, we're not like that, don't worry," Liv reassured her. "It'll be okay, you know you have other friends. There are lots of other people here." Her expression was kind and encouraging, and relief began to flow through Aurora. Perhaps it would be okay in the end. She would survive, she told herself, just put one foot in front of the other.

She experienced a wave of anxiety every time she entered her block until she was safely in her room with the door shut. She learnt to steel herself before entering and mentally blocked any noise emanating from the hall. She was nice to everyone else, but she totally ignored Paige, who no longer existed in her world. She didn't have much to do with Annabel and Sophie either, who had obviously allied themselves with Paige as they sat in the dining hall, whispering and looking over, huddled together conspiratorially. Aurora ignored them and carried on, head held high, keeping busy with schoolwork, playing ultimate frisbee and working on broadening her circle. She avoided shooting for now. Counselling began; it would be a lengthy rebuilding process, not a quick fix.

She reached out to Diana and confided in her, talking things through over a cup of coffee in a Clifton café one afternoon.

"Well, all of those girls never gave off good vibes, so I'm not surprised that you've had problems there. They were never big fans of mine," she said, raising her shoulders in a sweet hunch. "I don't know what I ever did, but they made that clear."

"You were the enemy running against Sophie, remember?" Aurora laughed as she said it, conscious that it was the first time she had spontaneously laughed in weeks.

"Oh my God, seriously?" said Diana, rolling her eyes. "Message me, you know, whenever you want to have breakfast or dinner. You can eat with us, don't worry, I understand dining room anxiety syndrome."

Spending time with her was soothing. It felt like she was slipping on a pink, fluffy angora jumper, soft and comforting.

"I hate walking in alone, it's the pits, everyone turns and looks at you, it's excruciating," Aurora said, shuddering.

"Uh huh, and I understand bitchy girls too, they made high school a nightmare for me. I totally hated it," Diana said softly in her South African accent. "I'm still traumatised by high school."

Their friendship grew and Aurora got to know Liv better as well. Liv, a confident social butterfly who flitted from group to group wherever it suited her, was open and friendly. Although her and Diana were best friends, they were not exclusive with it. As they sat eating dinner one night in the dining hall, Liv confided that she had talked to Paige.

"You know, I listened to Paige's side of the story the other night, Aurora. She insisted on telling me. I wanted to hear both sides anyway, I was curious and wanted to hear what she had to say. You know, as she explained her view about what happened, I was gobsmacked. I felt like interrupting and asking her how old she was? Like, grow up, you're not fifteen," Liv said with a disbelieving expression on her face.

"I'm sure she believes she's totally in the right, how else could you live with yourself?" Diana added.

Teddy, James and Winnie walked into the dining room as the girls were talking. The girls were on the other side of the dining hall, but the boys spied them and made their way over after serving themselves heaped plates of teriyaki glazed salmon with seaweed and rice. It was the best meal the kitchen put on and it brought every student into the dining hall whenever it was on the menu.

"So can we join the hot girl group tonight?" quipped James, looking at Diana across the table.

Liv turned her head to the side, looking up at him. "Gee, James, I don't know, do you look like a hot girl?"

"Absolutely!" he responded, shaking his long blonde locks as he plonked his tray down.

Teddy threw his long legs over the bench and sat

next to Aurora. She hadn't had a conversation with him since she had returned. Winnie had messaged her often following the ball, so Aurora could only assume he had filled him in.

"So how are you?" he said in a gentle tone as he sat down, looking expectantly at her.

"I'm okay, did Winnie tell you what happened, why I went home?" Aurora felt the same feelings rise up in her whenever he was near. The attraction, the chemistry was still alive and kicking as she returned his gaze.

"Yeah he did. It sounded like you've had a tough time with the girls and all," he said as he commenced to eat.

"I'm still licking my wounds, but I have no regrets about the choices I made," she answered. "I thought Paige was out of order and I still do. Let's not even mention Flynn, I can't fathom his behaviour." She felt embarrassed and mortified just talking about it and hoped they would move off the subject rapidly.

"He's obviously a complete twat, Aurora," he said darkly. His demeanour was kind and non-judgemental, which she was grateful for.

"I guess the whole situation has splintered the little social circle we had going," she said, acknowledging she wouldn't be a part of that group any more. "I'm definitely out now."

"The only reason any of us hung out with those other three was because of you. Well, I know for me it was," he said, lifting his eyes up from his dinner, turning to look at her. As he said it, she felt like they were the only two people in the dining room, the intimacy unmistakable. "You were a package deal, if you recall."

"But we all hung out together quite a bit, didn't you guys enjoy their company?" she managed, stunned by his statement.

"I think we had our moments, but Winnie and I won't be continuing to hang out with them," he said, leaving it there. It felt nice to know she had such support, she wasn't expecting him to really have a view. She knew from talking to Winnie that she could count on his friendship, but she didn't have any expectations that Harry, James or Teddy would feel the same.

He was a strange guy, she thought, a predator with a heart. Sometimes he showed this heart and soul that was warm and deep, and when he showed this side she really struggled not to fall under his spell. How could you trust boys, she wondered? Flynn had been talking to her and acting keen for ages and then bang, out of nowhere he changed gears. How would she know if Teddy was different?

"So, girls, what are you up to this evening?" asked Winnie. "Come to the pub with us?"

"Where are you going?" asked Liv.

"Steam, it's two-for-one night and it's good on a Monday," James answered, looking hopefully at Diana.

"I'm in," said Aurora, getting behind their offer, hoping it would encourage the other two girls.

"Okay, sure, just for a little while, I have some work I should do," said Diana cautiously.

"I'll come for a bit too," said Liv, who could never resist an invitation.

They met downstairs in Tudor after they all changed and Harry joined them. They walked across the Downs in the dark. It was March now and the days were getting longer, another couple of weeks and it would be light later, but it was dark as they set off now.

It wasn't far to the pub, a fifteen- minute walk in the cold. Although it was spring the air was still freezing and they huddled down in their padded coats.

"You have to be careful walking across the Downs after dark," Diana said nervously. "Another girl was attacked last week."

James took the opportunity to sidle up to her, saying, "It's okay, we're all here." It was cute to watch him in pursuit without his usual bravado.

"The Downs have one of the highest rates of rape in the country, you know," said Liv bluntly.

"Alright, that's not helping, Liv," said Harry. Diana looked spooked and moved closer to James. Liv shrugged, unbothered; a fact was a fact in her eyes.

Teddy changed the subject. "Snow is forecast this week," he said, looking up at the sky. He was wearing a tight black beanie with a black North Face jacket. His handsome features stood out even in the dark, his profile etched against the streetlights behind him in the distance.

"I hope it falls in Val d'Isère then," said Winnie excitedly, his hands deep in his jacket pockets. "I can't wait, not long now."

"Who's going out of you guys?" asked Liv.

"All of us," answered Winnie. "It's gonna be great."

"Are you girls all going?" asked James hopefully, looking around at them all.

"Yes, we're all staying together," said Liv, smiling. "We may catch you on the slopes then," she said vaguely, taunting James.

"Forget that, you're skiing with us, end of discussion," said Winnie.

The Ryanair flight touched down at Lyon airport, the flight jam-packed with students on the trip. Anyone else who had booked this particular week at Val d'Isère would be devastated when they all descended that afternoon. Buses transported them up to the resort, a long drive as the mountain passes were busy at this time of the year. After their 7 a.m. flight, most were sleeping through the bus trip. Paige and Co. were on Aurora's flight and bus, their presence still haunted her. She avoided them all as much as possible, but it wasn't always possible, especially when they had organised to be on the same flight. They sat a few rows ahead talking and giggling loudly while she travelled solo. She inserted AirPods and tuned them out. Aurora prayed they would not be in the same accommodation. Paige still whispered conspiratorially whenever she was around, casting furtive glances, and it made her feel self-conscious and insecure, even if she wasn't actually talking about her, she felt like she was and she couldn't shake it off.

The bus dropped her off out the front of her lodge and thankfully Paige, Sophie and Annabel remained on board. *So at least they are not staying here, thank God.* The accommodation was in large chalets, some directly on the slopes. After she unloaded her bag from under the bus, she walked into the reception area and ran directly into Winnie, throwing her arms around him like she hadn't seen him for months. "Are you guys in here?" she asked, delighted.

"Yep, we're on the top floor, looking straight at the slopes. Do you know what floor you are on yet?"

"No, but hold on I'll find out," she said, walking to the check-in desk.

As she walked back towards him, she held up a key, jangling it. "Top floor, baby," she said jubilantly.

He smiled broadly. "Ohh this is going to be great! Come on, I'll help you upstairs." Aurora wondered what she had done to deserve his friendship really. Everyone liked him, that was true, but he was also astute when it came to people. He could read them, and as a good judge of character and a social being, he could manage them well too. Teddy appeared to be his best mate, that must mean something, Aurora thought. She had never discussed Teddy with Winnie, she hadn't actually discussed Teddy with anyone but her mum, but his friendship with Winnie gave her pause for consideration. It certainly spoke in his favour, as to his character.

"What time did you get here?" Aurora asked. "You must have caught an even earlier flight because you weren't on mine with the girls," she said, pulling a face.

"Really? That's shit. We caught the dawn flight at six, only just made it, it was brutal. We were out last night till late and now the others are all sleeping, preparing for tonight." He grinned at the prospect of another night out.

As they stepped out of the lift on the top floor, Winnie pushed her case along on its wheels. "Harry and James are in there and that's our room," he said gesturing to a door with "303" on it, referring to himself and Teddy, "and you guys must be nearly opposite if you're 302, right?"

"Yes, here it is," she said, putting the key in the lock.

"I'll let you get unpacked. When will the other girls get here?"

"They're on the bus, so probably an hour or so, I guess."

"Are you going to the welcome drinks?"

"Yes, I'm sure we are. How about we catch you up there?"

"Great. Val is so good, you're going to love it. We come here every year at Christmas, so I'll show you around," he promised.

They all met up a few hours later at the first event Bristol had scheduled, which was the welcome drinks. Hoards of students had migrated to the Fall Line, a bar in the centre of town on the edge of the square. It was rumoured to be great for après, with wooden picnic tables outside and the bar inside. It had snowed a couple of days ago, so tonight there were banks of snow ploughed up around the edges, but that hadn't deterred people from drinking outside in the square all the same. It was teeming with life as Aurora, Diana and Liv made their way inside and joined the rest of the cohort. The bar was at the back, timber-topped and faced in stone, standard mountain decor. They said hello to Reuben, who was already really very merry.

"Ladies, ladies, where have you been? We started hours ago, you have to catch up," he said drunkenly, raising his glass high, before draping an arm around each of their shoulders and whispering, "You two girls are my favourite committee members, you know?"

Winnie had messaged an hour ago and said they were inside somewhere, so they extricated themselves and pushed on further into the rammed venue. They made slow progress as they said hello to various people, finally getting to the bar and ordering their drinks. Eventually they spied Winnie and sundry others in the rear left corner, where there was slightly more breathing space, and moved in that direction. Everyone was in high spirits and circulating fluidly. Liv disappeared, chatting to girls from her hockey team, and James, seeing an opportunity, moved immediately to welcome Diana.

Aurora could see Paige and Sophie on the other side of the room talking to a group of guys. *Excellent*, she thought, *at least she is over there for now. Hopefully the slopes of Val d'Isère will be big enough for the both of us*. Teddy came and stood next to her, following her gaze as she stared at Paige. "So now do you believe me?" he asked.

"I'm much more inclined to," she said, turning to look at him, but not wanting to give away too much.

"Good, can we go back to where we were then?" he said, bumping up alongside her lightly and playfully, making physical contact while smiling down at her. *Damn, he has this off-hand confidence which enables him to be flippant and casual, and it's so enticing.*

"Teddy, we are friends, what are you talking about?"

"Good, because I think we'll be skiing together a lot this week." He looked and gestured in the direction of James, who was busy chatting up Diana, his beer raised in one hand as he talked animatedly. She looked like she was enjoying the conversation, totally invested in whatever he was saying.

"Looks like he's making progress." Aurora smiled.

"Yeah it does, good for him."

"I think they're good together, she's so sweet and smart and he's just smitten. They look like a pair of bookends, blond wavy hair and all. Beats me why he slept with Sophie," she said, shaking her head.

"Come on, Roars, not everyone is playing for keeps all the time."

"Clearly," Aurora said sardonically, raising one eyebrow at him.

"So, have you skied a bit before then?" he asked, changing the subject.

"Yes, my family love it, we go every year if we can. We've spent quite a bit of time in Japan," she explained.

"I've heard that it's great for powder skiing."

"Yeah, not that that's my thing, but it is great powder. Culturally it's great too and the Japanese are so polite. There's no pushing in the queue for the lifts. You just have to watch out for the Aussies coming down the last run at the end of the day. What about you?"

"Yeah, I've skied all my life, although my dad is now into his sixties and slowing down a bit, so I prefer to ski with friends rather than my parents. After Christmas I went with some guys from school to Zermatt, that was a great trip." His face lit up at the memory, she could imagine what they got up to.

Aurora realised she knew so little about his life away from university. She'd learnt a bit when they went to his home; he obviously lived a very different lifestyle from most, it was like nothing she had ever experienced. That whole weekend now seemed like a lifetime ago, although in reality it had only been a few months. For a moment in time she'd felt like she was in a movie, instead of watching one. She'd been swept up and along and just gone with it, until she came crashing down that is. Come to think of it, spending any time with him always felt like a bit of an out-of-body experience, every sense was heightened, even just standing here talking to him, and she always felt special when he shone his light on her. Everyone else disappeared. Tonight he was head to toe in blue, wearing a navy three-quarter zip jumper with dark denim and Timberlands. She wanted to tell him she liked how he dressed, but instead she said, "So, these friends are from your boarding school, I'm guessing?"

"Yeah, all from school."

"How long were you there?"

"I boarded from Year 9, so we've been mates for a while, before that I went to school in London, we were based there until my mum retired from the city."

"Did your mum practise law then?"

"Yeah she worked as a lawyer in London and now helps Dad run things."

"So, that will become your job at some point, running things?" She figured he would just be walking into some cushy family job. *Nice to have it all laid out for you*, she thought.

"Well ... Yes. If we want to keep the estate, my life is mapped out for me, that's it, no choice, no freedom. It's a bone of contention between my parents and I. I don't really want to think about going on to run anything just yet, I've got years of it."

"Fair enough."

"I didn't want to do law either, I wanted to do zoology, which I'm far more interested in," he confided, taking a sip of his beer. She had begun to see another side of him with his horses and dogs, his affinity with nature. "As you can see my parents won that round, but they won't win every time."

"Where are you going to put your foot down exactly?"

"I'm going to travel after uni and spend time in Africa, I hope, on a reservation helping to protect the elephants from poachers or something like that, something very different."

"Well, I can see why that would terrify them, only son and all." She couldn't imagine his mother being happy to put him on a plane to Africa, but she could see him there, doing his own thing.

"I know. I haven't told them yet, but I'm doing that before I come back and get locked into anything."

"I don't feel sorry for you, though. I can see that it's a burden and you haven't been able to choose your own path, but God you get to keep something so amazing going. I don't think I've ever seen anything more beautiful than your home. It supports a lot of people in the process too, I'm guessing the village as well. If your life's work was to pass that on, then it sounds like a great life, how satisfying."

"So, you enjoyed being at Esslemont then?"

"Well, of course I did, who wouldn't, it was breathtaking," she said warmly.

He looked very pleased. "You'll have to come back in summer, that's when it really comes into its own." He seemed to suddenly check himself. "Well, you know the riding is better, tennis is a summer game and you actually feel like using the pool."

"I'm sure it's great," she replied, thinking it was unlikely to happen. "You know I love Oscar Wilde, he was an aesthete, do you know what that means?"

"Yes." He smirked, feeling somewhat patronised. "Someone who appreciates the beauty of nature ... and beautiful things."

"Yes, someone who is very sensitive to beauty. I think I'm an aesthete.

Anyway, he said, 'Beauty is a form of genius - is higher, indeed, than genius, as it needs no explanation.' It cannot be questioned." She was feeling the effects of a few hours of drinking now and was losing her inhibitions.

"We're on a ski trip and everyone around us is getting smashed and you're quoting Oscar Wilde to me?" he said smiling, greatly amused.

"Maintaining something as beautiful as Esslemont has to be a worthy occupation. Protecting the elephants from poachers and preserving Esslemont are not inconsistent, they're compatible. Great estates are in danger of extinction, just as the elephants are, both could disappear from the earth forever if not protected and preserved."

"But estates aren't living, breathing creatures that can be wiped out and never brought back, are they? It's not the same thing." He was a bit surprised by her argument, and thoughtfully took another sip of his beer.

"No, and people may not agree with estates as they were, but they are a part of British history and they still support a lot of people in the countryside. Everyone wants to protect the countryside, if they don't they should because if it disappeared ... My God, what a tragedy! It's part of what makes Britain so great."

"You've really thought about this then, I can see you're fired up," he said, studying her face and smiling.

"At home I guess we talk about what we love about each place we live in. We talk about the culture, the people, the place in general. Not that we study it, but when it's different from anywhere you've ever lived before you notice all the subtle variations, you learn about it because you're immersed in something totally new. Perhaps you're more objective. England's countryside is unique and very beautiful," she said simply. "I've decided, my whole life is going to be dedicated to the pursuit of beauty, either in the fashion or art world." It was a firm statement, a declaration of her passion.

"Well, you are a wonderful advocate and embodiment of aestheticism," he said, flirting.

She pulled a face back at him, acknowledging he was mocking her.

"What are you two talking about?" interrupted Winnie, catching the end of his sentence. He'd noticed the intensity of the conversation.

"Roars is quoting Oscar Wilde to me," Teddy answered for them both.

"A man ahead of his time," commented Winnie, "but really, Oscar Wilde now?"

"'A woman is meant to be loved, not understood,' Winnie," she replied, quoting Wilde again.

"Okay, all for that, but your drink is empty, woman,

so I'm going to the bar," Teddy said, gathering up their glasses.

Harry joined them, followed by James and Diana. As they stood talking and planning where they would ski the next day, she could see Paige manoeuvre herself next to Teddy at the bar, looking up at him, wriggling and giggling, twirling her hair and leaning into him. Teddy collected his bottles and glasses and made his way back to them, handing them bottles of rosé. "I'll be back in a minute, Paige has asked me to help her carry her drinks back."

"I'll bet she has," Winnie commented cynically.

"Am I imagining it or does she seem to feel the need to try and take away whatever attention she perceives me to be receiving?" Aurora said quietly to Diana.

"Nope, it does appear to be a pattern," said Diana, who was looking especially pretty in a pale blue wraparound jumper, with skinny jeans tucked into her boots. "First Flynn and now Teddy. I'd say there's a pattern there."

Paige proceeded to latch onto Teddy's arm, laughing and introducing him to the others in their circle, obviously hoping he'd remain. Occasionally she looked over her shoulder at Aurora to see if she was paying attention. He stayed for about ten minutes before making his way back over to them, immediately pouring himself a glass of wine. Aurora could hear Winnie talking to him behind her, in a somewhat agitated tone.

"Don't you dare tap that, don't even think about it! She's been a bitch to Roars."

"I'm not going to, trust me."

"I swear to God, I bloody won't live with you next year if you go near her. You know what she's playing at."

"Mate, to be honest, I'm a little offended you think I'd go there. I know I've made a few mistakes, but I'm not remotely interested," said Teddy. He was clearly irritated and defensive.

Winnie softened his tone and relaxed: "Okay, okay, I just could see that panning out."

Aurora was relieved. She had to admit she would hate to see Teddy go off with Paige, even if he wasn't hers, she didn't want him to go off with Paige, not even for a night. She was enjoying his company. She found herself wanting to get to know him better. She wanted to trust him, to believe he was genuine. She was also touched by Winnie's loyalty and support. In her experience, such loyalty outside of your family was rare.

The rest of the night played out without drama and they all walked home together, keen to get to bed at a reasonable hour, so they could get a full day's skiing the next day. Ski jackets on, hands in pockets, snow falling gently, encouraging them home as they wandered down small alleyways lit up by the odd lantern, the soft glow occasionally illuminating their faces.

Aurora walked beside Teddy, both of them way beyond tipsy, quoting Wilde for him upon request.

"Come on, give me another one …" he demanded.

"'Crying is for plain women, beautiful women go shopping,'" she recited.

"What the hell?" he said finally, "Did you study him for English or something? This isn't normal, you know that, right?"

"He's so funny, I love him. He speaks to me."

"About shopping?" he said, a quizzical expression on his face.

"No, about life. He's a genius, he understands humanity better than anyone ever has."

They came across a late night pizza shop.

"We have to get food," Harry said, ever hungry with his tall, thin frame, always looking for the next good meal. Not waiting for anyone, he went inside to order and they all obediently followed. After they finished eating, their stomachs full and ready for sleep, they set off up the hill to their apartments. The village of Val d'Isère, picturesque at any time, would be even more beautiful later tonight as a fresh layer of snow covered the buildings and streets. Teddy and Aurora fell in together again, bringing up the rear.

"Why do we always end up alone at the back?" Aurora asked him, noticing the trend.

"Maybe because subconsciously we want to break away on our own," he suggested.

She looked up at him walking alongside her. "You do hear yourself, don't you?" she said sarcastically.

He went on unperturbed, staring straight ahead with his hands in his jacket pockets. "I know exactly what I'm saying."

She decided to try another tack. "Right, well, if you're going to talk like this, tomorrow on the slopes I'm just going to have to leave you in my wake."

"Great. I'm happy to chase you around the playground all day."

"The suspense is terrible. I hope it will last."
– Oscar Wilde

They sorted their ski hire after breakfast and got out on the slopes mid- morning. It had snowed off and on through the night so there was a layer of fresh powder even where the groomers had been. It was still overcast with poor visibility, but the snow was good. It was a dull grey day, threatening to snow, but not forecast to. Not a day to be out on a terrace up in the mountains, but just being outside in the cold air skiing would be enough of a treat. Their plan was to spend the day roaming the resort with Winnie as their tour guide. Teddy had been here before, but he didn't know it as well as Winnie, who skied at Val d'Isère every year.

As a group, they were of mixed skiing ability and it became obvious that half of them were on another level, but it didn't matter, they enjoyed each other's company and a bigger group was much more entertaining. Harry, more of a latte skier, was constantly requesting coffee breaks, which annoyed James and Teddy enormously: they were keen skiers who just wanted to go hard.

"Guys, I think we should stop here for lunch," Harry said, reading the menu outside a restaurant near Solaise. "This looks great, steak frites, moules frites, boeuf bourguignon, non?"

"Tu es mouillé!" Winnie rattled off in French.

"Quoi?" Harry answered, looking lost, his French somewhat limited.

"It means you are wet, Harry," Aurora interpreted, "although I'm not sure that translates, Winnie." Her grandmother was French Polynesian, so she understood a decent amount of the language. Winnie didn't care, he'd made his point. "Tarte au citron, do they have that, I have to have that while I'm in France," Aurora said keenly.

"I just need a bottle of red." Winnie preferred a liquid lunch when skiing.

"I suppose we can stop again, Harry, but only because the weather is shit today. Where's your bloody stamina, man?" Teddy's irritation was breaking through his affable exterior.

"I'm hungry, what can I say?" Harry was unphased, looking at the girls for backup.

"Sure, fine," Liv decided for them all.

The restaurant was large and bustling as the French rolled in in droves to stop for lunch. Their passion for food unmatched by any other nation, the ritual of eating so sacred in France meant that the restaurants were always full at lunchtime.

The boys insisted on buying the drinks, and Teddy had already bought coffee earlier; it appeared that money was no object for the guys. For Liv, Diana and Aurora, who were on a budget, it seemed extremely decadent and they felt a little guilty accepting, but the boys insisted.

Harry appeared to prefer the discourse over lunch and coffee to skiing. Dissecting the merits of certain films, philosophising and talking art with Aurora and Diana was much more his pace. For the more athletic boys, it was frustrating to spend so much time talking and eating. They all got antsy after an hour.

"Shall we have coffee?" Harry asked hopefully after dessert was cleared.

"No, you've had enough coffee, just finish your wine and let's go. At this rate it will be time for après and we won't even have skied a run after lunch," Winnie said bossily, rolling his eyes.

Harry ignored him. "You know, Roars and Diana, you guys should come to the Edinburgh Fringe Festival this year. You'd love it, Edinburgh has some great vintage and charity shopping."

"I'd love to, Harry." Aurora was eager, keen to see the beautiful city she had heard so much about.

"Me too, that sounds like so much fun," Diana agreed. Teddy and James didn't look so thrilled at the prospect of a future trip between Harry and the girls in Scotland.

"I'd be having fun now if I was out skiing," James interjected, applying more pressure.

Harry took the hint and reluctantly downed the rest of his glass of red. They paid the bill and left. As they thumped their way towards the door in their heavy, clunking ski boots, Teddy nimbly jumped ahead to pull open the door for Aurora, gallantly holding it open. He did so naturally, like it was second nature: he wasn't trying to win points, it was a reflex.

"Thank you," she said appreciatively as he nodded in response. She liked the fact that his manners were impeccable and understated. He didn't brag or blow his own trumpet, he was humble. Confident, yes; cheeky and flirtatious, yes; but he never talked himself up.

James was torn between showing off, flying down the runs, over jumps and through the trees, and making sure he continued to show Diana enough attention. There seemed to be an internal struggle going on within him. He was a dog who wanted to chase deer but knew he should stay with his owner. In the end he couldn't help himself. He had deliberated between boarding and skiing, eventually giving in to peer pressure from them all and agreeing to ski. He would go off one day with his surfing mates and board. Diana looked very pleased that he'd decided to ski and they often disappeared down a run together, her leopard-print jacket following his bright orange one out of view.

Aurora had no trouble keeping up. A keen skier, she had always loved the mountains. She tended to keep pace with the boys up front. Dressed in the outfit she had managed to convince her dad she had to have a season ago – a short, white, biker-style cropped jacket and fur hood, with matching white trousers, both of which had black zippers and black stripes down the inside seam – she looked like a pocket rocket on the slopes. Teddy was never very far away, carving left and right, disappearing through trees only to suddenly reappear and cross her path. She felt an involuntary thrill whenever it happened and he often turned to smile back at her. She had no doubt he could outski them all. She enjoyed just watching him move, powerful and stable, the skis appeared to be a part of him. He was dressed in all black kit, but his skiing style made it easy for her to spot him.

Winnie was their undisputed leader. Knowing "Val" like the back of his hand, he determined their course. They cruised around, trying to avoid the crowds and get a feel of the place that first day. They bumped into friends occasionally, but never the other girls Aurora dreaded. Every time she saw them, it felt like someone was touching an open wound on her body.

Liv spent the morning with them, but she had to share herself around, so many friends were keen to spend time with her. To tie herself to one group of people would probably lead to boredom for her, she needed variety. Aurora's presence would mean Diana didn't have to follow her rigorous social schedule if she didn't feel like it, and Diana appeared to be very happy remaining with James.

Late in the afternoon, Teddy and Aurora stopped at the side of a particularly long, steep slope and found themselves momentarily alone, catching their breath. They were coming down a difficult black run from the Bellevarde chair and the run had split. They waited for the others, but soon it became apparent they'd taken the other red run down.

"We're alone," he said matter-of-factly. It was eerily quiet as only the mountains in snow can be, the snow acting as a sound buffer, absorbing waves. The run was empty, there were no telltale swishes from oncoming skiers. It felt like they had stepped into another reality and Aurora was suddenly nervous. "What do we do now?" she asked apprehensively.

"Well, we're not going to panic," he said, smiling at her, sensing her anxiety. "I think I've got this." He was unnerving her again. Alone with him like this, she felt unsure of herself and a bit out of control. She managed a faint smile in response.

"You know, anyone would think being alone with me made you nervous?" he said, raising his brows.

"You do rate yourself, don't you?" She tried to say it scathingly, but her voice wasn't convincing, lacking some of her usual edge. She leant forward, resting on her poles. Her boots were hurting her shins now. He was standing next to her and she was easily knocked off balance as he leant into her, sending her falling onto her side in the snow. She squealed and laughed and he fell down next to her, lying by her side.

"It's so quiet," he observed, echoing her thoughts. He sat up on one elbow, looking at her, legs stretched out, completely at ease and in command of the situation.

"I love the stillness, it's like it's amped somehow, there's a clarity to it," she commented. *At least I have my helmet and goggles on to protect me*, she thought. He commenced to take his helmet off – *There goes that*, she thought – and then his goggles, cleaning the snow off with the microfiber cloth in his jacket.

"Give me yours and I'll clean them," he offered.

She had snow and water all over her goggles from the fall, and looking through them everything was blurry. With some trepidation she took the gear off. "Thank you," she muttered, handing them to him. She could always knock him back if he made a move, she told herself, but the problem was, would she? When he was this close she was totally unnerved, her heart rate increased and her pupils dilated.

She wasn't feeling robust after the whole thing with Paige, she really wasn't. He could potentially rock her world and she didn't even want it to sway. She wanted it to remain steady and stable and the emotions he generated were the exact opposite.

The sound of someone coming down the run drew their attention and a group of five came into view over the rise. They were struggling with the steep and bumpy terrain, traversing quite a bit here and there. As they passed by, a girl in a hot pink jacket nearly fell as she stared at them and Aurora recognised Paige's small, sharp chin and petite frame. No doubt she had clocked Teddy lying by her side and cleaning her goggles.

"That's Paige and the girls," she said after they had passed by, a cloud falling across her features.

"You know, it's been a good day, hasn't it?" he asked, handing her back her goggles, looking at her and waiting for a response.

"Yes, it has," she agreed, returning his gaze.

"Well, I'll take that," he said, standing and holding out his hand to pull her up. "Come on, the others must be waiting for us at the bottom. If we hurry, you can burn Paige."

"That does sound like my kind of fun," she admitted.

"I know it does. I've played tennis with you." She smiled and he pulled his goggles down and set sail.

As they took off, Teddy went full tilt, straight into fifth gear, and she rode his coat tails, flying in tandem, so fast, totally committed to the speed and the slope. There would be a price if she were to fall now. Instinct had taken over, there could be no hesitation, reservation or self-doubt skiing like this. At this speed you had to trust your body. She was aware when they flew past Paige and Sophie, but the exhilaration of skiing with him at this pace overpowered any satisfaction she might have felt in simply beating the girls, it was surprisingly unimportant.

At the bottom, Winnie watched them come down together. "What happened to you guys?"

"We were waiting for you, mate," Teddy answered, offering no other explanation and looking away.

Winnie searched his face for a few seconds before saying, "Come on, let's go for après, quite a few people are there already and it's nearly 4 p.m. Thomas and Jasper have been messaging me for the last hour." Winnie was often at the centre of any plans being made and they all relied on him to keep the rest of them up to date.

"Sure, I don't mind, let's go, we're down anyway," Teddy agreed. As the weather wasn't great, après were on down the hill by the lifts instead of up the mountain. They arrived at the outside bar, which was heaving, music blasting with a swamped bar, overrun as skiers flocked to it. It was a carnival atmosphere already, raucous and intemperate. They found a space to congregate and Aurora offered to go to the bar: "It must be my turn, so I'll go."

"No, I'll get it," Teddy countered.

"No, it's my turn," she quietly insisted.

"Okay, but I'll help you with the glasses, you won't be able to carry it all."

As they made their way through the crowd to the bar, she saw Emma and waved, shouting, "I'll come see you in a minute!", excited to see her again. She felt Teddy's hand on her back as he guided her through the crowd, occasionally putting a protective arm out to shield someone from stepping into her. She had to admit he sure knew how to treat a girl; no wonder he was so successful.

Aurora made her way over to Emma, glass in hand, and hugged her. "How are you? It's been too long," she said warmly.

"I know, where have you been? I haven't seen you in ages?" Emma asked.

"I went home for a couple of weeks and then didn't feel like going shooting for a while," she confided.

"Did that business with Paige have anything to do with it?"

"Yeah, actually, everything, it blew up into a shitshow to be honest and we aren't friends any more."

"Did she double down on it then, the whole you can't be my friend and see my ex's friend?"

"And some. Let's not talk about it, it's depressing and I'm having a good day."

"Is that because you spent it with Teddy Talbot? I saw you walk in with him and he's currently keeping an eye on you," she said, looking over Aurora's shoulder at Teddy.

"We skied as a group, it was fun, that's all."

"Well, I think he'd like it to just be the two of you. I've noticed him watching you before."

"We are just friends," she assured her.

"Well, watch him, he's a bit of a player. He was with a friend of mine briefly and she still won't stop talking about him."

And there it was, the warning again. She couldn't get away from it and it was disappointing to hear, especially when he'd been so lovely all day.

"Why won't she stop talking about him, what happened?" Aurora was keen to understand the background.

"She had a real thing for him. She said he was so lovely to her, so charming, a real flirt, but then went cold. Nothing came of it after they were together a couple of times and she was pretty cut up."

"Right, well, I'm experiencing the charm offensive, I think."

"Better to be aware, huh?"

"Yes, much better, thanks." It didn't feel better, though. Aurora wasn't happy to hear the story. The guy she had spent the first day with had been great company, kind and considerate, warm and genuine. The way Emma described him, he was a predator. They continued to chat for a while before she rejoined her friends.

The expectation was that they would après for a good few hours before changing and going out to a club later. It was a gruelling schedule for the body and the girls knew that they had to have some downtime, stop drinking and preferably sleep before going out in the evening or they would never make it. That was to be their daily routine for the week and Aurora wondered how they would go the distance.

"The only way to get rid of temptation is to yield to it."
— Oscar Wilde, The Picture of Dorian Gray

Two days later, Diana and James were officially a couple. Their romance had blossomed and his bad boy surfer dude image was totally shot. Around her he lost all credibility, totally whipped and so obviously walking on air, doting on her. She was a serene person to start with and now she glowed, lit from within.

"So, you and James are together?" Aurora asked tentatively as the girls came in from après.

"Yes, it just happened," Diana answered happily, flopping onto her bed by the door.

"He's been besotted with you for a long time," Aurora informed her, "it didn't just happen, I can assure you." Aurora sat on her bed under the window and crossed her legs, ready to listen.

"Well, he grew on me, you know, he's very cute and funny." Diana was beaming, clearly chuffed at the situation.

"Yes, James is funny, in a naughty kind of way." Liv smirked.

"He just makes me laugh, I guess. I like to talk and he seems happy to listen as well."

"I have no doubt he would hang off your every word, Diana," Aurora said.

Liv lay on her bed in the middle, arms behind her head, and turned to Aurora. "What about you and Teddy, he's totally into you, Aurora?" she probed.

"He's generally into girls, he doesn't specialise," she responded cynically. Liv and Diana both looked unconvinced. "I like him, but he's just a friend. I couldn't trust him, even if I wanted to."

"Aurora, James is a player too in that case. None of them are angels, it's always a risk, sorry, Di, but you know what I mean?" Liv said.

"Sure." Diana appeared unbothered.

"There's a difference between not being an angel and being a devil, and Teddy's a devil when it comes to girls. I've seen him in action and I've been warned by friends. No, I don't need the drama, I really don't." She was firm and a little defensive in her response. Looking down at the ground, avoiding eye contact with the two other girls.

"Okay, fair enough. He mustn't mean that much to you, though, or you wouldn't be able to help yourself," Diana added. "James has a history, I know that, but I trust his feelings towards me are genuine. I suppose it's a leap of faith at the end of the day."

"But he is so obviously in love with you, Diana, it's different," Aurora admonished, dismissing her point.

"It's easy to be objective and courageous with someone else's feelings, Aurora," Diana argued.

"I think it's a very similar situation, Aurora, I really do," said Liv, unmoved by her argument.

Aurora mulled over the conversation later while they got ready to go out and watch an open mic event in a club. The last two days had been pretty cool, she had to admit. Sunny weather, good snow and great company.

They finished each day up at La Folie Douce for après up on the slopes.

It was a non-stop party. Teddy had been flatteringly persistent without crowding her. He seemed to sense the line and when not to cross it, but he was charming, generous and let's not forget bloody good looking. He was making it hard. She reluctantly had to admit that Diana was right, it was easier to be objective about someone else's feelings, much harder when your own were at risk.

Later that night, they stood at the bar together, bodies sore and tired after another long day skiing. The boys were downing beers and Aurora was sipping her champagne. Diana and James were coming out later, preferring to be alone in the room. The decor at the venue was cosy American ski lodge, and in the centre of the nightclub was a sunken lounge area with chairs and tables and a stage area raised up in front. The long bar was along the left wall, glass backed and filled with bottles of liquor and glasses. Booths surrounded the sunken area on the other walls, raised up to the same level as the bar. A couple of guys were on the stage at the front, busily setting up amps and a couple of microphones for their weekly open mic night. Winnie had wanted to come as his band were going to perform, just for practice, and it was rumoured to be a great night. It was filling up as Bristol Uni took over the venue and students chatted about the day on the slopes and began the second part of their day, the night. Paige and her followers were already seated at one of the tables in the sunken area, drinking their white wine, dressed in virtually matching outfits. They followed the Bristol dress code, but they wore all designer labels.

"Testing one, two, testing one, two," said the compère as they did their final checks. People had to register their interest so they could organise the time slots and the equipment was provided in house. Winnie was off talking to the other two guys he was performing with and was getting jumpy in anticipation, chatting and bobbing around on the balls of his feet.

"He bounces around when he's excited," Teddy observed.

"Yeah, he does," said Aurora with a laugh, "but he seems excited and happy, I'd be feeling sick."

"You don't fancy being a front woman?"

"I can hold a tune," she said, raising one eyebrow, "but I'm not one for being the centre of attention, it scares me silly."

"Yeah, me too, I'd hate it. I hope he's good so I can honestly tell him that and I know you couldn't possibly give false praise."

"What do you mean by that?"

"I mean you're honest, not rude, but you tell people what you really think."

"Is there a better way to be?" she asked.

"It's just different, you're really forthright, it's a bit direct for your average Englishman."

"If you can't take the heat ..." she trailed off.

"I can take it," he answered suggestively.

Right, so now she was too direct. Oh well, they would all just have to get used to her as she was. It was too exhausting trying to dial herself down all the time and be a chameleon. Australians are known for being straight and blunt. She didn't challenge him, didn't retaliate and let it pass. It had been a lovely day and she didn't want to take up arms against him. "Well, I'm pretty sure he'll be very good, you've heard him sing," she stated.

"Yeah, he will be. Then he'll have all the girls in here falling all over him tonight, except for you."

Aurora wondered what he was getting at. She assumed he was referring to Winnie and her friendship, or did he think she fancied him, so she wouldn't be open to any other offer? That thought bothered her more. She was considering asking him, but Winnie had returned for his beer.

"You nervous?" she asked.

He nodded. "Yeah, I am a bit. The room is pretty full, it's more than I've ever played for before, school concerts aside," he added ruefully.

"You'll be great, Winnie, your voice is special, it really is," Aurora said, pumping him up.

"Don't worry, mate, if you miss tonight, we can just get slaughtered," Teddy offered.

"Thanks for the moral support, that's a consolation," Winnie said sarcastically.

"I've got your back, don't worry," Teddy assured him, patting him on the back. They were good mates, Aurora had observed. Of all the guys, they appeared to have formed the closest bond.

Harry arrived still looking sleepy from his post

après and dinner nap. "So, have I missed anything then?" he asked, adjusting his glasses and yawning. "Too much drinking all day. Wow, Roars, you look nice," he said, admiring her outfit. "Who are you pulling the stops out for?"

"No one, I just got sick of T-shirts and thermals," she said in a somewhat prickly tone. She'd decided to wear a cropped, one-shouldered, emerald green silk shirt, with an exaggerated puffy sleeve, and black jeans that tucked into her après boots. Teddy was smirking, enjoying her discomfort.

God, she wondered, *am I subconsciously dressing to impress him?*

The compère for the evening came on and began to introduce the acts one at a time. A guy did stand-up comedy, a trio of girls sang, then more comedy, some of it good, some of it very bad. The general atmosphere was jovial regardless of how good or bad the act was. Most people recognised it took courage to get up there. After an hour or so, Winnie's band was announced to lots of cheers; he had a following just because of his personality, most had never heard them play.

"Wish me luck," he muttered, before striding up to the stage and grabbing the guitar. They were performing their own song.

Their sound was decidedly indie, akin to the Kings of Leon, perhaps a bit retro for the age group, but very good. He had a great voice and the passion, which really is the force behind most success, and everybody could appreciate the quality of sound. He looked great on stage too, tall and lean, Prince Harry as a muso. They finished to resounding applause and euphoria, undoubtedly the greatest reception of the night.

He appeared to enjoy every moment of it, returning

to them at the bar, receiving pats on the back along the way, to clink glasses with Teddy and Aurora.

"I like the song, mate, it's good," Teddy affirmed. "I'll be your manager."

"Sure thing. Now can we get totalled? I've been holding off all day." He breathed out a sign of relief as he said it.

"God, you guys you don't have to get smashed every night, you know?" Aurora pointed out.

"We don't, but tonight is definitely the night to get smashed. There's a blizzard forecast for tomorrow, so no skiing," Teddy asserted, downing his beer. "Right, spirits or red?"

A few acts later, Diana and James wandered sheepishly in.

"Thanks for the support, you two, you missed our band already," Winnie said derisively.

"Sorry, mate, but you're lucky we turned up at all," he said, smiling at Diana, who looked a little embarrassed.

"Well, they were great," Aurora advised them, smiling proudly. "They brought the house down."

Diana was glowing, holding James' hand as she trailed into the club after him, cuter than ever. Her trademark look was felt shorts over tights with a big jumper, her legs on show in her short black boots. Aurora envied her: she had the look of love written all over her face, relaxed and content.

Her study of Diana was interrupted as she suddenly heard her name being read out as the next act. "What?" she said, turning to look at the compère.

"Aurora Bond," he repeated.

"What's going on, did you guys do this as a joke?" she said angrily, rounding on Winnie and Teddy.

"No, no, we didn't," Teddy answered, looking baffled.

"I promise we didn't," Winnie said, backing him up, looking concerned.

"Aurora," Diana said, tapping her on the shoulder. "I think Paige did, Aurora." Diana was staring at Paige and her group in the middle of the sunken lounge, right in the centre of the stage. "She's just in fits of giggles."

"I can see," Aurora said stonily, following her line of sight. She took a moment to think.

"Aurora Bond," the compère said again in his clipped French accent. This time Paige pointed her out to him.

"For fuck's sake!" said Winnie.

Aurora turned intently to him. "Winnie, can you play guitar for me?"

"Yeah, within reason, but what are you thinking?"

"Gabrielle Aplin? My piano teacher taught me to play and sing 'Home'. I can't play it well enough, but I can sing it."

"You can?" Teddy exclaimed, looking worried.

"Sure, I'll look it up, I know the song you mean. Quick, just go and see the guy, they'll give us a minute," said Winnie.

Ten minutes later, he had it sorted, enough time for Teddy to return from the bar with a shot in hand for Aurora. "Are you sure you want to do this, no one would blame you for bailing?"

"Yep. She wants to see me squirm and have to explain why I can't sing. I'm not going to give her the satisfaction," she said, determined and impassioned, eyes flashing.

"Okay, well, throw this back and go kill it," he said sincerely as he handed her the shot.

She walked to the stage. Winnie took a seat with the acoustic guitar on his lap. He lowered the microphone on the stand in front of him. "So I can back you up in the chorus," he said, smiling up at her, trying to be reassuring. She just nodded at him nervously, too tense to say anything.

She centred herself for a brief moment and thought of her family and her mother's words: "Remember we are with you, urging you on." She felt like they were; she felt like something was anyway.

The compère came back and announced her again, quieting the room, which was noisy and raucous. She stood at the microphone and took a breath. "This song is called 'Home', wherever in the world that may be for you," she said in a small voice. She began to sing along with the gentle strumming of the guitar, "*I'm a phoenix in the water...*" Her voice had a sweet, gentle timbre, with a lovely quality to it. It wasn't strong and her nerves showed, but the song didn't require a big voice. People were still talking but it was a low buzz now as they started to listen and take notice. When she got to the chorus, Winnie's voice joined hers softly and gave it more depth and resonance. He was a powerful ally and she turned to smile at him and acknowledge his support. She grew in confidence as she became aware people seemed to be listening and enjoying it.

Aurora sang the song with her eyes closed for the most part, partly to garner the emotion she needed to sell it, but also to block the crowd out. However, when it came to the second stanza where the song talks about overcoming adversity, she instinctively opened her eyes and looked in the direction of Paige, Sophie and Annabel, staring right through them coldly. The emotion flowed out of her as she sang and she lost herself in it, the identification with the words made that easy, the alcohol serving to aid the process as tears welled in her eyes. She felt like she was fighting for her dignity, fighting against the victimisation. She didn't fully belong in any one culture any more, home was where her family was. It was a poignant rendition and the room felt it.

The song gathered momentum throughout and as she approached the end, there was a slight lull before it built up to the final chorus. It was here that Winnie encouraged the crowd to join in and they erupted in unison with her.

As she finished the last few words, the applause had already started and she mentally returned to the room. With an outpouring of gratitude and relief, she hugged Winnie right on the stage. "Thank you so much, I just couldn't have sung without you."

"Bloody hell, you showed them," he said into her ear, "I wouldn't have missed it."

She returned to her friends and Teddy wrapped her up in a full embrace, the emotion of the past ten minutes was becoming overwhelming. "That was great," he said quietly to her. She felt like crying, her emotions were building like a wave, threatening to engulf her. He released her to shout to James at the bar. "James, James, get some champagne!"

As friends and acquaintances told her how good her performance was, she calmed down, but she felt raw, the emotions lying just below the surface, ready to spill over. So far it was a rollercoaster of a night. She wanted a moment alone to process her feelings and just get a grip. She decided to slip outside. Grabbing her coat, she said to them all, "I'll be back in a minute, just getting some air."

She leant up against a wall around a corner of the building alone, hiding away, taking in the cold air, looking up at the stars. The sky was still clear, with no sign of the front predicted to roll in by morning. Teddy followed her outside about ten minutes later and stood next to her, saying nothing for a moment.

"I could point out the constellations, would that be too cliché?" he finally said.

"Please don't, I'm enjoying them as they are, I don't need to analyse them." It came out a little harsher than she intended. She knew it wasn't fair, but she had been enjoying his company far more than she had ever intended. He was getting to her, she thought he would have gotten bored by now and looked in another direction, but he hadn't deviated one bit. Coming to check on her now, another example of his dedication.

"Come on, Aurora, soften up."

"Why do you keep pushing me?" She rounded on him. "I haven't encouraged this, but you keep coming back like a hungry, stray dog. I keep holding you at bay, but you keep coming and coming, and to quote Holly Throsby, 'You can't see where your friends stop and your lovers begin.' There's a room full of bimbos inside, go and take your pick," she said, waving him away.

"Holly who?"

"Forget it, it's a song my mum plays, you won't know it," she said dismissively.

"I don't know why," he said, dropping his head. "I can't help it. I sense it takes effort for you to resist, that spurs me on."

At least he was being honest, she thought. "I think you like a challenge, you like the chase and the minute I give in you'll be off."

"I don't think I will." He shook his head

emphatically and moved to position himself directly in front of her.

"Really, well, I don't want to take the chance. The risk isn't worth the reward, not for me," she said flatly.

"See, I think you do. I see it when you look at me, you can feel the energy between us." He gestured between the two of them. "You know it would be great," he stated confidently, edging closer.

She scoffed at him pulling a face.

"What's happened to you, who hurt you so badly?"

"Nobody has. I've just seen you and your type in action over and over again!" she retaliated, angry he had made the connection.

"My type, my type, I don't have a type." He was agitated now, brows drawn together in a scowl, hands in his pockets, frustration etched on his face. "Am I supposed to be celibate until I fall in love? Maybe I just didn't want to be in a relationship with any of those girls. Love is a risk, haven't you heard?"

"But with me it's all different?" she said sarcastically. "Really? I'd be a colossal fool to fall for you. 'Love is a losing game', just listen to Amy Winehouse," she said sharply, turning her head away to avoid eye contact.

"What's with all the song references?" he asked, puzzled, breaking into a grin. "Can't you just talk in your own words?"

He was bad, he really was, unflappable, seemingly able to take the sting out of their argument and lighten the mood. She couldn't help it, she smiled and looked up at him standing in front of her. It was enough to break the tension and that was all the encouragement he needed.

He grabbed her around the waist with one arm and

pulled her into him, the other went to the back of her neck, forcing her to kiss him. Shivers ran up her spine. It was daring, forceful, ardent. She was tired of resisting, it was hard work always pulling away, he was gorgeous and it was exhausting when the full force of her inner being was so compelled and drawn to him. Her body and mind in constant conflict was wearing her out. He pushed her back against the wall and she was pinned, unable to escape. His fingers were in her hair, then touching the side of her face and all the while his lips pressed firmly against hers, his whole body leaning against her. His charisma overwhelmed her and she gave in. He felt it immediately as she let go, felt her submit and go limp against him, felt her respond, kissing him back. Thoughts were whizzing through her brain, maybe she should just get it out of her system, maybe just put it all to bed, go to bed, be done with it, all of it went through her mind. They kissed long and passionately and she knew she was in real trouble right here, right now if she didn't halt proceedings. He was well behaved but it wasn't reasonable to expect that to last. Unchecked, they were headed in one direction. And then he surprised her. He put both his hands either side of her on the wall, pushed back and pulled away, releasing her, and stood catching his breath for a moment before giving her one last kiss on the head. "That's enough for now," was all he said in a subdued and husky voice. It was not without effort, that was obvious, but he did it and she was left burning, with a million tingling sensations and her heart racing. Before he walked around the corner, he turned and looked back at her, smiling.

Cheeky shit! He did that just to show me he could. No wonder she didn't feel safe, she felt like he'd pulled her out into a deep, deep ocean and then left her there alone treading water. He'd totally disarmed her and he knew it. She had no option but to follow him back inside, but she waited as long as she could. With the clear skies above, the temperature was plummeting, even in her ski jacket she was freezing. He's made his point, she thought. He was right of course, the chemistry was undeniable now, but that wasn't the issue: where did they go from here, what was he offering? Diana was also right, at some level it was a leap of faith.

When she went back inside, a DJ was playing music, all the acts finished. She rejoined her friends and found Winnie, busy chatting to his fans, highly engaged and animated. Diana and James only had eyes for each other tonight, standing alone together at the bar, talking intimately.

Liv approached her. "Hey, do you mind Harry being in our room tonight? Diana wants to stay in with James. I suspect we might have him in with us for the rest of the week," she said, glancing at the pair of them cosying up at the bar.

"Sure, that's fine, he'll feed us if nothing else and he doesn't look like a snorer." Aurora was still feeling somewhat stirred and exhilarated. It had been a heady hour or so and emotions were bubbling away under the surface. *I'm watching how much champagne I drink from now on.*

"Hey, you okay? That looked like a pretty intense situation." Liv stood scrutinising Aurora's face.

"Sorry, what do you mean?" Aurora visibly recoiled at the reference. *God, did she come outside too, did she see what happened?*

"Up there on stage, don't tell me you've already

blocked it from your memory?"

"Oh no, yes, it was," she said with relief. "I needed to get some air outside for a bit after. I thought I might cry for some bizarre reason."

"Fair enough, you sang with a lot of emotion." Liv appeared to be none the wiser and Aurora relaxed.

Teddy came over and handed her a glass of champagne. "Cheers," he said, clinking her glass. "That was quite a moment."

"Wasn't it?" agreed Liv. "I was just saying that."

"Yep, full of passion, you poured your heart and soul into it," he said with a smile playing about his lips, looking directly at Aurora as he took a sip of champagne.

He was enjoying himself now and was way too confident.

"Thank you. Well, when you get put on the spot, what are you gonna do?" She shrugged as she said it and flashed him a look which said *don't go too* far as she toyed with her necklace.

"Hidden talents there, Roars, you've been holding out on us all." He was smiling and happy, exceedingly jovial. It made her feel warm all over, she felt like she was radiating heat.

"Aurora, that was great," James said, coming to join them with Diana. "I thought you were going to crash and burn and Di didn't breathe for a full minute, I swear, but then you pulled it off."

"Yeah, it surprised the hell out of Paige, I think. I was watching her through part of it," Diana added, "she looked shocked as she realised her stunt had backfired, and then you glared at her too."

"I didn't glare at her, I just looked at all of them, that's all."

"Oh honey, no, you did not," Liv assured her adamantly, shaking her head. "It was an icy cold, withering glare."

"Okay, well, clearly I'm more transparent than I think." Aurora glanced around the room to see where Paige was, but couldn't locate her.

She watched Teddy talk to various other people as they both inevitably mingled. She saw the girls come and go, some flirting with him, but he kept returning to her side. She too had lots of admirers, guys she did and didn't know, who came and told her she'd been great on stage and lingered, but his way of looking after her champagne glass and his presence circling around her soon sent them on their way.

Harry was scrutinising her through his black spectacles. "You're glowing tonight, you must feel good, huh?" He was astute for a guy, sensitive and aware of others.

"Yes, Harry, I do," she said simply.

Paige made herself scarce early and Aurora relaxed and enjoyed her victory. She didn't want to be in a war with her, didn't want to engage, but sometimes you have to stand your ground and push back, enough was enough.

Winnie became entangled with a pretty brunette, rounding out his night. He'd been talking to her for a couple of hours.

"Who is she? I don't know her from anywhere?" Aurora asked him when she got the chance.

"She does Fine Art, her name's Tabitha."

"Well, she looks quirky and very cute." The girl was petite. Dressed in black, skinny jeans and an oversized sweatshirt, anchored by après boots that appeared far too big for her delicate frame. At first glance she could have been an elf or a gelfling. Dead straight black hair cut into a sharp bob with a fringe, her ears ever so slightly peeking through the curtains of black. Aurora noticed lots of piercings, a multitude of friendship bracelets and chains; she pulled the alternative look off well.

"She just came up and started chatting about music, asking me about the band, etc. She is cute, isn't she?"

"She is."

The evening was over way too quickly. As they all walked home, Liv was so smashed she needed Teddy on one arm and Aurora on the other. The life of the party was coming down fast. Harry went off to get takeaway and Winnie was well occupied with his girl up ahead, who was obviously going back to his room.

Together they put Liv to bed and Aurora suddenly realised she had a problem. With Tabitha in Teddy and Winnie's room, where would Teddy sleep? Harry was taking Diana's bed, but they couldn't very well leave Teddy out in the hall. The rooms were small and compact, typical of ski lodges in France. They had three single beds and the floor was covered in bags. *Shit, shit, shit*, she thought. *I can't make him sleep with Harry, two six-foot guys in a single bed*. Liv was already passed out, not that it would have been fair to ask her to share with him.

Teddy was looking around the room. "So, which bed is ours?" he said, way ahead of her, smiling broadly. "I'm guessing it's this neat one under the window?" He sat down, bouncing on her bed, before proceeding to take off his boots. He had achieved his goal for the night, he was very merry. "Come on, sit down," he said, patting the mattress.

"You can stay, but only if you promise to behave

yourself. One false move and you're on the floor, you understand?" she said firmly.

"Can I sleep in my boxers?"

"No." *Oh God, where is Harry?* she thought. *He will unwittingly keep him in check.* "I'm getting into my pyjamas," she said, going to the bathroom. "Remember what I said, one false move!" When she came out of the bathroom, Harry was back with French fries and burgers. She ate some fries with them and they sat talking, having their afters, the drunken babble at the end of the night.

As they finally settled down, it was nearly dawn, the front bringing the storm had finally rolled in and it was snowing heavily. Aurora looked out the window before getting into bed, the large flakes were highly visible in the glow of the lampposts, swirling and whipping wildly around in the wind. It looked tempestuous and turbulent outside, reflecting her emotions indoors.

22

"Everything in the world is about sex except sex. Sex is about power."
– Oscar Wilde

As she came to the next morning, it was a gentle awakening. She was aware of someone holding her, warm and close, reality merging with her dream of someone kissing her neck ever so delicately. It was electric and her body was responding instinctively. As she came out of the dream, she realised what was happening and who it was. She rolled over to face him. "You are supposed to be on your best behaviour, remember?" she whispered.

"I'm trying, but you're making it difficult. I think I'm still drunk," he admitted with a happy grin.

She could feel his bare legs next to her. He'd gone to sleep in his jeans, but now they were definitely not on his body and he was under the duvet with her.

"You promised and now your jeans are off."

"It was uncomfortable, that's all, no ill intent, I promise," he said softly. It was still early, no sound of any movement. Outside it was a total whiteout, there would be no action on the slopes today. He leant forward, they were only centimetres apart anyway, and kissed her gently. It was soft and tender. It felt different to last night, his lips were beckoning to her today, asking her to follow him rather than demanding, and she so wanted to go, but they were in a roomful of people and she was with the most notorious philanderer of her year.

He rolled her over onto her back, his arms either side of her as he looked down at her from above, playing with her hair, blue eyes blazing as he searched her face. "You're even more beautiful in the morning," he said sincerely.

"You're good, you know, you really are." She said it with sarcasm, tinged with begrudging admiration.

He ignored her and kissed her again, one hand in her hair, the other one grabbing one of her hands. She felt herself drifting along with it for a while, but as he upped the ante, she put both hands on his chest, pushing him back. "Whoa boy, easy now." In the cold light of day, her resolve was stronger. He lay back down next to her, expelling a big sigh.

"You're making this tough."

"You can always lie on the floor if that's better for you," she reminded him. She reluctantly had to admit to herself that having him even just lying next to her felt wonderful. Her stomach was filled with nervous excitement and all, but this had happened so fast. Yesterday they were friends, he had been pursuing her for sure, but they were still just friends, and now a line had been crossed.

They dozed off and on for a few hours, but neither of them could really sleep and when he got the all-clear message from Winnie, he prepared to go. He stood and put his jeans on and leant down to kiss her again before leaving. She was sitting up in bed now, her mind filled with thoughts flitting around inside her brain, trying to assess his behaviour and her feelings.

"Stop, someone will wake up," she whispered, pulling herself away.

"Does it matter?"

"Yes. I feel awkward."

"Why?"

"I don't know why," she said honestly. There was a brief pause before she added, "I'm just not sure." She was deep in thought, unsure of what she did or didn't want to have happen.

He looked a little confused, a little hurt, then he slipped away back to his room.

Aurora was grateful Liv and Harry were still sleeping as he closed the door behind him. She nipped into the bathroom, showered and then dressed in comfy clothes. Her favourite loungewear was an oversized eponymous Ralph Lauren hoodie with a pair of leggings. She felt a little giddy, her stomach still had butterflies. She wasn't hungry at all.

As she came out of the bathroom, Harry was gone and Diana was back, chatting animatedly with Liv.

"Morning, so how was your night?" Aurora asked suggestively.

"It was good, so good!" she said, beaming. "It's just

so natural, you know, so easy. He makes me happy," she said, smiling ear to ear. "He told me he organised for us to be in the same lodge as all of them. He knows someone on the committee who was doing the accommodation, so that's how that happened."

"I thought it was a little too convenient," said Liv wryly.

"So, what about your night, Aurora?" Diana said returning the favour, raising her eyebrows questioningly.

"Come on, spill, what's going on?" Liv was straight in, no subtlety.

"I would, but honestly nothing's going on." Why didn't she want to tell her friends, include them and share it? Somehow she wanted to hug it to herself; it wasn't real yet, it wasn't something to be shared. No one had seen anything, she didn't need to kiss and tell. "Liv, we had to put you to bed like a baby, you don't deserve to know what you missed," Aurora said, throwing her socks at her, before turning away from them both to put her pyjamas and toiletries away.

Liv caught the socks. "Thanks for that. Gotta admit I don't remember anything after we left the club, probably before actually," she said as she stretched out in bed, arms above her head, staring up at the ceiling, trying to recall what she could.

"You aren't going to get off that lightly Aurora, dish!" Diana was adamant, looking at her sternly, sitting on her bed by the wall. "I can see it written all over your face."

"And Teddy Talbot almost never goes home alone," Liv added.

"Thank you, girls. And there you have it, he never goes home alone, that's the problem," Aurora finished.

"He's not that bad," Diana said, trying to reassure her.

"And now you're making excuses for him. Let's be honest, Teddy has, shall we say, a voracious appetite. I suspect it's not likely to be satisfied with just one girl. James is different, he's so obviously in love with you, Diana, since he first saw you, I think." She sat down on the bed, facing Diana on hers.

"Aurora, you don't see what we see," said Diana.

"It's not about what he's doing now. I'm questioning what he'll be doing after we leave here, maybe even sooner," she said defiantly. She had no confidence in anything he said or did.

"Yes, I get that, but Teddy looks pretty besotted to me. He's spent the whole time with you."

"And his friends," Aurora added as she shifted uncomfortably. *Why are they cornering me like this? Why do they care? They just don't understand, they haven't been there, they haven't been kicked in the stomach and winded by emotional, gut-wrenching pain.*

"He's following you around, come on, we've all watched it. I think Winnie is a little put out he's lost his two friends," said Liv, pulling off her jumper. "Ugh, I can't wait to get out of these. My clothes feel disgusting and my teeth are all furry." She was still fully dressed under the covers and wrinkled her nose with displeasure.

"He's putting in all the moves, I agree with you, but that's not what is making me nervous." She was beginning to feel panicked inside, old feelings making their way to the surface again. *Why do I feel so irrational about this? It's not worth getting worked up over. God, what is wrong with my stupid emotions?* "I don't just want a one-night stand, or a thing for a while. He's a friend now too, and he's Winnie's best mate and Winnie's mine, it's all so close," she said, pointing exasperatedly in the direction of the boys' room.

"Why are you getting teary?" Liv asked, brows furrowed in concentration.

"What's the matter?" Diana asked, looking concerned.

Aurora wiped away a few stray tears that had escaped. *I think I know what this is about, but can I trust these girls, we don't know each other that well?*

She decided that she had no choice, the tears were coming anyway, she may as well tell the story. She took a tissue proffered by Diana and wiped her eyes again, wondering how to tell the tale. She figured blunt and straight to the point was easiest.

"The first guy I ever had sex with was called Callum. He was the captain of the rugby team of this big private school in Cambridge, really cute, funny, smart, the whole package. We were going out for a while. He pursued me like Teddy is, like Flynn did, and I really fell for him, you know. Then, when I slept with him, well that was it. Finished. He broke it off the next day and just moved on. It was all an act, it was all about the conquest, he didn't care about me, but *I* really thought he did."

"God, that's awful," said Diana, shocked.

"I was blindsided and humiliated. It almost traumatised me somehow." Aurora looked away out the window to try and gain some control, wiping her eyes quickly again.

"Somehow? I can easily see why it would, but you are so not alone. It happens to lots of girls," Liv sympathised, pulling herself upright.

Aurora put a hand to her forehead. "Gosh, my head hurts, I need water, I'm dehydrated. Anyway, I haven't really liked anyone like that since, so nothing was at stake, but now ... now ... I'm scared."

"Of course, anyone would be," said Diana.

"When that business with Flynn and Paige happened, I just spiralled down into some sort of a depression, I think. It's been hard getting out of it, and now I don't want to risk going back there, I ... I ... I don't feel strong enough." The tears welling in her green eyes overflowed and rolled down her face with the admission. "I've been seeing a counsellor ever since, and I'm all over the place."

Diana jumped up and went and sat down next to her, putting a slight arm around her shoulder. "I'm so sorry," she said, giving it a heart-felt squeeze.

"Guys can be such arseholes," Liv said, shaking her head. "Being pretty is almost worse, you're a target."

"I don't know about that, I only know how it felt and I couldn't handle that again right now."

"Aurora, don't do anything until you're sure, like really sure, he cares about you. If he gets bored waiting and moves on, then he was always going to. Make sure, especially if you really like him," Diana said earnestly, staring directly into her eyes.

Aurora nodded as Diana spoke, feeling like a small child. "I know, I know, I am." She felt better for having shared what felt like a dark secret, shame wrapped up in a ball of hurt that had been living in her gut.

"So, do you? Like him, that is?" Diana asked.

"I'm ... very attracted to him," she finally admitted, sighing. She couldn't deny it to herself or to her friends any more, she did like him. She wouldn't have spent so much time with him otherwise. She was embarrassed to admit she'd been talked round by Teddy. She looked up at the ceiling as she searched for the words. "He's not quite what I thought he was initially. That weekend we went away, when we were all at his place, he was really humble. My God, you should see it." Her eyes grew wide and were brighter now, her expression animated.

"A mansion, huh?" said Liv.

"Unbelievable, really, but he was so low-key and just so lovely and for the most part he's been so charming. That's the word I keep thinking of in my head, but he's very smooth, which is worrying, and he's a bit of a devil as well," she finished breathlessly.

"Well, isn't that what makes it exciting too? Otherwise it would be downright boring, wouldn't it?" Liv asked, looking at them both, deciding not to point out that Aurora was practically glowing as she talked about Teddy.

"Yes," Diana agreed.

"Now what happened?" Liv demanded, smiling like a co-conspirator. "He really is so fit."

"Liv, forget it! There's nothing to tell."

Aurora slipped out of their room, pretending to get breakfast while Liv and Diana showered. She found the internal stairs and slipped inside. She listened for a moment to make sure nobody was already on them further below, figuring she would hear if anyone opened a door. She needed to speak to her best friend, the one who had been there through the whole Callum fiasco. The friend who wouldn't sugar-coat anything, the friend who absolutely had her back. She called Chloe and explained what had happened the night before.

"What do you think? I'm so conflicted I can't think straight. Do I trust him?"

"He's got to earn that, no?" said Chloe.

"Yes, but I didn't rush things with Callum and it didn't matter. Teddy could do the same thing."

"To be fair to you, Callum was patient, almost calculated, but Callum isn't like most guys. I never trusted him, remember?" Chloe spoke with the authority of one who is right with hindsight.

"I remember, but he was saying and doing all the right things? I wasn't a complete idiot, was I?" Aurora looked forlornly down at the concrete stairs as she spoke into the phone.

"He was just after a trophy, Aurora. With his huge ego, he was like some macabre, fucked-up collector. I know that's a horrible thing for me to say to you but, the harder the prize was to earn, the more he wanted it." Chloe spoke quickly, enunciating perfect English in her French accent.

"None of his other trophies came and warned me about him. Nobody said a word to me beforehand, only afterwards."

"Why would they? They all thought they were special too, but if it happened to you as well then they weren't the only ones to be suckered in. You know, misery loves company."

"Thanks, this is making me feel so much better," Aurora said sarcastically.

"Sorry, but he was a dickhead and it was all there if you had really looked. You didn't want to see it because you were already in too deep, you were flattered."

"Ouch, Chloe, what the hell?"

"It's harsh but fair, Aurora, tell me I'm wrong?"

"Okay, maybe I was, but I don't want to make the same mistake again, *which is why I'm calling you!*"

"I have never met this Teddy, I've not even seen a

picture of him, which is good because it would bias me, but so far he seems to have been genuine. He has been himself, he called you a 'convict and a savage', which is the exact opposite of what Callum would have done."

"Yes, he did."

"And the biggest thing in his favour is he's supported you after you and Paige fell out. That shows good character."

"He was a real dick to start with and then something changed after I called him out, like he's actually emotionally intelligent. How can somebody be both a dick and emotionally intelligent?"

"Some people use their emotional intelligence to be dicks. I would give him a chance, but go in with eyes wide open and take your time."

Aurora smirked to herself as she said, "Like you do?"

"But I'm French, it's so different."

"How?"

"You think your power is in giving boys sex, my power is taking it away."

They finished their chat and Aurora sloped back to her room. Everyone had slept in and after showers they regrouped. On the ground floor of their lodge was a large dining room, which flowed into a lounge and bar area. Students were congregating here while the storm blew through. There was a fire with sofas and coffee tables arranged around in conversational groups. The decor was basic and simple, just as the rooms were. The bar was at the far end and was the focal point of the entire area. Long, with as many as ten bar stools in vinyl lined along it, it was always busy and lively before they went out in the evenings. Today it was open and it promised to be a day of drinking, games and cards.

"Let's play Cards Against Humanity?" suggested James.

"Oh, I brought Most Likely To, it's great," said Diana.

"Thanks for putting Teddy up for the night," Winnie said as he came and stood next to Aurora.

"No worries. Good night?"

"Yeah, good night, very good night."

"She seems to have gotten to you a bit? Don't think I've seen a girl turn your head before."

"It was a good night," he enthused, nodding his head as he said it with a smirk.

"Okay, let's just leave it there, shall we," Aurora said, retreating from the conversation. "I don't want the details."

"Oh alright, but she really knows her music too, that's hot. A girl has to love music and be able to talk about it, or she isn't attractive, not to me anyway."

"Okay, Winnie, I'll remember that. I'm glad you enjoyed yourself. Will you see her again?"

"Maybe, I don't know. I'll see."

Boys are so disconnected from the physical act. It's so different for girls, who almost give their soul away, for boys it's like going to the gym, unless they're attached somehow. This is the scary fact of it all, figuring out when they are truly invested. She was determined not to let Teddy get too close, too soon.

"Let's play Most Likely To," Winnie shouted into the circle as they sat down, eager to get the games going.

Teddy arrived, having gone back to bed for a few hours, and joined them where they had snagged sofas close to a fire. He'd showered and was looking sober and brighter now. Aurora watched him as he entered the lounge; her heart skipped a beat, sending a wave of anxiety through her.

He stopped to engage with various people as he moved through the room in tracksuit bottoms and a T-shirt. He'd obviously just done his hair, still damp and curling, and beginning to form his trademark waves. He was well liked, she observed. He appeared to treat everyone he came across with the same benevolent air. She used to think of him as arrogant and smug, but that was a while ago now. His bravado and confidence was still there, but he never referred to his title, or talked about his home or where he went to school, unless really pushed by someone. He was at pains to play things down. He sat down opposite her, but didn't look at her and was quiet.

That's a bit odd, she thought, *it's not like him.* Normally he would be full of chat and flirtation, flashing her a grin.

They started playing as one card after the other was pulled out of the deck and they had to decide within five seconds who was most likely to suit whatever was written on it. The majority of votes would decide which person the card belonged with, and that person had to drink. Sort of a get to know you, come drinking game best played among a group of friends.

Thomas and Jasper also joined them, they were on another floor in the lodge. Aurora and James moved down to make room for them on the sofa. "So, did you arrange for them to be in our chalet too, James?" she quietly asked him archly.

"Maybe," he said, smiling cheekily. "Is that Teddy's hoodie you're wearing?" he asked in playful banter.

"Touché!" she responded. *Diana!* she thought. Clearly she was already discussing everything with James and was not to be trusted, damn. Don't worry, she told herself, all they know is that she was forced to let him stay in her room and that she was the one whose bed he'd shared, that's it. *Just play it cool.*

The first card to come out was drawn by Thomas. "Only has drunk game," he read out.

"Well, we know someone who spends most of his life in this state, don't we?" Aurora suggested.

"Ah no hinting, Roars!" James interrupted.

It pretty much unanimously went to Winnie.

"Pees outside when the bathroom is open. Eww really?" said Diana, pulling a disgusted face. The girls were all taking guesses, but the boys all gave it to Jasper; clearly they knew more.

"Will make a great cougar. Oh that's more like it," said Winnie. Diana was giggling as the majority went to Liv, who had this air of confidence about her, although Teddy nominated Aurora, which she was a little offended by.

James announced the next card, "Is pulled over for driving too slow."

"Where's Sophie when you need her," Teddy piped up at last.

And then "Has sex while watching TV," "She was made for this game," Harry said laughing.

Aurora pulled the next. "Being Facebook friends is too much commitment."

"Well, this won't be hard," said Harry, looking at Teddy. It went on, and Teddy ended up with various cards: "Is a total flirt", "Is going straight to hell", all of which formed an incriminating story and one which he didn't seem to be finding amusing as he drank from his beer.

"Come on, what's up with you today?" James badgered him. "Take your punishment."

"Mate, there's plenty coming your way too!" Teddy retaliated as he read out, "Is fucking stoked." James was always being ribbed by his mates for wanting to be a surfer, for growing his hair out and cultivating the surfie image.

When Jasper pulled out "Is destined to be a trophy wife", it unanimously went to Diana, who was offended. "I'm going to be an independent career woman, not someone's prize," she said with indignation.

Harry turned up "Watches *Planet Earth* for five hours" and quite a few of them seemed unsure, but Aurora knew that Teddy absolutely belonged with the card. As they all pointed to their nominations only she, Winnie and James had tagged him, but it was enough to give him the majority.

"Only your nearest and dearest know that about you, clearly," Liv said, teasing him.

Teddy finally looked at her then and she could see he was different today, something was off. Gone was the warmth and the carefree, flippant attitude.

"'Has a dark side'," read Diana.

"Well, we know who to give that too, don't we?" James said, looking at his mates, and the guys all pointed to Harry.

"Really? Harry, I don't believe it," Diana said, defending him. He just drank, saying nothing.

"He knows he's guilty," said Teddy.

"I thought you'd give that to me," Aurora admitted.

"No, Roars, this is you," said Winnie, reading, "'Has resting bitch face'."

"I don't, do I?" She was genuinely affronted. The girls were thinking about it, but the boys weren't.

"Yeah, you do," Harry insisted.

"Well, I'm scared of you," Thomas, who didn't know

her so well, admitted.

"You intimidate a lot of guys," James concurred. "The barman at Steam said he'd rather shoot himself than have a conversation with you."

"I've never had a conversation with him." "Exactly," replied James.

"Well, thanks for the feedback. Glad we're all learning about each other today," she said sarcastically.

"That's the idea!" Diana said, happy her game was being well received.

"'Could do a whole lot better'," read Thomas.

"Fuck me, that's just way too easy," said Winnie, looking at Diana and in turn James for his reaction.

James just shrugged his shoulders. "I'm good, I've got the girl," he said smugly.

They finished their game and agreed to have a break for a while. Aurora looked at Teddy, wondering what was wrong. He was so subdued and quiet. *Is that it now? No sex, so he's out?* She felt the familiar waves of anxiety building inside her, baffled by the change in his demeanour. She was aware that this was so not what she needed.

Afternoon slowly spilled into early evening as the snow fell heavily and winds buffeted the lodge. Snug and warm by the fire which burned slowly, the students were happy to have a rest day and sit drinking. A few hours later, they were deep into a poker game. Most of the players were bankrupted, which left Teddy, Harry and Aurora still in. People stood around watching as they played Texas Hold 'Em. Teddy seemed to be well practised, as did Harry, both having said they played in boarding school. They were good at reading people and bluffing. Teddy hadn't warmed up all day and Aurora wondered what had happened from the time he'd left her in the morning.

"Roars, how come you can play?" James asked, curious.

"We play at home all the time."

"Lady Luck has been with you today," observed Liv. Aurora still had a decent pile of chips in front of her. As they played the hand, Harry went out, Teddy taking the round. They were down to just the two of them now. A few more hands were played and it went back and forth, like a tennis match.

They were dealt another round and they paid the blind. The bidding increased rapidly as each card was turned over; there were two aces out now. After the river, Teddy deliberately looked across at her, calculating. She stared back at him, expressionless.

"I'm all in," he said intensely, shoving all his chips into the centre. "The question is, Aurora, what are you going to do?" He stared hard at her, a look that meant way more than the game in front of them. She knew he was talking about a totally different subject by the tone of his voice. It wasn't light, flirtatious or teasing, but intense and serious.

"Be patient," she returned deadpan, staring back at him.

Winnie's head shot up sharply, like a terrier after a rat. Thankfully most of the others were either too drunk, bored or distracted to have caught it. "Are we still talking about cards?" he tentatively asked, looking back and forth at both of them.

Aurora ignored Winnie, refusing to respond, as did Teddy. She elected to go all in, knowing she would probably lose the game. "I'm in. Let's see what you've got." She pushed her load of chips into the centre of the table with his. Teddy had three aces, she had two pairs, and it was game over.

As she got up from the sofa afterward, she knew she was going to have to find an opportunity to talk to him alone. She didn't have long to wait as it was dinnertime and everyone began moving into the dining room, most of them desperately in need of food. She lingered behind and went to the bar, where he silently joined her. He sat at one of the bar stools while she ordered.

"Teddy, do you want anything?" she asked, turning to look at this new version of him before her.

"Yeah, just a Coke, thanks."

She ordered and sat in the stool next to him, swivelling it to face him. "What was that?" she said with slight irritation.

"I don't know, Aurora, are you interested or not?" he asked, clearly rattled.

"Am I interested in what, Teddy?"

"Me? This morning you said you're not sure. I've been wondering what that means all day, so I put it out there." He was deadly serious.

"Uh huh, you did, and now Winnie's caught on something's up," she said, a little annoyed. "You asked me why I felt awkward about anyone knowing about us and I said 'I don't know why, I'm not sure,' that's all. I don't know why I feel that way, but I do. I don't want anyone knowing anything." She was adamant and not prepared to be pulled into something for which she was not ready.

"Well, I sort of took it that you weren't sure about being with me at all," he said softly. For the first time he wasn't full of game, he was a little unsteady, on the back foot, and Aurora could sense the balance of power lay in her hands.

"It's not no, it's just not yes, not yet anyway. I don't

know anything, I guess. It was no, but you forced that issue and overcame it last night," she said, smiling at him, referring to the time outside the club. "I don't really know *you*. I know the flirt and the playboy." She knew she was opening up the door now, encouraging him to continue.

"You know, I'm usually pretty good at reading people, but I can't tell what you're thinking most of the time," he said honestly.

"Oscar Wilde would say, 'Women are made to be loved, not understood.'"

"That I know how to do," he said ruefully, smiling again for the first time.

"Yeah, that's not really how it's meant. Then again maybe it is, but it's not what I meant." She wanted to reach out to him all of a sudden, to touch his face, his leg, anything to make physical contact, but was so conscious that they were in the middle of a ski trip with fifty of their friends eating dinner twenty metres away. She was forced to keep her hands to herself. "I did go all in when I should have folded," she said more gently, "and it cost me the game," she added with mock irritation.

"I know it cost you your pride."

"We both know I had you."

He couldn't help himself as he leant forward and grabbed her lower leg behind the knee, pulling her slightly towards him. "I'll happily take a rematch anytime." Shivers ran up her spine again as she looked into his eyes, and with that one move the power balance levelled out again.

23

"Never love anyone who treats you like you're ordinary."
— Oscar Wilde

The next day, they got an early start; with the promise of good weather and fresh powder to be had, they were eager to get up there first. The skies had cleared after the storm and the sun was out and shining. Aurora threw her skis down on the snow at the bottom of the chairlift, preparing for the ascent and the day, putting on gloves and goggles and kicking the snow out from under her ski boots before placing them in the bindings. The Alps were exposed in the morning light; it was a breathtaking view and she took a moment to take it in.

Winnie threw his skis down next to her.

"So, last night was weird." It was definitely a statement, not a question.

"How so?" she said lightly.

"The banter, it was just weird," he said, tackling it head on. "Was it?" she said innocently.

"Yeah it was," he said more forcefully. "With you and Teddy?"

"Huh, we didn't talk much, really?" She looked at Winnie now, being sure not to act furtively.

"All in?" he said quizzically, brows raised.

"We were just playing cards, that's how you finish the game, 'all in', usually that is anyway."

"Yeah, I know how poker is played, I'm not an idiot," he said, smirking. He wasn't buying it. "Teddy's different this trip."

"Is he?" she responded, looking puzzled.

"Don't be fucking coy with me," he said, smiling.

"I don't know what you mean?" she answered assuredly. She pulled her sunglasses down and skied off to the chairlift. He stood shaking his head as he clicked his boots in, watching her ski away.

After lunch, as they left an outside bar, Winnie ran into Tabitha, the girl he'd met and taken home from the open mic night, and stood talking to her. Aurora was putting her skis on with the other girls and Teddy and stood up, ready to go. Harry was skiing with his drama buddies and James was boarding with his surfing crowd today, so it was just the five of them.

As they waited to make their way out onto the slope, Winnie ran over in just his boots. "If you guys don't mind, I'm gonna ski with Tabby and her friends for a bit, cool?"

"So cool," Teddy said grinning, mocking him.

"Sure," the girls all said.

"Do you want to wingman me?" Winnie asked, directing the question to Teddy.

He hesitated before answering, "Do you need me to?"

"Ahhh no, I guess not."

"Okay, good, I'll catch you later then. Good luck, mate." Winnie looked slightly surprised and Aurora made herself busy talking to the girls, who said they planned to head straight down to the bottom and home. She was unsure of what to do when it was taken out of her hands.

"Diana and I are heading down," Liv announced to Teddy. "We've had enough and want to go shopping."

"Roars, come on then, it's just you and me now," he said, not skipping a beat. Aurora threw her a dirty look as she skied off following him. Liv was mouthing, "You're welcome," as Diana stood next to her, beaming like a proud parent. *More alone time*, Aurora thought, well, *this ought to be interesting*. His confidence was back today. He seemed to have something particular in mind, so she followed as he took her up one chair after another, skiing in between where necessary. She wasn't interested in reading maps, content to go anywhere.

"Where are we going?" she asked as they boarded another chairlift, with just the two of them on it.

"Tignes, where we might have more space."

"Okay, the other resort?"

"Yeah, we went over very briefly the first day, but there's a couple of good runs and a nice place I want to take you to."

They were climbing to the top of Val d'Isère and then would ski down into Tignes. It was a beautiful sunny day, heaps of snow and not too crowded with it being a weekday. She looked up at him beside her, back in good spirits, although more considered in his conversation.

"Winnie is suspicious," she stated.

"Yeah, he'll know something's up now I didn't go off with him." Teddy took his gloves off and checked his phone.

"Will he talk to you about it?"

"No, guys don't talk like that. He won't ask me outright."

"Well, he already has with me."

"I have no doubt you can handle him," he said confidently. They got off the chair and skied down a green run which joined Prariond, a long blue one that ran into Tignes. "There's a couple of nice runs up these chairs or we go up on the funiculaire, any preference?"

"Let's ski a couple of runs, but where are we going?"

"Up to the Grande Motte glacier up there," he said, pointing to the top of the resort. You're an aesthete right?"

"I did say that, didn't I?" She squirmed as she remembered her drunken declaration. He grinned as they joined the queue for the next chair. *He must think I'm such a moron.*

They skied two more runs and as they came off the Vanoise chair went directly to the restaurant that sat up the top. Perched high above Tignes, with its lake below, it was a spectacular location on a beautiful day. *The European mountains are unique,* Aurora thought, stark, *bald faces jutting up into the sky, devoid of any trees here above the tree line, bright white against the deep blue of the sky.* The huge terrace was covered in deck chairs and skiers were drinking and worshipping the sun while they rested. It was such a privileged, elite sport, she thought.

"There's really nothing else like skiing, is there?" she asked him as she took off her skis. "I always feel so lucky to be here, so fortunate, you know?"

"Yeah, I know, it's unique. It's how I feel when I ride too."

"Yeah, there's nothing else like that either," she agreed.

"If we sit out here, it's not so private and I think you'll like it inside," he said, holding the door open for her.

They went into Le Panoramic past the interior design store, which Aurora thought she'd have to go into after, and made their way through the takeaway section and into the bar area. It was a beautiful venue with an obviously pricey restaurant, but they stayed in its bar area. It was a cosy, warm space. Wooden walls lined the rooms all decorated in neutral colours of brown, cream, grey and taupe. Sofas and pouffes covered in faux fur throws and cow hides were dotted around. A fire burned in the centre of the room. He was right. She did like it. He returned from the bar with a glass of champagne for her and a beer for himself. They sat in a corner tucked away. *Well, if we see anyone, we are going to look very guilty, hiding away in here, but he obviously heard me when I said I wanted to remain private. What am I doing, am I playing with fire? I'm engaging with the enemy now, not that he is still the enemy, but it sure started out that way at the beginning of the year.*

"You quoted a song outside the club the other night," he said smiling, "what was that?"

She struggled to remember what he was talking about for a second, then remembered and put her hand over her mouth, "Oh God, Holly Throsby, she's Australian."

"I don't know her?"

"The song is 'Things Between People'. It's an old song my mum likes," Aurora said, trying to dismiss it. She didn't want him to be offended if he listened to the words, which he definitely would be. "It's not very flattering to you, don't listen to it."

"Now I have to," he responded.

"No, don't, I didn't mean it, really."

"You seemed to at the time?" He put his beer down and slid his jacket off.

"I was feeling pretty wound up and emotional when I said all that! It just came out ..." she said quickly.

"Yes, you were," he agreed, nodding as he sipped his beer. "Okay, I'll drop it, but what about the song you sang the other night? It's special to you isn't it?" It was a question she could choose to expand on or not.

"Yeah, for me home is wherever my immediate family is. It's not Australia any more, it's not Singapore, Manila or the UK. When I go home to Australia, I'm aware that I don't quite fit."

"So, nowhere is home?" he asked, trying to understand, looking confused.

"Home is wherever my family is, hence the song choice. I'm Australian first and foremost, my parents are Australian. I guess it's just that you never belong fully, you always feel like an outsider to some degree. The definition of a third-culture kid is where a kid has lived outside of their parents' home country for two or more years, so I more than qualify. We're going back to Australia for a trip when I get back from skiing. We haven't been for a few years."

"You are?" he said, looking a little surprised, but

recovering quickly. "I'm sure it'll be great."

"Only for a month for the Easter break." She studied his face, trying to read him.

"A whole month?" He looked disappointed as he took the news in.

"Yeah, three and half weeks."

"The timing sucks. When you come back, we have exams. I have all of mine then, law doesn't sit halfway through the year, they're all at the end."

"Wow, that will be tough."

"I have to pass. If I fail, my mother will kick off, Dad too. He's low-key and easy-going until I fuck up."

"Do you 'fuck up' often?" she teased light-heartedly.

"Not often, no. Well, not so they know." He grinned cheekily. She suspected he didn't. He was no doubt a 'Cedric Diggory' to his parents, their fine son. "But I haven't worked hard this year," he said as a shadow fell across his face.

"Really, I am surprised to hear that," she said sarcastically.

"I know, I know, it's just been too tempting to go out all the time and not get up for lectures."

"So, wasn't your boarding school a bit the same?" she asked.

"Not really the same, you have very little free time at school. Every minute was just about scheduled."

"And what was it like?"

"Radley? It's a posh twat school, I'll admit it, but I had a great time, home was close by and everything was laid on. It's just that I don't want to be defined by it."

"I don't think anyone wants to be pigeonholed by anything. That's what I like about being Australian here, I don't fit into your class structure. Well, apart from being called a convict," she said archly, taking a sip of her champagne.

"Yeah, I really am sorry about that," he said with genuine remorse, looking at her for forgiveness. She smiled, indicating a truce.

"But in Australia that just doesn't exist, it's irrelevant to us, we Australians genuinely don't care."

He nodded in agreement. "People either have class or they don't, it's innate, a part of them. It's about individual integrity, not where you went to school or who your father is," he said thoughtfully, looking away while drinking his beer.

Teddy's uncharacteristic statement caught her by surprise. "Wow, well, I have to agree." She was surprised to hear him talk like this.

"My dad taught me that class isn't something you're born into. It's who you are as a person, your conduct and how you treat others, whether you have honour and integrity, are you genuine." He didn't appear to be completely at ease as they talked, the subject was close to the bone.

"Still, where we're born has a great impact on who we are, our opportunities and quality of life. I used to think about that in the Philippines. The only difference between me and the orphans living in the cemeteries of Manila was my birthplace."

"I know, I know, I'm very fortunate, very privileged and it's not a burden for all it offers me."

She thought back to his Georgian mansion and the land it was on and decided that was an understatement. "When we were at your place and we went into the pub, the local people there were almost deferential to you, weren't they?"

"That's because we own the pub, and yes, I'm the heir," he said with some reluctance. "I'll get you another drink." He obviously didn't want to dwell on the topic.

As he went to the bar, she was going to offer to buy the round, but he wouldn't accept it she knew, not today. He'd dropped the flirtatious chat for now and she was beginning to see more. She had never heard him speak about being an earl's son and she had certainly never broached the subject, not even at his place that weekend. She had seen others try and he didn't like it, which she could respect.

He returned with their drinks and sat down closer to her on the L-shaped sofa in the corner. They were tucked under the staircase and out of the way.

"You're getting me to open up, I don't usually talk about this stuff or about myself in general."

"I know, I've seen you in action. I heard you doing that to a girl the night we met, I couldn't see you, but I could hear you. You asked all the questions and just got her talking. It was just before we were introduced."

He smiled at the memory. "Okay, so that makes more sense."

"How?"

"You really had it in for me from the beginning," he said, shaking his head.

"You called me a convict almost immediately and a savage later on," she pointed out.

"I did, and I've regretted it ever since... You have heart though, when you sang the other night, that's what I took away, it was brave." He was staring at her intensely as locks of his hair fell across his eyes.

"Did I conduct myself well?" she asked facetiously, momentarily distracting him.

"Exemplary conduct. Lady Trentbridge would have been impressed."

"Thank you," was all she could manage before he

leant fully across the space between them and his lips met hers. He held the kiss for just the right amount of time, not too long, enough to make her want more.

As he pulled away she said, "So, I have to ask, how does being a womaniser fit in with honour and integrity?" A smile played on her lips.

"And you were being so nice until now," he chastised. Reluctantly, he looked at his watch. "We had better go or we'll miss the last lift." The time had flown by.

As they put their skis on, he looked really worried. "We're going to have to gun it to get over there in time."

She took off before he was ready, giving him something to chase down, knowing he could catch her. She pulled up at the bottom of the hill for the next lift and turned back to look for Teddy just as he came screaming in, screeching to a halt and coating her in a wave of powder in the process. She threw back her head, laughing.

"Thanks for waiting, you deserve that," he said, smiling.

"What? Couldn't keep up?"

"You're so competitive," he said, shaking his head.

"I'm sorry, I can't help it."

"Don't be sorry. I like it."

They just caught the last chair, the crucial one that would take them into the next valley. The area by now deserted, everyone on their way home already. The liftie was shaking his head at them as they boarded. The sun was very low now and the temperature was plummeting. Aurora looked up warmly at Teddy as he put his arm around her shoulders.

24

"The very essence of romance is uncertainty."
— Oscar Wilde, The Importance of Being Earnest

They'd missed après up the hill at La Folie and came straight down into the village. As they came off the snow, Teddy pulled out his phone again. Winnie had been messaging him for some time.

"How's he getting on?" Aurora inquired as she released her bindings.

"Okay, I think. He's suggesting we go out for fondue. What do you think?"

"Got to say I'm sick of the food in the chalet," Aurora said disparagingly as she lifted up her skis. Stew every night was wearing thin.

"Me too. I think he wants to bring this girl and go to

the club later." Teddy put his phone away and took his skis off also. They began to walk off the snow into the village, skis over one shoulder, poles in the opposite hand.

"Where is it tonight?" Aurora said without much feeling. She had lost interest in the clubs a bit by now; a different venue most nights, but it was always the same.

"Someplace called Dick's." Teddy didn't sound overly enthused either.

They got back and found everyone in the hallway chatting about what to do for dinner, whether to blow off the paid-for chalet food or go out for fondue. Fondue won in the end. They would get ready and meet downstairs.

Aurora chatted with the girls about their shopping and her afternoon skiing, leaving many details out as they showered and dressed. She decided to wear her tight two-toned jeans, particular favourites she had snagged at the Portobello Road market. Grey denim on the outside and black down the inside, they were skintight and a statement on their own. She wore a short, tight sleeveless velvet top with thick straps that tied into bows. Everyone put up with the cold outside, wearing just their ski jacket over the top, as the clubs were so hot once inside.

As she left her room and walked down the hall to the lifts, Teddy came out of his, surprising her as she walked past, his eyes lighting up. "You look hot," he said, grabbing her hand and pulling her into his room. He hurriedly shut the door. His aftershave engulfed her with its heady scent, the way it does when it first goes on. "This is what I've resorted to to get you alone." He pulled her in close and kissed her.

She pulled back. "Where's Winnie?"

"Downstairs, don't worry," he said, pulling her back in. "When we get back to Bristol, I wondered if you wanted to go out for dinner on our own?"

"Teddy, are you asking me out on a date?" she taunted.

"I am," he said, sitting down on the bed and pulling her onto his lap. He was back in blue denim, a loose, white, well-washed polo and a navy fitted beanie. She did love his fascination with beanies. She put one arm around his neck and one on his chest. His arms were already around her and he was tightening his grip.

She pulled back. "Wow, you're pulling out all the stops now?"

"Well, you are setting me quite a course," he said.

"You don't have to participate, you know, nobody is forcing you."

"Oh, I'm not complaining at all, I'm happily in pursuit." She just smiled at him, he was boyish, charming and a bit of a rogue all at the same time. "'The essence of romance is uncertainty'," he said soberly.

"You looked up Oscar's quotes, didn't you?" she said, her eyes widening with surprise.

"I did," he said, smiling, pleased with himself and her reaction.

She decided he'd earnt a bit of encouragement and leant in to kiss him as she sat on his lap. He responded rapidly and, before she knew it, had pushed her back down on his bed, looking at her from above again, half on top of her. *Thank God I'm in jeans so tight I can hardly breathe*, she thought. He proceeded to kiss her again. Her heart was racing, his passion was so intense. It was what she had always sensed: he was dangerous, things could escalate so fast. His hands were beginning to move, it was so tempting to just go with it. He'd clearly had lots of practice and it would be so nice to just stay in here with him, let the others all go out, but afterwards, what then? The fear would kick in, the uncertainty. *Am I just another one, will he still want me tomorrow?* She would tighten up and would he still be the same? She couldn't, she knew what would happen, she understood the risk and the repercussions.

She pushed him back. "We will be missed and they will add it up," she said softly.

"Are you embarrassed to be with me?" he asked, clearly confused. "Is that it?"

Had this never happened to him? she wondered.

"Teddy, you have a reputation, that's it. That gives me pause. I don't want to be just another ..." She was struggling to find the right word and looked away as she thought. "I don't want people saying she's his next target, now it's her turn. It's not very flattering and it doesn't instil me with confidence, so I guess it is a bit. I am a bit embarrassed, it's why I want to remain private."

"These are the consequences of my actions, I get it. Consequences, fuck. My dad is always banging on about the consequences of my actions!" he said, shaking his head.

"Yes, essentially. I need time." *God, I only have to get through another day and then I'll be away for a month. We will see when I get back if he has any staying power.*

"You go out first then, I'll be down shortly, I need a cold shower anyway," he said ruefully.

She smiled at him as she left, leaving him lying on the bed, his beanie on the floor, looking up at the ceiling and pondering the consequences of his actions.

She checked her lipstick in the toilet before she entered the bar; all looked okay. When she arrived at the bar, she ordered a Prosecco and joined the others. She had showered last of the girls, so it was fair she was late. Teddy joined them five minutes later and they all walked up to the fondue place.

As fate would have it, she sat next to him and had Diana on the other side. Winnie's new love interest, Tabitha, arrived a few minutes later.

Winnie jumped up from the table and pulled the chair out next to him.

"Hi, so I think you met everyone the other night?" he said, looking around the table.

"We didn't meet," said Diana, smiling up at the girl who was still standing. "I'm Diana. We left early the other night, remember?" she said, turning to address James.

"Hi, I'm Tabby," the girl said, smiling sunnily back.

James was looking mildly uncomfortable, and seemed to be having trouble meeting Tabby's gaze.

"Oh James and I know each other, don't we, James?" Tabby prompted, looking directly at him.

"Ummmmm," he pondered, offering her a wan smile.

"How do you two know each other then," Liv interjected, curious to understand the connection, sensing something from his reaction.

"It's been a few weeks, hasn't it?" Tabby asked James, looking at him for clarification.

"I can't seem to recall meeting you before now," James replied, visibly squeamish.

Tabby ploughed straight in then. "James, you shagged my flatmate a few weeks ago, remember?" she said bluntly.

Diana visibly stiffened. "Oh wow, what a small world. How nice!" she said, calmly addressing James. James was massaging his temples, looking down.

Tabby proceeded to sit down next to Winnie and opposite Aurora. She was a bit like an edgy elf, with her fine features, tiny upturned nose and sharp black bob. She could clearly hold her own and Winnie seemed to be very interested, which was a first.

A little while later, Aurora struck up a conversation with her. "Tabby, whereabouts are you from?" She found herself unable to resist asking the obvious question to start.

"I'm from Essex." She looked around self-consciously as she said it, to see who had clocked it.

"Me too," said Aurora brightly, "we're outside Cambridge in the countryside."

"Wait, you're both Essex girls?" jumped in James, grinning with amusement. "Where are your mini skirts?"

"Okay, here it comes," said Tabby, her chin jutting out stoically, ready to weather the storm. "Not all of Essex is like that."

"You guys and your stereotypes, the world is so much bigger than that," said Diana scathingly, always ready to champion the underdog and angry at him still.

Aurora decided to wage in and attack his weak spot. "James, if you really want to be accepted by the surfing crowd, you're going to have to pretend you're not a privileged, private school boy. I'd leave that part out of your life story. The surfie scene is definitely not your set, you know?"

"I will, Roars, but I can see why you don't advertise you are from Essex."

"I'm not 'from' Essex, but please define an Essex girl

for me," she said cynically.

Winnie jumped in here. "Well, I believe it's a girl who wears mini skirts, has fake boobs and lips, but most importantly lots of fake tan." He was setting James up, knowing the girls were poised to strike.

"And is generally not considered to be intelligent," Teddy added, to make sure he was really served up on a platter for them.

"Uh huh, that's what I thought, so really I'm struggling to see the resemblance?" Aurora was alternatively pointing at herself and Tabby as she spoke, fixing James with a look.

"You would look cracking in a mini skirt and white boots though, Roars." Teddy said under his breath into her ear. Aurora pretended she hadn't heard him.

"I'm not saying you two are stereotypical Essex girls obviously, it's just funny that you're from Essex," James said, still smirking.

"No, no, you don't get to back out now. That's exactly what you were insinuating." Tabby was holding him to account as he now looked to backtrack, grateful she had Aurora as an ally. Teddy was grinning, watching James having to defend himself after he'd stirred the pot.

"You've got to admit it's true, they turn out a certain type there?" James countered.

"I would love to send you out surfing in Australia with my cousin James and watch how you get on. We're all stereotypes. Whether it's positive or negative just depends on where you're sitting at the time of judgement." Aurora raised her brows at him as she spoke. She wasn't letting him off lightly; she felt for Tabby, who was new to their circle. Diana was in between them, sitting back in her chair, encouraging her.

"Okay, okay, jeez you girls are so touchy, lighten up."

Diana was in an unforgiving mood. "James, you asked for that, and we aren't touchy." He understood her meaning and shut up, deciding it was best not to argue with her while he was still on thin ice.

As the night progressed, Aurora found herself talking more and more to Teddy next to her. At one point she felt his hand on her leg, squeezing it absent-mindedly as he talked across the table to Winnie. She flinched a little, but he continued. She left it alone, it felt nice.

As they left the restaurant and walked to Dick's, they were a boisterous group. They had really bonded on this trip together, not just because some of them were in couples, but as a group they were beginning to hum. Her mum said when a group of people come together there's a sorting out process and then after a while it settles down and begins to purr. They were purring now.

Winnie sidled up to Aurora while Tabby was busily engaged, talking to Liv. "Teddy is different on this trip, and you're the difference," he stated knowingly.

"Okay, Winnie, just because you're falling for someone doesn't mean the rest of us are. Some of us are just friends," she deflected.

Winnie turned his head to the side, looking at her with a bemused expression on his face. "Ever seen *The Wolf of Wall Street*?"

"Yes, I think I have?" she said pensively, recalling the film and wondering where he was going with it.

"Well, you're Margot Robbie, he's Leo and you two 'were never going to be friends'," he said, quoting the line from the movie.

"Okay, whatever," she said, waving him away with her hand, refusing to get into it.

"You're not fooling me."

"Okay, Winnie."

A few hours later, they left the club. As they walked up the main street, everything looked so beautiful, the lampposts covered in snow, everything dressed in white. One more day and they would return to reality. As usual they were at the back, Teddy and her. She had enjoyed being the object of his attention again all night. It was such a large crowd, there were so many people neither of them knew that it didn't matter so much. He had started to put a hand on her whenever he thought nobody could see. An intimate, possessive touch here and there. It was actually reassuring.

"You'll be gone a whole month," he repeated to himself. It wasn't a question.

"Is that an issue?"

"No, I don't care," he said jokingly. He knew she was referring to whether he would be his usual promiscuous self if she wasn't around. "It's just a long time."

Aurora reminded herself they were not a couple, they were nothing at this stage, at best a holiday romance, not even a fling.

Before they got back to their chalet, he pulled her down the side of a building into an alleyway and kissed her again. Reminiscent of their first kiss outside the club, his passion and eagerness so obvious, and she struggled to hold the line again.

"This creeping around is killing me, but I gotta say it's also kind of hot," he observed. She smiled up at him. She was falling in love, she probably had long ago if she was honest. He was clearly in lust, but she wondered if it was love for him. How could she know?

"Some things are more precious because they don't last long."
— Oscar Wilde, The Picture of Dorian Gray

She woke before anyone else. It was the last day, after today they would leave this playground that was exhilarating and hedonistic and return to reality. A trip home to Australia would be a very different pace, siblings to deal with, family to visit, her time would not be her own and of course he would be absent, no longer filling up her senses every five minutes. They had been some heady days, she reflected. She felt like she was in a constant state of excitement and nerves, it was at times thrilling, just lying next to him now she was feeling it. They were close, side by side in the single bed, even though it was uncomfortable and he wouldn't have much space up against the wall, it was thrilling and neither of them even thought about complaining.

Unable to help herself, she rolled over to look at him sleeping beside her, studying his features, his mother's long Germanic nose, his lips, not excessively large, but full enough. His hair! His hair was always falling across his eyes; sandy blonde, naturally textured, his hair was sensational. But what made him so attractive was inside for her now, it was his essence.

He sensed her and his eyes slowly opened. They were now somehow psychically connected she thought. She had tried her best to avoid this, damn it. For much of the year, she had been avoiding this moment, being totally invested in him. It didn't matter whether they did or didn't have sex, now she was vulnerable regardless. Now she was emotionally invested, she was exposed and it was way too late to get out unharmed. She had fought him, then herself, and had lost. Now he had the power, whether he knew it or not. The question in her mind was whether he was invested too? Was he hooked as well, or was it the chase for him?

"I was really struck by you the first time I saw you, did you know that?" he asked, moving her hair off her face.

"I didn't know it, but I remember it well. It felt like we looked at each other for a long time," she conceded.

"I couldn't take my eyes off you, I'd never experienced that before." He continued to play with her long hair. "You have the most beautiful green eyes by the way."

"Thank you. Your eyes are my favourite shade of denim blue and I think I was a little taken in by you too."

"You never showed it," he whispered.

"You were with another girl, but I still clocked your attributes all the same."

"Good, that's how I like it," he joked. "This is our last day."

"I kind of hoped we would all ski together again to finish off. I feel like we've all grown close in the space of a week."

"We have," he said, putting his arms around her under the covers. She went to look over her shoulder. "They're still out to it. Harry's a deep sleeper anyway and Liv was smashed again, she won't be up too soon." It felt like she was in a cocoon, a safe and fully contained habitat that she didn't want to leave. He pulled the covers over both their heads.

"Just because the covers are up, doesn't mean we are invisible," she reminded him.

"I really don't give a shit, not this morning," he said, kissing her again. His lips parted hers, soft at first, increasingly becoming more demanding, pulling her into another world and it was on again, she was drifting off with him. It was like he was the Pied Piper and she was following him in a trance. It was torturous pulling herself out and it was becoming too much for him, she could tell. This situation was unsustainable for them both. He had to sleep in his own bed tonight. She ended the kiss.

"If I have to have another cold shower I'm going to get frostbite."

"You asked me who hurt me the other night and I lied. I said no one, but you were right, I have been hurt, back in high school, and after that thing with Flynn and Paige I got real low, you know what I mean?" He nodded, comprehending what she was saying. "So, that's also why I need to slow it down."

"I'm sorry, I didn't mean to make you feel guilty for, I don't know, I suppose denying me," he said gently.

"It's okay. I'm just a bit gun-shy."

"I understand. I'm just a guy." He squeezed her hand. "Do you want to go out and get breakfast or some decent coffee and then come back? It's only eight and I think we've got a couple of hours before everyone's up."

"That's a good idea," she said with relief.

He dressed in his clothes from the night before and she threw on jeans and a light jumper. They went to a café chatting easily; conversation, it just flowed.

"I've never known an Australian girl before," he said thoughtfully as they walked down.

"Well, we are direct, but you've spotted that already, and we don't suffer from the British reserve. We threw that off with the yoke."

"I have noticed that."

"I don't like my accent really, I'm self-conscious of it, especially in the UK."

"See I love it," he said, smiling at her.

"Yours is charming, it's a weapon in your arsenal," she told him matter- of-factly.

He laughed. "Are you flirting with me at last?"

"Huh, maybe I am," she said with a shrug. "Remember that dinner at your place?"

"How could I forget? My mother made that stupid comment," he said, shaking his head. "I couldn't believe she could be so ignorant."

Aurora could tell Teddy felt awful and moved on. "Well, I was sitting next to Bill Macfarlane in conversation with him, his dulcet tones, sophistication and art collection."

Teddy cut in: "Yeah, I kept wanting to join your

conversation while my mother was in my ear." She laughed at the memory.

"I gotta tell you I was intimidated. Then there was your mother and father and the whole English aristocratic thing that I still don't understand, and everybody else around the table has grown up in these elite boarding schools ..." She paused for breath and let out a large sigh as she finally explained, "I was well out of my comfort zone."

"You made quite the impression, you know. Bill was enchanted. His wife was chiding him later, according to my mum."

"I did?"

"You did, you were not outclassed if that's what you were worried about."

"I was worried I came across a little rough around the edges," she admitted.

He laughed outright. "You have no idea, do you?" He was just looking at her, looking into her soul almost.

"It's hard to be objective about yourself, isn't it?"

"You see, guys just don't think that much, it's so much simpler."

"Sometimes I wish I was a boy. I could lose my cool and people wouldn't bat an eyelid. If a girl gets angry, it feels like it's a crime."

"Don't they say there's a million negative names for women, but hardly any for men?"

"It's so true! I always feel like I should be dialling myself down and I really try, but when I'm angry sometimes it just comes out."

"You have to be who you are, you're generally harsh but fair from what I've seen." His assessment was correct, she thought, but she needed to learn not to react in the heat of the moment, to just take a minute to cool off a little.

They entered a tiny coffee place, very quiet at this hour, and ordered from the bar. They found a table in the corner and Aurora sat on the bench seat, Teddy joining her rather than sitting opposite in a chair.

"Did you talk about me with your mother then?" *He probably thinks I'm self-centred.* "Only she made a comment about my coming from a big family which I thought was funny at the time because I didn't tell her that," she hurriedly explained.

Teddy nodded, flipping the lid on the sugar canister on the table as he played with it. "She knows me, she thought there was something special about you, so we had a chat, yes."

She felt herself glow with warmth from the praise. A young Frenchman brought their coffee and pastries. "Did you ever feel lonely being an only child? Your mother kind of alluded to that also?" She pulled a part of her croissant off and dipped it into the coffee.

"God, you like getting in and probing around, don't you?" Teddy said as he finally left the sugar alone.

"But it's okay for you to ask questions?"

"Okay, okay." He was mildly uncomfortable but he answered the question. "Yes, bottom line, absolutely. I envied people with brothers and sisters. I was always allowed to have other kids over, my parents encouraged that, but at the end of the day it was just me. It's okay, it's what I'm used to after all." He smiled over at her. "We've had very different experiences growing up, I think."

"That's for sure and we come from very different backgrounds." She shook her head just thinking about it. "My family is the antithesis of that, lots of bickering and sibling rivalry, and I'm hardly ever alone at home.

If you get the house to yourself, it's a treat."

"I think I'd like that, though." He looked thoughtfully over at her as he sipped his coffee.

"But it's annoying. We drive each other crazy at times. You would think we were heathens."

"Have you seen who I hang out with?" he said dryly.

"Huh, they aren't heathens, trust me."

"I'm attracted to spirited creatures."

"You're smooth. Did you have to work on it, or were you born with that too?"

"You just make it easy," he said, lowering his tone. His voice still captivated her, its resonance at times took her back to that first night she overheard him speak, and without checking herself she moved over, cosying up to him on the seat.

They returned to the chalet and joined the others, kitted up and got out on the slopes about mid-morning. It was a cloudy day, but they would make the best of it. As they sat eating lunch later, Winnie started talking about music; he and Tabby had discussed little else, it seemed.

"So, I've just found a new song I really like," he announced as Teddy left the table. "Roars, you might know the artist, she's Australian."

"Who?" she replied, half listening, as she sat eating a burger and fries.

"Holly Throsby, do you know her?"

Aurora nearly choked on her burger, looking up at him, unable to suppress a smile.

"So, you do know her, I thought you might," he went on cheekily. "I think I might learn to play it. It's folk, but you know I'm always open to expanding my horizons."

"I like folk music," Diana enthused. "It's so lilting

and tells a story."

"Yes, it does tell a story, doesn't it?" Winnie agreed enthusiastically, grinning at Aurora.

He was a bugger, but it looked like he was only interested in making her uncomfortable, not really blowing their cover. How the hell did he get hold of Holly Throsby and "Things Between People"? Teddy wouldn't talk, she knew he wouldn't, and he certainly wouldn't mention that song.

Later on when she got hold of Winnie at après, she asked him the question. "How the hell did you come across Holly Throsby? She's not exactly current and certainly not your genre."

"I don't know, that's unfair. Her last album was not that long ago, she's probably about to release something else and I'll have you know I listen to all different types of music." He was amusing himself no end. "Are you broken yet?" he challenged, grinning, so pleased with his effort.

"Come on how?" she demanded.

"I saw Teddy listening to it, so I was curious. I can tell you I was well rewarded for my curiosity. I played it and got the gist of what's going on."

"Well, you have to let him back into his room tonight. He can't stay with me again, it's not fair."

"Okay, okay, I get it, I'm sorry, I'll make sure it's not a problem. So, you're not keen?" he asked. He was still grinning from ear to ear.

"Winnie, I'm not discussing it with you, talk to him yourself."

At the end of the day they were up at La Folie Douce for the last time. The crowd was massive for the final day. The DJ was up high on a platform in the centre of the L-shaped building. Wooden picnic tables covered the terrace area in front and people were dancing on them now; not really dancing, more like bouncing up and down, where they had been sitting eating lunch only a few hours earlier. It was an exuberant, high-spirited crowd. Outside on the fringes, away from the loudspeakers, their own group gathered. It had been a tiring but great week, so much fun, and Aurora and Diana stood apart having a download.

Aurora looked around at the gathering and caught Paige, staring at her from the far side table.

"She's always watching me," Aurora said to Diana. "I don't know why and I don't understand her at all. What does she want?"

"She's been put back in her box a bit, I think. You've just carried on and left her to it, haven't you? I mean you haven't spoken to her at all?"

"No, I haven't spoken to her and she hasn't come near me. I'm a pretty black-and-white person and when I'm done, I'm done."

"You never confronted her, though. Why not? Weren't you angry?"

"Yes, I was so angry, furious, but underneath I was, well, I still am so hurt. It felt vicious and vindictive. I slept in her room on the floor for two nights after she broke up with her boyfriend, and that's what she thought of our friendship, that's how she repaid me."

"Yeah, not great." Diana was at a loss as to what to say. Her eyes, though, were sympathetic.

"I'm not comfortable in all-girl groups, I don't trust them."

"I hated girls in high school too. I never learnt how to navigate the bitches either." It was uncharacteristic of Diana to speak so fiercely.

"You had a hard time with girls, you've said before?"

"I was bullied, they made my life a misery. I needed to be tougher, I'm just too soft, so I was an easy mark."

"I can confront guys easily, tell them off, stand up to them, they're usually pretty straight up, but girls are different, they have sharp teeth, and they hunt in packs, like velociraptors or lionesses."

Diana was laughing with the identification. "I know but we need our girlfriends too."

"Good friends, yes," Aurora said looking at Liv and then back at Diana, "but she clearly wasn't a good friend. She crossed a line. I'm not going to be friends with her now. If she had apologised, I would have forgiven her. I'm trying not to resent her, but it's a tall order."

"You've been distracted this week, though, haven't you?" Diana prodded with a suggestive smile, looking at Teddy, who was talking with another group closer into the centre.

"Uh huh I have, that I can tell you," Aurora said.

"He's cute, Roars, he is. I see him looking after your drink, checking where you are, all the while trying not to give too much away. I also see a lot of girls trying to engage him, get his attention, but he only has eyes for you."

"James is a bit the same, isn't he? I mean with other girls. That long blond hair and all."

"I guess. It's not a problem when we're all here together, but I wonder how it will be when we're not around and they're out, as a group of boys and all. Tabby's comment the other night reminded me of what James gets up to, but what am I going to do, worry?"

"No, but it goes both ways, doesn't it?" Aurora pointed out. "I think you have to keep them honest. They are just as vulnerable, maybe more so, only as girls we don't usually think like that."

"Make them jealous, you mean?" Diana didn't look so sure.

"I don't think you want to let a guy get too comfortable. It's a bit of a power play after all." Aurora stared at Teddy, who was talking in a crowd with the guys.

"You mean play games?"

Diana's question brought her back to the conversation at hand and Aurora smiled slightly at her. "No, not play games, just remind them who you are."

"And how do you plan to do that from Australia?" Diana asked.

"I don't, we aren't together, but if he's with someone else, he won't be with me. If he can't wait a little bit over three weeks, then you know, it was never really there for him."

"Is that what you think, he'll go off as usual when you aren't here?"

"I hope not. Anyway, everyone will be home for Easter, he'll only be back at uni a couple of weeks ahead of me, but at this stage it's a long time. We'll just have to see what happens."

Reuben joined them, chatting about his week and what they had to do for the JCR and the remainder of the year, in particular the final ball: the Founders Ball, which was held the night their exams finished. This ball invited students from all the other Stoke Bishop halls, so it would be a much bigger undertaking. As they talked, the music proceeded to rise in volume. Reuben, a warm, touchy-feely sort of person generally, but especially after some drinks, put his hand on Aurora's shoulder, then her back as he leant in closer to hear what she was saying. Five minutes later, Teddy had joined them and Diana smiled to herself.

They went through the same routine tonight that they had for much of the week; dinner, sleep and then out later. Aurora packed as well, she had an early start to catch her flight from Lyon in the early afternoon. She was dreading the back-to-back flights. Lyon to Stansted on the Saturday, London to Sydney on the Sunday, all on the back of a week's skiing. It would be a tough couple of days, followed by jet lag once she got to Sydney. With a bit of luck, she would sleep well on the flight there.

They didn't stay until closing tonight, leaving by 1 a.m. As they walked up the hill to their chalet for the final time, Teddy put his arm around her. "Nobody cares at this stage of the night," he assured her. It was beginning to feel comfortable between them, less giddy, more real, his arm around her just felt right.

"No, they don't," she agreed. Small flakes were falling again; they had been so lucky with the snow, but it needed freshening up again. He was quiet tonight and she sensed he was in a reflective mood. "You're quiet?"

"I'm just thinking of what's ahead now."

"You said you were going away with your parents for a week?" she said, looking up at him. He kept his gaze forward, looking further ahead of them.

"Yeah, I'm flying up to Paris to meet them there."

"You'll be taking in the cultural sights then? It will be strange after this week, which has been such a party and so intense. We've been in a bubble here, which is probably why we all feel like we've grown close."

"And you'll be busy and in another time zone. I'm not really much of a social media user, so I guess we won't have much to do with each other for a while. I don't usually non-stop message girls and all that shit."

"That's okay, you don't need to explain." She got it, he was saying he wouldn't be communicating with her, the future was uncertain.

"I'll say hi and all, but I don't chat that much," he said bluntly.

"I get it," was all she replied. It didn't bother her, she wasn't a big fan of endless virtual chat. Flynn had loved to talk and flirt online and it didn't mean a thing.

He pulled her away in the lobby of their chalet, down a hallway, and kissed her long and passionately. "What time are you leaving in the morning?" he asked.

"It's a 9 a.m. bus."

"Damn." They said goodbye at her door and she went in. She immediately felt a sense of loss.

The next morning, she was running late as usual, rushing to make the bus. She said goodbye to Liv and Diana, who had the luxury of a later departure, as did all the boys. Unfortunately, she was alone again, the same way she had arrived. As the bus pulled in, she stood in line ready to load her bag into the undercarriage. As she went to hoist it up, it suddenly became weightless and was taken out of her hands. She turned to meet Teddy's eyes and he proceeded to load it for her. She was touched, a wave of emotion sweeping through her. He looked exhausted and sleep deprived but he had bothered to get up and come out. It sent a thrill through her. She put her arms around him and they hugged goodbye.

"Whatever happens going forward, I had a really nice time," she said wistfully into his ear.

She took a mental note to remember how it felt to hold him. Whatever was going to be, would be, but this felt good, right here, right now. He stood in only a hoodie and track pants, obviously just thrown on. He was still warm from bed and she could feel his body underneath.

"I'll see you in a month," he said unwaveringly.

"The only difference between the saint and the sinner is that every saint has a past, and every sinner has a future."
— Oscar Wilde, *A Woman of No Importance*

Aurora arrived back in halls in the afternoon, quickly climbing the stairs up to her room. The familiar anxiety was rising and she hoped she didn't encounter Paige. She could manage Sophie and Annabel: they were just followers, there wasn't the same sense of betrayal, and they avoided all eye contact one on one. Both had at some point asked her how she was when she encountered them alone on campus or in halls, but the conversation had felt superficial and false and Aurora had no interest in rekindling the friendship.

She dumped her bags. Her room was musty after being shut up for so long and she threw open the windows. She just had time to unpack before meeting Liv and Diana at a favourite coffee place of theirs at the top of Whiteladies Road. She lay on the bed and looked at her collage of pictures by her bed, many depicting beautiful young couples, all the models dressed in jaw-dropping outfits. *Are they inspiring, or in reality are they all just advertising a fantasy?*

She spied her Oscar book of quotes and lay on the bed, opening it at random. She liked to do this sometimes and use it as a reading. The page opened at: 'We are all in the gutter, but some of us are looking at the stars.' She took it as an answer to her question. It was a matter of perspective, she decided, and she would choose to dream on every time. She had to believe that romance and love were within her grasp as much as the next person. *Even if it's a lie, I want to believe it.*

The sun was out and warm, and she wondered how the next couple of weeks would play out as she walked across the Downs. She had to get her head down and study hard now, she was late back to uni, having missed a full week, and exams were starting in less than two.

The trip home to Australia had been a welcome break and distraction as she re-engaged and reunited with family. They were constantly busy seeing relatives and spending lots of time on the beach, her favourite place to be. Nothing else would ever compare to Australian beaches, not in her mind. It was the little things she'd noticed and missed, things that called her back to her early childhood: the afternoon sun on the beach, the crickets in the evening, and in particular the birdsong. The currawongs' call as it echoed along the riverbank, and the lorikeets' screeching as they came down to feed off her grandmother's balcony. These were inherently familiar, as was the sense of belonging to such a large family. The time hadn't flown by like it usually did: even though they were busy, she'd felt the passing of each day.

Teddy had been an ever-present thought, an unanswered question, a possibility but not a certainty. He crowded her dreams and was her first waking thought. He made sleep elusive even at the end of a full and tiring day. She craved the sound of his voice most of all. He messaged her daily, and as promised he was economical with his words, but at least it was something. He knew she would be back today, but had not arranged to see her.

As she arrived at the café, the girls were sitting at a table near the front and they greeted each other like it had been a year.

"It's so good to see you guys, I've missed you!" Aurora gushed.

"We missed you too," Diana responded.

"So, how is everything? How is James?" Aurora was eager to catch up on all the news.

"He's good, all is good, I'm still really happy," Diana enthused. "He might drop in and say hi later after he finishes studying. He never really seems to do all that much, to be honest."

"Yeah, that's James, though, isn't it?" said Aurora.

Diana nodded in agreement. "We've been studying together, but it's obvious I work so much harder than he does."

"Yeah, he admitted he does what he needs to do, no more, no less," Aurora confirmed.

They were interrupted as their coffee arrived. "And how is young Theodore?" Liv asked suggestively as the waiter walked away.

"Is it Theodore, or do you think it's Edward?" Aurora asked.

"You don't know?" Diana asked, surprised.

"I have no idea!" Aurora said, stumped. "It never came up and he's hard to get info out of, he doesn't volunteer a whole lot." He had opened up a bit away in France, but obviously there was a lot missing still.

"Definitely Theodore." Liv was emphatic.

"Well, I haven't seen him yet, I just got back, so I don't know? You tell me, how is he?" Aurora lifted her latte up and drank, looking expectantly at both of the other girls.

"We have been watching him for you," Liv assured her. "I've been subtle, but I've kept my eye on him when I've seen him out, which hasn't been often."

"James wouldn't say anything to me, even if there was anything to tell, he's not stupid," said Diana, "and we couldn't really ask Teddy how he was coping either, so we can't say."

"I'm a bit nervous to see him actually. You know he got up and saw me off on the bus, which was so lovely, and unexpected. I just hope he's the same, really."

"Oh my God, he's almost courting you, like old-fashioned courting you?" Liv said with surprise, her eyes open wide. "That's almost weird, nobody dates any more." Aurora looked a little bit taken aback.

"No, that's so sweet," Diana cooed. "I love that he did that. Can I tell James?"

"No, you cannot tell James! You can't tell James anything, Diana, nothing," Aurora said firmly.

"So, has anything, you know, gone on?" Liv asked, always wanting to know the state of play. Aurora shook her head in denial. "Come on, where are you up to?" Liv persisted.

"All I'll say is that we are more than friends. He said he'd take me out for dinner when we got back here, so we'll see."

"So, those nights he was in our room you're telling me nothing happened? He kept his hands to himself?" Liv asked with her mouth open.

"Like I told you, I'm scared. I'm just worried he's in it for the wrong reason. I didn't want to go there with him, I swear it's almost a phobia." She said it lightly but she knew in her heart she really meant it.

"You'll probably see him at dinner, won't you?" Liv pried.

"Probably, oh please say you're eating in tonight?" Aurora pleaded, suddenly realising she couldn't bear to sit there alone hoping to see him.

"Yes, we are, and we have a JCR meeting also," Diana reminded her. "Things are really hotting up for the ball, and there's still a bit to do".

As they sat down later in their usual place at the far side of the dining hall, away from the food and on the edge of it all, Aurora was filled with nervous tension. The butterflies were dancing in her stomach, and the anticipation was making it hard to eat.

"I can't eat," she said to Diana.

"James said they'll be here soon, they've all been in the library together, so sit tight," Diana said, looking down while reading her phone.

"I'm liable to be cold and standoffish now because I'm so tense," moaned Aurora.

"Just smile, no one wants your resting bitch face right now," Liv pointed out grinning. She was enjoying the drama.

They all walked in a few minutes later and Aurora's

heart flipped over at the sight of them. It was genuinely so nice to see all the guys all come in, they were her friends and she had missed each of them. Teddy, however, was not among the group, and a cloak of disappointment fell over her heavily. She was all keyed up and suddenly she felt flat. *Is he avoiding me? That wouldn't really add up, though*, she rationalised.

Winnie came running over and hugged her. "So, how was it? I can see you're even more tanned." he grinned broadly. He immediately set her at ease.

"It was great, I'm still a little jet-lagged but it's much easier flying back this way. How are you? Anything new?"

"Well, I am still seeing that girl from the snow. We're having a thing, you know?"

"Great description, Winnie, a thing?"

"Look, let me just get some food, we're coming over." He rushed back to pile food onto his plate. Tonight was lasagne and salad, which always went down well. The caterers had managed to nail that.

He sat down and launched into question time, asking after her family, her holiday and then talking about the aftermath of the ski trip. He said it took him a full week to recover. Tabitha was still more than holding his interest. Eventually he got round to Teddy as he finished his meal.

"So, have you seen him?" he asked, turning to face her on the bench.

"And by him you mean your best mate?" she returned.

"Yeah, that one."

"Well, I just got in today, so no. I thought he was with you in the library?"

"Oh yeah, of course you wouldn't have seen him. He

was, and still is in the library. He's under a lot of pressure, hasn't done enough all year." Winnie looked guilty, he had played a major role in Teddy's current predicament.

"No, I gathered as much and law is a tough course. They sit all their exams for the year now, he told me, so his day of reckoning is upon him and all that."

"His first one is in a week, I think," Winnie explained. She knew this was what Teddy meant when he said it was shit timing. She had her own study to get busy with anyway, but then once exams finished it would be the end of the academic year. They didn't have much of their first year left.

After dinner she dutifully went to the JCR meeting, although she hardly felt like it. It was largely about the Founders Ball, and they were told what their final assignments and tasks were. Everyone had to help out with the setting up of the room, which was always held at the completion of exams. Paige was there of course and as vice president she had a lot of say.

"I hope we're sitting together," Aurora whispered to Diana.

"Leave it with me. I hope she's not organising that part, but I'll make sure we are together."

"Of course she will be! She'll want to control who sits where." Aurora was pretty confident she wouldn't like the seating plan.

At the end of the meeting she checked her phone and there was a message from Teddy. "Meet me in the bar when you're done." Someone must have told him where she was. She was pleased that she would get to meet with him alone, it would afford them some much needed privacy.

She went straight down at the conclusion of the

meeting, checking her hair and makeup in the bathroom on the way. She saw him immediately, seated at the same table they had sat in back at the end of January, when he had tried to convince her that Paige had gone into his room uninvited. As she walked towards him, the usual shudder of excitement went through her. *So that hasn't changed*, she thought. She had to force herself to look at him as she remembered Liv's words, "just smile", and she offered up the sunniest smile she could muster. She hoped it didn't look creepy because she felt a tad uptight still.

He stood to greet her. He looked good, a bit worried or nervous, but then it didn't detract from his looks at all, he still looked fit, like he always did. He stared back at her, the corners of his mouth were turning up and the way he was staring was mesmerising as usual. Gone were the heavy jumpers and coats of winter, he was just in his jeans and a grey T-shirt, his pendant around his neck. He liked plain T-shirts with no pattern she had noticed.

"Welcome back, how are you?" he said, giving her a hug, very much like a friend, she noted with concern.

"I'm pretty good, a bit tired still, but good. How was Paris?" They sat, neither of them drinking anything tonight.

"Quiet, but we had a good time. Lots of eating out, museums and shopping. How's your family?"

"All the same. It was great to see everyone, the weather was good and I loved being on the beach." She felt like the conversation was not the one they needed to have. She struggled with the formality after the intimacy they had shared. "Winnie tells me you're pulling all the stops out for these exams?"

"I'm in a bit of trouble, I think," he said, running his

hands through his hair. She'd noticed he did this when he was stressed. "I've left my run a little too late, I hope not, but I might have." He looked like a naughty schoolboy.

"So, you're putting in some hours at the library?" she asked.

"Yes, a lot." There was a pause in the conversation and Aurora felt the panic inside her beginning to rise. She could see he was a little tense. *Is he trying to work out how to let me down? Has he had second thoughts now we're back?* His voice suddenly cut through her thoughts as he continued, "Listen, can we go on that date after exams are finished?" he asked, looking earnestly at her.

She felt the tension drain out of her body. She didn't care what he said after that, it didn't matter any more. They were still on course, he didn't want to pretend none of it had happened, he wasn't looking for an out. "Teddy, just do what you need to do, I'm busy too," she assured him.

He looked relieved, but it was different to their time in the snow. That had been so carefree and hedonistic, and now it was almost the opposite, life had intruded. It felt serious and there seemed to be expectation floating around in the air, a weight that had been absent before.

"Well, the night after Founders then?" he suggested.

"Okay, that's fine, but we'll both be very hungover," she said, reminding him.

"Yes, but we still have to eat, don't we?"

They chatted for an hour or so after that, and it felt like they were returning to where they had left it, once he'd established when he would be taking her out. As they left the bar he looked left and right down the hallway. She prepared to say goodbye and walk in the direction of her block when he suddenly grabbed her hand and dragged her out through the main front entrance. He kept going, past the birch tree, walking further into the garden, holding onto her hand before whipping her into him, pulling her into an embrace. She was laughing up at him in the twilight, confident they wouldn't be seen. The familiar scent of him was everywhere again, the feel of his muscles under the thin shirt. It was all as she had replayed in her mind over and over for the past four weeks.

27

"Behind every exquisite thing that existed, there was something tragic."
— Oscar Wilde, The Picture of Dorian Gray

The week went slowly past and Teddy was largely absent from the dining room and bar. Aurora was in the library a lot and saw him sometimes, often with the boys or friends from his course, but she left him there alone, saving only to say hi. She didn't feel she could just intrude, and she knew she wouldn't be able to concentrate around him. The following week Teddy's exams started and Aurora's quickly followed. It was so easy to forget that the whole point of uni was to study, and it all came down to this at year's end.

Aurora felt hers went well, and when she finished

she celebrated with friends from her course in the pub after. They went to the Spoons on Whiteladies and it went on until well into the evening. She decided to leave shortly before 10 p.m., having had enough socialising, worn out from the mental strain of the exam. At the bus stop she checked the timetable and saw the next bus wouldn't be for another twenty minutes. It was virtually still light at this time of the year, the summer solstice was not far away now, so she decided to walk, it was still relatively early. She strode up Whiteladies and crossed over the road onto the Downs. She had her music in, blasting as she walked. Her pace was quick as she thought about the coming ball, her anxieties, hopes and desires.

At the top of the Whiteladies, Teddy was in the Kings Arms pub. He had studied hard and, with one exam to go, was having a beer with mates from law. He planned to study some more in his room after. As he stood talking and drinking at the tall windows which framed the street below he caught sight of Aurora walking past.

It was light for so long at this time of year that Aurora decided to walk directly across rather than around the perimeter of the Downs under the streetlights. She had been warned numerous times not to do exactly as she was doing, but it was still twilight, she rationalised. She stepped onto the grass, cutting a diagonal path straight across the park to the lane opposite, making for the back entrance of Tudor. It was right on dusk. The light was dim, the sun had set, but its after-effects lingered, preventing the sky from being pitch black. She increased her pace, it was only four hundred metres across or so, she would be quick.

As she strode through the centre of the park, she

began to regret her decision. It was far darker here away from the streetlights than she had expected, and she began to feel jumpy and nervous. It was quite cool in the centre of the park and her imagination was active. In the shadows she began to see forms take shape. The bushes became dark, menacing, hunched-over figures waiting to spring. She turned off her music, she needed all her senses. Fear swirled around her like a floating spectre trying to steal her away, and the sensation that she was being watched settled upon her like an unwelcome companion. The hoot of an owl nestling in a tree sent a chill racing up her spine, but she didn't jump, she didn't pause, she marched on. *This is all just my imagination, get a grip.*

She was anxious to get to the other side now, and only relaxed as the houses on the other side of the road came out of the gloom to meet her. Bordering the road was a line of lovely old horse chestnut trees which proudly formed an avenue; a row of sentinels, she thought. As she approached the trees she had always admired, she noticed that tonight they looked sombre with the starless evening sky.

Now only fifty metres more and she would be crossing the road. The streetlights were flickering, calling her home, and just as she began to feel safe, a hooded figure emerged from behind a large trunk and stood stock- still, obstructing her path. A wave of anxiety swept through her body. She paused for a second and assessed the dark form in front of her. He was tall and burly, a fully formed man, not a student, his presence no accident. She felt every hair on her body stand on end, every fibre of her being suddenly on high alert and screaming at her. She turned to her right, preparing to go around him, attempting to act as if nothing was out of the ordinary. Hurriedly she moved away from him, making a sharp right-hand turn, keeping her head fixed forward, glancing left out of the corner of her eyes to keep an eye on him, resisting the urge to just run.

She had only taken a few steps before he moved to block her path and fight-or-flight took over. She bolted, sprinting as fast as her legs would go, frantically trying to escape the boundary of the park, desperate to reach the brightness of the road.

It was futile. She didn't make it far before being grabbed from behind, a big meaty paw taking a hold of her jacket, jolting her forwards. Instinct kicked in and she fought with everything she had, lashing out, twisting and turning to wrench herself free. She thought, saw and felt nothing but her struggle. She managed to pull him slightly off balance as she wrestled with him, enough to delay his passage forward as he stumbled, and they both fell, but still he did not release her.

Rising back to his feet, her attacker's grip became more violent and determined as he grabbed her arm and dragged her upwards and then a moment later Aurora felt them take a sudden blow from the side, which sent both of them flying, forcing him to relinquish his grip on her. She heard a loud scream, only realising it was hers as she landed hard on her back, having been flipped over. The force of the landing winded her badly. She strained for breath as she scrambled to safety, crawling across the ground on her grass-stained knees and dirty hands. She collapsed onto her front and rolled over onto her back, glancing to see if she was being chased, hardly able to see through watery eyes. She made out a struggle between two figures wrestling in the grass metres away. One gained the upper hand, sitting on top of the other, landing a blow to his adversary's face. Her attacker managed to free himself from the other's clutches, kicking out with his feet before fleeing. Aurora, still gasping for breath that just wasn't there, continued crawling backwards in terror when her hand slipped and her head hit the ground. As she lay prostrate on the damp turf, she heard a car squealing away.

And then he was there, he had her, he held her as her breath returned. "Roars, it's me, it's okay, I've got you. Are you okay?" Teddy had his arm around her and clasped one of her hands.

"I don't know," she said stunned. "What just happened?"

"He's gone." Teddy was struggling to catch his own breath.

"Oh my God, oh my God." She went limp as she realised she was safe and the adrenaline left her system. He got to his feet and helped her up, his arm around her waist supporting her weight.

"It's okay, it's okay, I've got you. Come on, we need to move."

"It just didn't seem dark when I started to cross," she whimpered.

"Do you think you're alright? Can you walk?"

"Yes, I'm fine, I'm fine. I was just winded, that's all."

"Come on, we need to report this," said Teddy, taking her hand and walking directly to the car park. He put her in his car and drove to the police station while she stared out the window in shock. He looked across at her often on the drive there, placing a warm hand on her knee, his brow furrowed and creased, a pained expression on his face.

He was in command when they reached the station, he took control, giving his version of events. She responded to the questions directed to her. She had very little intel to give them. She could tell them her attacker's height and build roughly, but little else. She'd had no clear look at his face, it was a vague description. Teddy helped fill in some gaps, supplying some facial features.

She had no obvious injuries, but she would be changed by the event. In the end, she didn't feel violated or scarred, the attacker hadn't stolen a piece of her. However, the threat of an assault, far graver than anything she'd ever experienced before, would stay with her forever.

The young female detective was talking to Teddy now. "Your girlfriend might be in shock, she needs to stay warm."

"Okay." He was a bit spaced out and didn't feel the need to clarify she wasn't his girlfriend.

"Preferably not alone," she explained.

"I'll take care of her," he said solemnly. Now that the immediate danger had passed and the authorities alerted, it all began to hit him.

"Just keep an eye on her. Call 111 if you're worried." The police officer continued to study him for a moment. "Are you okay?" she asked, sensing his emotional state. "You fought the guy, so it must have been quite disturbing for you?" She could see he was shaken.

"I'm okay," he said. He could still feel the throbbing in his chest, from where he was kicked.

"You might have a shiner developing there," she said, hinting at the cut under his left eye.

"It's nothing, I've suffered much worse on the rugby pitch," he said with some chagrin.

"You may have saved her life, you know?" she said, looking him in the eye. He nodded, acknowledging the accolade, still feeling hopelessly inadequate.

As he drove them back towards their halls in the trusty old Defender, Aurora was awake and restless in a manner she couldn't quite comprehend. "You can't be alone, Roars, do you want me to call your parents, take you to Diana's? What do you want to do?"

"No, my parents will drive here through the night if I tell them, I don't want them to do that, so I'll call in the morning. I'm okay now, but I don't want to go back to my room alone. I'd like to stay with you," she said gingerly, looking across at him. She couldn't face her room up there alone in the nest of vipers. He had been through this with her, they were in it together and she wanted to remain with him.

"Of course, of course, I just didn't really want to be the one to suggest that." He squeezed her hand as they pulled up outside the Asda. "Are you hungry? I really need food, and I'll get tea or something to drink. What would you like?" he asked gently.

"Tea is good, but can I have a swig of something strong in it too?" she asked with a wry smile as she pulled her jacket tightly around her to protect from the chill of the evening air. She was cold, strangely cold and she just wanted him to wrap her up in his arms.

"Sure, I've got that covered."

She had never been into his room before, had no idea where it was even. He and his mates were in the first block by the bar, she knew that. His room turned out to be on the ground floor, near the kitchen, which was handy. It was now past midnight as he opened his door and showed her in. Like hers, it was large and spacious. Unlike hers, though, he had a double bed instead of a single.

"And how did you manage that?" she said, gesturing to the bed under the window.

"Being the future Earl of Trentbridge has to be good for something, doesn't it?"

"I'm sure it is." She could tell the linen and tasteful selection of cushions were all his mother. His duvet cover was white, no doubt Egyptian cotton, bordered with a neutral taupe linen.

"So, who decorated your room for you?" she asked with a faint smile. She was beginning to feel a bit more grounded, a little more normal. *It's all okay, I'm okay, thank God he was there.*

"I'm not answering that." He smiled, embarrassed, leaving the room to go to the kitchen.

She kept her jacket on and looked around the room. He had photos of his horses and one of the dogs in wooden, nondescript frames on the mantelpiece. She picked up the photo of Dorian, the horse she had so enjoyed riding at Esslemont all those months ago and exhaled deeply. So much had happened since then, so much continued to happen. *Why is there always so much to deal with? I just want a break, I want it to be easy... easy just for a while. I don't want to struggle any more.*

The rest of the room was filled with necessities, the pinboard by his desk covered in schedules for polo and various uni social events. A narrow bookshelf lined the wall next to the fireplace, books filled the shelves, many law and study related, but novels as well. She had never pictured him reading, had never guessed he was an avid reader, clearly she'd missed that. On the top shelf was his bar, bottles of various spirits and a couple of glasses and measures. He had a compact record player on the end of his desk as well, and a pile of vinyls. She felt safe, she felt comfortable, like she was home. She sat down on the bed.

He made them some toast and tea in the kitchen and brought it in.

"Here, toast is my speciality," he said, handing her the plate and a mug of steaming tea. He then took a bottle from the top shelf. "Rum? It's good with English breakfast, it will help."

"Sure," she said, holding out the mug as he poured a shot into it.

"Are you cold?"

"I am a bit still."

"They said you had to stay warm, get under the covers." She put the tea and toast down on the bedside table and dutifully took her denim jacket and white trainers off, gratefully getting under the warm duvet.

He added some rum to his tea as well, shaking his head. "I was worried I wasn't going to get you in time," he confessed, sitting down on the edge of the bed. They hadn't talked about the details, they hadn't had a chance to process it and they needed to. "I could see it playing out in front of me, but I just couldn't move any faster."

"How far away were you when he came out from behind the trees?"

"About a hundred metres."

"It's not your fault, I shouldn't have cut across, but I thought it was light enough, no one was around, it looked clear," she explained, a guilty expression flickering across her face. She'd been warned about the danger, they all had, she felt like a silly little girl who'd caused unnecessary trouble.

"You were fighting like a tiger, and you slowed him

down. I described his build and the van for the police, but I tackled you both side on, I didn't think it through and you got winded and he got away before I could see his face properly. I should have chased, but you couldn't breathe, so I stayed with you." The words were flowing out of him rapidly, like he'd made a mistake, like he needed to explain, like he was somehow deficient and to blame for the situation.

"Teddy, you were there, you were there." She gripped his forearm. "And I don't know how or why, but I'm so grateful you were. I'm so sorry."

The tears were welling up in her eyes as she spoke. Her heart swelled with emotion, a mixture of gratitude, love and remorse.

It seemed to pain him to look at her, and he looked down at the floor sadly as he responded: "I saw you walk past the pub, I was having a beer with the guys on my course. I just wanted to catch you up and walk back here with you, but you were walking so quickly, so far ahead ..." He trailed off in regret.

"I started to get a bit scared crossing, I knew I shouldn't have, really." The tears rolled down her face. He moved closer to her and wiped them away, wrapping his arm around her shoulder. They sat there for a while in the lamplight, just processing.

"You shouldn't have to even worry about walking home in the dark."

"But girls do, and I knew that, I ignored the danger."

"You're not to blame," he assured her.

"And neither are you."

She turned her face up to kiss him, and he kissed her gently, pulling away before long. He had a concerned expression on his face.

"I have to study and you need to rest. Why don't you try and sleep while I do that?" he said kindly. She nodded, feeling a little rebuffed. He moved to his desk and began pulling books out of the backpack he'd carelessly thrown on the floor nearby.

She was aware that she felt powerfully drawn to him now, an almost overpowering need. She continued just watching his movements. "You still have another exam, this is hardly good timing." She smiled apologetically.

"Despite how distracting you are, I don't think your presence will make the difference. I'm trying to make up for a year of not really doing enough."

"Okay, do you mind if I have a hot shower?"

"No, of course, I'll get you a towel." He pulled a white towel down from the top of the wardrobe and handed it to her.

"And do you have a T-shirt I can sleep in, the grey one maybe?"

"That's specific?" He looked at her with a grin, awaiting an explanation.

"I know your wardrobe, the grey one please," she said, rolling her eyes.

She was done with pretending to be ambivalent.

"Sure," he said, smiling to himself, rummaging in his drawer before throwing it to her. "The bathroom is down the hall on the left. It sounds quiet, don't think the guys are around." He went to the door, opened it and looked down the hall. "Coast is clear."

It didn't seem important who saw her any more. After the events of the evening, that all seemed so insignificant. He went back to his desk opposite the bed and prepared to study.

She showered for what felt like ages, just letting the

hot water run over her. Her body sucked the heat in and it was comforting. She returned in the grey T-shirt, clean and warm, finally warm all the way to the bone.

She tried to settle down and sleep. The bed was soft and comfortable and the sheets felt smooth and expensive. She could get used to this. She dozed and drifted in and out of consciousness for a while. Her mind woke her up as it replayed the attack over and over and every time she opened her eyes he was still there at the desk. From the bed she could lie there and just look at him. It was like she was worried he would disappear, that she would be alone, so she kept a watchful eye. She needed to know he was still there.

A small desk lamp was on, the only light in the room which he'd turned to face the wall to lower its intensity so she could sleep. He looked drained and tired. The weight of the world on his shoulders, his fun-loving nature somewhat obscured of late. His room had the same half-panelled walls and fireplace as hers. It was dark and sombre, apart from the desk where his handsome face was illuminated in the golden light, as he poured over pages and pages of notes, his hair falling forward as he hunched over.

"Why are you studying now?" Her voice came out of the gloomy light, out of nowhere, surprising him slightly.

"I work better at night, when it's quiet," he explained, smiling gently. "I was just going to do a little bit, but it's never-ending."

As she lay awake watching him concentrate, she realised she no longer cared what happened between them going forward, she wanted to be with him now; irrationally impatient, she was done with waiting. She got out of bed and he turned to look at her as she walked towards him. His piercing gaze still felt like it went right inside after all this time.

"You can't sleep?" he asked with concern.

"No," she answered as she sat astride him in the chair. He sat bolt upright now, still and rigid, as he backed away, so unlike him, his hands on her shoulders. She put her arms around his neck, her hands moving in his hair as she kissed him, revealing her intent.

He pushed her back gently. "I don't want to be that guy," he said resolutely. "You know how I feel, you know how badly I want to, but I don't think now's right." He was uncomfortable and conflicted.

"I don't care any more, Teddy, nothing matters now, I could have died tonight. All we have is now." She leant forward again and kissed him, ignoring his request.

He turned his head to the side and away from her. "Please, don't make me be that guy," he begged. She kissed his neck, her hair falling across his chest, pausing only to take off his borrowed shirt, her gold necklaces and underwear all that was left. She redoubled her efforts, and this time she felt him capitulate, as honour and integrity gave way to passion and desire. His arms wrapped around her, moving up and down her back, and then he rapidly stood up, bearing her full weight, her legs instinctively wrapping around his waist as he moved them over to the bed, and placed her down gently.

He stood back up, taking his shirt off as he looked down at her. "Neither of us are getting any sleep tonight," he said with surety, shaking his head.

28

*"We are each our own devil, and we make this world
our hell."*
— Oscar Wilde

They did sleep eventually, but it was not for long. Teddy awoke with a start, his subconscious breaking through, a sudden jolt through his exhausted, foggy mind, not a gentle rise to consciousness.

"Aurora, Aurora, I've got an exam, it's at ten, I have to go," he said, gently shaking her awake. "Shit, shit, I need coffee!" he said anxiously as he dived out of bed, pulling clothes out of the drawer rapidly, carelessly throwing anything on and jumping into his jeans. She watched, wishing he didn't have to leave.

She could see his mind calculating rapidly, working

319

out what he needed to do to get out the door, totally focused on the next task. She felt so guilty; his final exam and she had forced his hand. What had happened? Why did she do it? She didn't regret it, come what may it was done, but she was sorry she had put him in this position.

"I'm so sorry, this is my fault," she managed to concede guiltily.

"It's okay," he said, throwing things into a bag, a pencil case, textbook, not looking at her.

"I shouldn't have forced the issue, I don't know what happened?" she said, perplexed. It had come over her like a wave, this intense, selfish ache.

"Don't be sorry. My God, I have no regrets, it was intense," he said, looking over at her. "It's nature, life-threatening situations spur animals on, we're mammals," he said, grinning.

"Basic instinct then? I'm not sure that makes me feel better."

"It's just one exam. If I fail I'll claim extenuating circumstances," he said with a smirk, coming over to the bed and kissing her warmly. "I have to fly, I'll see you later."

As the door closed softly behind him, she lay back, enjoying the warmth of his bed and the smell of his room; he was everywhere still. She fell back asleep.

When she woke hours later, she contemplated the previous evening's events, staring up at the ceiling. Her feelings were all over the place. She shivered as she remembered the terror she'd felt when she was dragged in the grass. All alone and without Teddy to distract her, it was harder to throw off the after-effect of the night before. She knew she should probably alert her parents. The ball was tonight, she didn't want to miss that, and she didn't want to open up about anything that had happened in the last twenty-four hours immediately. *I'll call them tomorrow.* No questions, no reflections, she wanted to just keep going forward. She could get out of helping on the JCR probably, given the circumstances, but the activity would occupy her, which would no doubt be a good thing.

She replayed the events of the night with Teddy in her mind, choosing to focus on that instead, and felt waves of yearning again. She didn't want to come down from the high, a high she had never experienced before. *"Intense", he said. Well, I'll take that.*

After a while the room felt empty without him, and she crept out down the hall and outside. She made for her room, having taken his grey T-shirt with her, which she was wearing over the top of her ripped denim jeans. She couldn't bear to leave it behind, she wanted to hang on to it.

She messaged Diana and Liv and suggested they go out for food and coffee, where she relayed the events of the attack and Teddy's miraculous arrival on the scene.

"Oh my God, he saved you?" asked Diana.

"He came from nowhere. Well, I had headphones on until I was nearly across the park, so I didn't hear anything, but he was chasing me down apparently. I don't want to think too much about it today if possible, but I've never been so terrified, never even close. I can't explain the fear." Her heart raced as she described the scene and relived it in her mind and she became agitated, playing with a ring on her finger, pulling it on and off rapidly.

"Did you talk to your mum and dad?" said Diana, looking concerned.

"No, I don't want them to freak out, and I'm fine,

just a little shaken up is all. Besides, the ball is tonight." Aurora's face brightened at the prospect of the event.

"It's okay, don't if it's distressing now, but you will have to talk to them about it, won't you?" Liv gently prodded.

"Yes, I will. I'll tell my parents of course, but just not today. I don't want it to spoil tonight and other things."

"What other things?" Diana inquired, intrigued.

Aurora smiled, unable to suppress her pleasure, her joy at the memory of being with Teddy from the night before, bursting to share it with her friends now.

"Of course you did." Liv surmised what had transpired, nodding knowingly.

"I couldn't help it, he didn't want to, but I insisted really," she admitted. "I just wanted him so badly, nothing else mattered." Her face lit up at the recollection.

"Weren't you upset after, you know, going to the police station and all that?" Diana was confused by the course of events.

"Yeah, did you feel like that really?' Liv probed.

"It was weird, Teddy said it's a phenomenon in the animal world." "I'm sure he did," Liv said dryly.

"No, it wasn't his doing, I can assure you. I've been resisting him for so long it feels like, and I thought what for? Why am I still tormenting myself when I really want him? I've been running from these feelings all year, and it's like nothing I've ever experienced before."

"So it was good?" Diana asked.

"It was amazing. I just realised that all I have is now, and only fear was holding me back."

They were understandably concerned about her mental state given what had happened. So far she appeared to be stable, somewhat buoyed up by the romantic turn of events. However, there were emotions that would have to be dealt with at some point in the future.

By the afternoon, however, the bliss of the evening before was beginning to wane, giving way to mild anxiety. There had been no message from Teddy, no call, no text, nothing to say how the exam went, how he felt in relation to her, just radio silence. She wasn't unduly concerned but she had expected to hear from him.

Her assignment for the JCR was to decorate the marquee, which had been put up in the quad earlier in the week. As she worked with Diana, she began to express her doubts and fears.

"I haven't heard from Teddy all day and it's the afternoon," she said as they began hanging fairy lights.

"What were you expecting? You know, what did he say?"

"He said, 'I'll see you later.'"

"Okay, casual, non-committal, but honestly he was rushing, late for an exam. He's been showing all the right signs, right?"

"Yes, but, Diana, one week on a ski trip of ... well ... forcibly restrained good behaviour does not reform someone, does it?"

"He's been consistent, Aurora, calm down. He's just doing his exam and now they'll be in the pub. Relax," Diana reassured her.

As they placed centrepieces on tables over an hour later she could no longer take it, and she resorted to messaging him. A simple, 'How did your exam go?', keeping it light. There was no response.

As she returned to Tudor later, after having been

down the road to have her nails done, she glanced in the direction of his block, scanning the building. She now knew the exact set of mullioned windows which belonged to his room. The curtains were still drawn, just as she had left them, no clue as to his mindset to be gleaned from that.

She showered and dried her hair. She planned to leave it down tonight, just curling the ends. Her dress was a "showstopper", even by her standards. She had bought it as soon as she saw it in a magazine. Mid-length, in steel blue, it was a halter-neck, backless dress, covered entirely in fringing with a handkerchief hem. It was striking against her Polynesian colouring. Her Aussie tan had deepened her already olive skin, and her long, dark hair contrasted well with it. She checked her phone again; no acknowledgement, no response, nothing. After three hours, fear and dread took up residence in the pit of her stomach, refusing to dislodge. She tried reminding herself he wasn't good with his phone. She mentally went through their interaction, checking for signs of warmth, his care, devotion, interest, all of it she scanned thoroughly. Their brief history together; she went over and over it again in her mind. *Did I get it wrong again? I can't have, surely, I felt the connection, it was real.*

She packed her makeup and took her dress and shoes with her to do the rest in Diana's room, where they had arranged to meet.

When she got to Diana's she was beginning to seriously doubt him. It was 6 p.m., drinks were starting at 7 p.m., and she began to panic. She hadn't eaten enough all day, now she felt too nauseous, self-doubt flooded her system like a poison.

"I can't do this!" she admitted to her girlfriends. "I

don't think I can face this without knowing what he's thinking. I can't bear it."

"I'll admit it's strange," said Diana, "but I can't believe he would do that Roars, it's just not possible. Especially on top of what happened last night."

"He has been so lovely, so charming and so believable!" Aurora said forlornly.

"Come on, that would be evil," Liv stated. "Hang in there, it doesn't make sense."

"If you only knew how many times I've said that about people, guys in particular. It doesn't make sense. It doesn't have to make sense, it usually doesn't make sense! People are a mystery all the time. Look at Paige, that didn't make sense, not to me, I'm still dumbfounded."

"This is different, he's a good guy, I'm sure he is. James says he's a solid friend, and I agree it would be wicked to do that to you." Diana was trying to allay her fears.

"I did it, though, in the end, I did it, I made it happen finally. Perhaps that lets him off the hook there?"

"No, it doesn't, it would be more than shitty still!" Liv was unmoved.

During the course of the afternoon Aurora had progressed through bewilderment, confusion and frustration, which now quickly transitioned into anger. Her anxiety was ruling her now. She began to feel furious as the doubts in her mind became reality to her, reinforced by his silence. She grabbed her phone in fury, typing, "You can't even be bothered to answer my message? So you got what you wanted ... you asshole!" pressing send immediately.

"Who did you just message?" Diana said, catching

her furious typing action.

"Him," she said through gritted teeth, eyes blazing.

Liv grabbed the phone. "Okay, let's just cool it on the texting, not right now, just hold off, there's plenty of time for that if he really deserves it."

Aurora's makeup was done, her eyes dark and smoky, lips pale; her favourite look. She wore long crystal earrings, vintage, which stood out against her hair, and strappy, wraparound shoes. As she stood looking in the mirror she couldn't understand why others seemed to find love and relationships so easily. Why was it so hard for her? What was wrong with her?

"I can't go tonight, I don't think I can face this," Aurora bemoaned. Trauma was beginning to raise its head.

"We've got you, Liv and I, we're here." Diana hugged her. "Don't let fear stop you going tonight. Look at you, you know who you are, don't let it take over. It will be his problem, not yours, all his."

"What is it I do, why does this happen to me?" she asked, beginning to lose it, her face in her hands.

"Aurora, we're not going there, we're not, this is his shit. It's not a reflection on you. His shitty behaviour doesn't define you!" Liv was now pissed off on her behalf.

It was 7 p.m. already, drinks would have started. The enormous marquee stood erected in the quadrangle, filling it completely. Inside it was separated into a bar area which then went through into the dining room, where round tables were set out in an organised fashion, with name tags corresponding to Paige's well contrived seating plan. Jazz and swing were playing as people began arriving. The event was black tie and would be well attended by all the halls in Stoke Bishop, the biggest event of the year. Strands of lights were hanging across the ceiling in all directions to give the effect of stars. As the sun finally went down, they would come to life.

They entered the bar area. Aurora scanned the room, locating Winnie, James and Harry standing together, but there was no Teddy. The girls immediately went to the bar, getting into the Prosecco before joining them.

James was admiring Diana's dress, a short wraparound number in pastel colours. She usually liked her cocktail dresses short, showing off her legs.

"You look beautiful tonight," Aurora could make out him saying before he kissed her. It looked so easy for them both, there wasn't any insecurity, no struggle. She checked her phone again, both messages were showing read now, but without a response.

"Have you seen Teddy?" she turned to ask Winnie, unable to stop it from coming out of her mouth. It was a loaded question, she was better off not asking him, but her overwhelming need to know eclipsed her desire to play it cool.

"No, I haven't seen him, I knocked earlier but he didn't answer. He finished today so he's probably been in the pub." Winnie seemed completely unperturbed, he was waiting for the delightful Tabitha to arrive, scanning the room himself.

They posed for photos, everybody was having their photo taken with someone. Reuben sauntered over, asking to have a photo with her. As they posed by the side of the marquee, she forced a smile and stood making small talk with him afterwards in a group of his friends. He was a nice person, funny and warm, and she tried her best to be engaging.

"I have to say, Aurora, you look absolutely beautiful," he said smoothly.

She failed to answer him immediately, her full attention suddenly taken as she saw Teddy had arrived. Unfairly handsome in his tuxedo, chiselled cheekbones, hair styled in full-on heartthrob mode, he strode through the crowd purposefully. She felt like his energy immediately charged the atmosphere, people reached out to stop him and say hello, girls' heads still turned. He ignored them all now as he made his passage through the crowd.

"Thank you." She smiled up at Reuben, attempting to convey as much warmth and gracious charm as possible.

She stood in a circle talking in a group, perhaps eight of them, boys and girls, when from the far side Teddy excused himself between two of them and extended his hand to her. She openly glared at him. No message, after all that had happened last night. Here he was, all fine, why? She was hurt, but the anger was all you could see on the surface. He grabbed her hand anyway and pulled her through the centre of the circle and out the other side; she pulled against him, making it difficult, a show of non-compliance. Reuben protested, "Hey, Teddy, what are you doing?" It was ignored.

Teddy turned her to face him, holding both of her arms above the elbow firmly, not squeezing, but like she was a small child who needed to listen to what he had to say. He looked seriously frustrated. People all around them were watching, sensing drama, but they were in their own little bubble of two.

"You're with me now, we're done with all this," he said looking around the room as he tried to explain himself. "We're done with all this creeping around, this pretence, it's finished," he said firmly, and then he kissed her tenderly, still restraining her arms so she was in no doubt of his meaning. The room could talk. Public displays at the end of the night were expected; at the beginning of a night, they were not so common; emotional connections and public displays were even rarer still.

As their lips parted, her eyes filled with tears. His features softened now as he relaxed, taking it all in, watching her closely as he let go of her arms. The fear that lay underneath everything within Aurora ebbed away, taking the anger with it, leaving behind the essence of the girl. He wrapped his arms around her and held her close for a minute, kissing her head.

"Why didn't you respond?" she asked him, her head now lying on his chest.

"I got back to my room at about two. After the exam I went to the pub and then crashed out. I just slept, and I should have messaged you, I'm sorry, I just passed out. I was so tired after everything, studying, the police station, staying up all night and then the exam. I woke up like five minutes ago and saw what you'd sent. I got ready and came down, it was easier to show you."

"I started to panic, I thought …"

"I know what you thought," he said, cutting her off, "which is why I needed to show you. Aurora, I'm sorry but you're stuck with me. I'm not going anywhere." She looked at the gorgeous young guy in front of her and almost felt her legs give way. Relief flooded through her like a river, and she suddenly felt so drained. He was sure, he had her and he wasn't going anywhere, she didn't have to hold herself any more.

"You get me," she said simply, feeling a little

embarrassed by her behaviour now. She smiled faintly.
"Yes, I'm afraid I do," he said with a smile.

29

*"Always forgive your enemies; nothing annoys them
so much."*
— Oscar Wilde

It was already time to go through for dinner, and as
they looked at the seating plan together, Aurora saw she
was at the back, at a table with Diana and Liv. *At least
I'm not alone*, she thought. Teddy found himself at a
table with his mates, down the front by the stage, his
back to Paige on the adjacent table. *So convenient*, she
thought.

"I'm at the back here with the girls." Aurora pointed
at her table.

"No you're not, you're with me, someone will be
moving," he said authoritatively. He took her hand,

pulling her along again. He was a force to be reckoned with tonight and he rearranged the table to suit them. Jasper and Thomas and another guy, Louis, agreed to move to the table of girls at the back, swapping with Liv and Diana, who came down to the front. Paige came over to say something, and Teddy intercepted her, it was a short discussion. What was said, Aurora didn't know.

As they sat with all their friends, Aurora could see Winnie across the table clocking everything. He smiled, saying, "It's going to be a good night!", shouting over the rumble of voices. After the main course, he came and chatted to them both. Liv and Diana had already spoken to him and relayed the previous night's drama before they had even sat down to dinner. Word of what had transpired the night before would be passed from person to person through the course of the evening, it was inevitable. He sat in Liv's empty chair next to Aurora, bringing his wine with him.

"So, I hear you had a close call?" he directed to Aurora, looking concerned.

"I don't know what it was that I escaped exactly, but I was terrified, is all I can say."

"You got to swoop in and save the damsel in distress?" he said, now directing his gaze towards Teddy.

"I didn't feel like a hero, nothing prepares you for a situation like that," he said, shaking his head at the memory, all the while looking at Aurora. He put his arm around her and she instinctively moved in closer to him, enjoying the position she found herself in. She looked at him beside her and her heart swelled with joy. That she was so delighted given the circumstances of the last twenty-four hours was a miracle, almost madness, and yet two hours ago she was distraught. Crazy and ridiculous, emotions were so powerful, so turbulent. Her friends were all around and there was a buzz in the room, she felt almost euphoric, all the while knowing it was inevitable that she would fall from this high.

A friend of Teddy's interrupted their conversation to talk rugby and Winnie took the opportunity to lean in and whisper quietly to her. "I was onto this," he said, gesturing to the both of them, "way before you guys were. Like I said, you two were never going to be friends." He seemed very pleased with his insight from months prior. "I can read people better than they can read themselves," he said, smugly raising his glass to his lips. "Maybe I should go into intelligence or something?"

"Really? Well, you never let on that you were so clever, not until the ski trip?" she said quizzically.

"No, it wasn't my place to get in between you both, you're my mates, but it was obvious."

"Obvious! I hated him at first, he was so rude and obnoxious."

"Yeah, but the sparks flew. That first breakfast, it was on, from that point it was on. It was just a question of when. God, even the night before, when I introduced you two. You made him sit up and take notice, you challenged him. There must have been some twists and turns because I thought you'd get together so much sooner, but then it's probably better this way," he said, looking at Teddy. Aurora guessed he meant that Teddy had had to work for it.

"Well, Paige put a damper on things way back at Teddy's place that weekend, and his reputation did the rest. I wasn't sure and I didn't really trust him."

"Ahh, good old Alvin. How's she been since we got back from the ski trip?"

"I haven't seen her in our block, I see her working the tables in the dining room, and I can see her over there now," Aurora said, looking across the room to where Paige was standing between two girls at another table chatting animatedly. "It's like she's always networking."

"She is, she lives for it. She loves manipulating people, she's made for it. You must hate being surrounded by them upstairs?" he said, looking sympathetic.

"Well, I'm almost done, the year's over, but I'd like not to worry about bumping into her in the hallway. I'd like to be free of that."

"Let it go, Roars, it's not worth it." They began to serve dessert and he returned to his seat, musing on his cleverness.

After dessert, Aurora excused herself to go to the bathroom, which was located back inside the bar area. As she came around the corner, she came face to face with Paige, just the two of them, all alone. She knew that after the discussion with Winnie, coming face to face like this in a chance meeting was fate, an opportunity not to be missed. In all the time since the fateful night of the ball, she had never bumped into her in the hallway, never been alone with her. There had been no accidental encounter ever, and had there been, she doubted that she would have been ready to speak to Paige about what had happened. Too wounded, too vulnerable, and outnumbered. On top of that there had been too much charge around the event to address it appropriately, until now that is. She needed to confront the still weeping wound that would not heal until cauterised. She needed to take her power back.

Paige looked set to ignore her totally and walk straight past, avoiding any interaction, but Aurora addressed her head on.

"Paige, you and I both know what you did," she dived in. Paige looked like a deer caught in headlights, unable to take her eyes off the car bearing down on her. Without an entourage behind her she was meek and timid. "You know I tried to resolve the issue between us. You know I tried to talk to you and sort things out the night before the ball, remember, when you said it was all okay? But then you went and stuck the knife in. I suppose that's your prerogative in the end." Paige stood still, not answering, so Aurora continued: "And let's not forget the open mic night on the ski trip, bonus points for that one. But just so *you* know, I forgive you. We won't ever be friends like we were, but I don't hate you. I'm not carrying that shit around with me. You carry on the way you have been if that works for you. Go back and gather your forces, plan another attack, bitch about me or whatever it is you do, but I don't care any more."

Paige was taken aback, at a loss for words. Her mouth was open, gaping, like she was trying to speak, but the words just weren't coming. Aurora shook her head as she finished her speech and walked off continuing on her path. As she was nearly at the door to the bathroom she heard Paige call out.

"Aurora, it was girls' code. You violated the girls' code. I told you I wasn't comfortable with you seeing Flynn and you were just going to carry on anyway, you didn't drop it," she said defensively, arguing her case. Aurora turned and strode back towards her.

"Paige, I tried to talk to you about it. The guy wasn't your ex, he was his friend. On top of that you spent all night with Flynn, after saying you couldn't bear to see him with me, it was psychotic. You wanted to just click your fingers and have me jump to attention, and when I didn't you went nuts." Aurora's eyes narrowed and flashed fiercely. She had reached her limit now and wasn't about to accept bullshit.

"In boarding school if someone calls 'girls' code', it's hands off," she stammered, trying to explain.

"We're not in high school any more. We're adults, we're in the real world now," Aurora said disparagingly. "Now it's just about whether you're a decent human being or not."

Paige looked like a little lost waif, like the rules had changed and she didn't understand the game any more. "So, you don't hate me?" she asked, looking puzzled.

"I don't hate you. If you had apologised we might have still been friends, but it's over now, I've moved on."

Aurora walked into the toilets and took a deep breath. A weight lifted off her shoulders, it was palpable. She was in a mood to face things; suddenly time seemed to be of the essence, the attack had given her a new perspective. She wanted to leave the shitty experiences behind her, she was ready to embrace the future ahead without any baggage, glad she had finally confronted Paige.

She returned to the marquee and to Liv and Diana, who were standing talking, preparing to go upstairs and change into more casual clothes for the second half of the evening. Outside in the grounds of Tudor, dodgem cars and a small carnival area had been set up. It was a warm summer's evening and would be light until at least 10 p.m. A Pimm's bar was waiting and they would party the rest of the night, moving between the marquee, with its bar and silent disco, and the carnival outside.

Aurora returned to her seat and Teddy, putting her hand on his knee, whispering, "I'm just going to change with Liv and Diana, be back soon." She leant in to kiss him and he grabbed her arm, not letting her go quickly. Aurora was glowing, she looked ethereal under the fairy lights in the twilight. Teddy was simmering all night, constantly reaching out to touch her, to feel her skin. His eyes followed her wherever she moved.

"Why don't you change in my room," he said, grabbing her other arm. "In fact just get clothes for the next couple of days."

She smiled at him, flattered at his eagerness. "Teddy, it's like twenty metres to my block, I think we can afford to be spontaneous."

"Good, let's go now then," he said, devouring her with his eyes. He got to his feet, offering his hand, "hold my hand so you don't float away."

As they left the room, heads turned, people had noticed all through dinner that they were an item. The news of the attempted assault had spread like wildfire. Some people surmised that the event had brought them together, others on the ski trip assumed their relationship had begun during the course of that week, but only their closest friend knew that the flame had been ignited long ago. If Aurora was honest, she would have dated it from the night she signed up to run for the JCR, when she first heard his voice.

Epilogue

*"You don't love someone for their looks, or their clothes,
or for their fancy car, but because they sing a song
only you can hear."*
— Oscar Wilde

It was with some trepidation that Aurora took Teddy home to meet the family at the beginning of July. Unwilling to be apart, he accompanied her home as boyfriend and rescuer. The police had launched an investigation into the attack and claimed to have some leads. All they could do for now was wait and see.

As they drove up the drive, Teddy had a nonchalant hand on her knee, tapping in time to the music, seemingly calm, while she sat next to him, worrying about whether he would cope with her unruly family and the informal atmosphere. She was nervous their frank and honest dialogue would be too much for him, would invade his privacy, and was terrified they might embarrass her.

"Are you ready for this?" she asked, looking up at him.

"People usually like me straight up, you know? You were the exception."

"My family take no prisoners, that's all. They won't be rude of course, but they say it like it is," she said seriously.

He laughed it off. "I can handle myself, don't worry."

"I know you can, I'm not worried about your manners, I'm worried about it being a baptism of fire," she said as she lifted up her sunglasses to fix him with a pointed stare. Teddy was unphased. "I'm just trying to prepare you is all."

Her family warmly received him in spite of her mother's initial prejudice and Aurora's fears. He worked hard to win them all over and they appreciated the effort, Ajax especially. Teddy sat at their large family table during the evening meal every night of their two-week visit, observing their interactions, and the sibling rivalry that often reared its head.

"Rafael is one of my boy's names, Bas, remember?" Aurora asserted one night. They had somehow ended up talking about what they would call their children, an old favourite game that always ended up in a fight.

"No, it's not, Aurora, it was always Sebastian's," Evie jumped to her brother's defence, scowling at Aurora.

"Swear it was mine, *Ninja Turtles*," Bas said, shaking his head, adamant he was correct.

"Are we really fighting about baby names?" Nicky questioned the table, looking unimpressed.

"Well, I'll probably be having children first so I'll just beat you all to it," Aurora said with superiority, forgetting herself for a moment. Teddy threw back his head laughing.

"Good luck with that," Bas said, looking at Teddy, who moved to place a restraining hand on Aurora's thigh, reminding her that she didn't need to compete, to retaliate or fight for position.

"Yeah, and you were the ugly baby," Lanna added,

grinning, attempting to provoke her sister. Normally Aurora would launch a counterattack, but not this time. Her mouth moved into a tight-lipped smile and she let it drop, catching herself in time.

He got her father's dry sense of humour and was respectful towards her mother, his main worry. Samantha was friendly but maintained some distance, circumspect about the relationship and the boy's intentions given Aurora's first assessment of him. She could see that Aurora was besotted, and it wasn't hard to understand why, but she wasn't about to be swept away by his charm. The fact that he had saved Aurora on the Downs was highly in his favour, though, and Samantha knew they were in his debt.

The males of the family, like most men, were territorial and protective of their girls. Aurora had played her cards close to her chest, unintentionally as she really wasn't sure they would be together come the end of the school year, so it was a bit of a surprise to everyone when she asked to bring Teddy home. Teddy eventually connected with Bas, hard to do coming into the household abruptly as the new boyfriend. Her brother, a superb athlete who excelled at any sport he tried, dreamt of making it to the Olympics for decathlon. It bordered on complete obsession, but then he was easier to live with if exercised, so everyone fanned the flame.

Teddy made the mistake of expressing a desire to go for a run with him. "I'd like a run, keep my fitness up for rugby," he said one afternoon.

"No, no, don't go out with Bas, he's training," Aurora warned.

Teddy was indignant. "It's okay, I can run, I'm not bad."

"Yeah sure, let's go," Bas encouraged.

"No, Teddy you don't understand." She placed a restraining hand on his arm with a concerned frown.

"I ran cross-country at school," Teddy asserted, looking insulted.

"He'll be right," Bas assured her as he patted Teddy on the back.

As they went out the front door, Bas turned and flashed Aurora a cheeky grin. He took him out for a blistering ten kilometres, which culminated in Teddy throwing up. When they returned home Aurora was furious, looking daggers at her brother, who of course had intentionally humbled his sister's boyfriend. After that they could be mates.

Lanna fell under Teddy's spell and was frequently caught staring at him, unabashed. When he said he was 6"2' she told him that was model height. Overloaded with confidence and charisma, she generally charmed her way through life. She giggled and flirted with her sister's boyfriend, which amused him no end, and irritated the life out of Aurora. She defended herself by saying, "What? He's pretty to look at."

Evie trailed around after the pair of them as often as she could get away with, attempting to engage Teddy in shooting hoops, playing croquet and jumping on the trampoline. He was good with her, obliging and happy to play. She worshipped him.

Teddy discovered the whole family was competitive as they played tennis together during the day, and cards by night. He hung in there through it all, determined to win them over. The young couple spent hours in the garden with the good weather and went for long walks with the dog. She discovered Teddy liked to laugh at himself, would always give as good as he got, but was usually good-humoured with it. Aurora allowed herself to let go, to fall into the deep, trusting she could keep herself afloat, that she wouldn't drown with him.

Deep into July she returned to Esslemont. This time she arrived with the heir in his summer convertible, the warm wind in her hair as they whipped up the drive to the mansion. Aurora hoped the transition would be seamless because the location was inconsequential. They were in love, and it mattered not where they were, so long as they were together.

Aurora added warmth and richness to the large, imposing house. She got to know Constance as best she could, making every effort to be engaging and polite, complimenting her cooking and showing interest in her hobbies and pursuits. His mother, who recognised the future had walked through the front door, began to let her guard down as she grappled with the change in her son.

His father applauded his son's choice, enjoying the conversation and the sport of watching his son fall under the spell of a beautiful young woman. It reminded him of his youth and brought life to their home. Aurora found Tom highly amusing as he mocked his son and teased his wife. He had a sharp wit, coupled with extensive knowledge, learned and good-natured.

In his presence, she always felt valued and at ease. She glowed and Teddy beamed as he showed off his new girl to his parents and friends who lived close by.

As dusk fell on another warm day, they led the horses out to the fields and released them for the night. They had ridden late and sat on the grass, watching the horses as they moved off and away to graze.

They would follow the horses' example and spend the summer in the same way, drifting here and there, going wherever the mood took them. They had plans to join their friends in Corfu, where they would all play hard for a week.

Teddy lay down and she followed his lead, lying next to him on the soft, cool grass, looking upwards as the night sky darkened. The stars were just coming out.

"Now can I point out the constellations?" he asked.

She laughed at the memory of her outburst outside the club in Val d'Isère. "Go ahead, I think I'm ready for them now."

"You were horrible," he said, wrapping his arms around her.

"I was, I can't believe you saw through me," she confided as she laid her head on his chest.

Life was good, for now all was idyllic, they were blessed and they knew it.

Acknowledgments

To my big, boisterous family who are scattered around the world, you are all in here somewhere and you all contributed in a multitude of ways, using your own unique gifts. Thank you for listening and putting up with my feelings of inadequacy. I honestly can never thank you enough. Richard, what can I say? Together we ride wild horses and walk the road less travelled, but you are also the stability in my life. Eliza, without your belief and encouragement it simply would never have been completed. You were instrumental. To Jack, I say thank you for sharing your talent with me. From re-writes and dialogue, right through the editing process, you held my feet to the fire and contributed so much. Susannah, your inspiration, on- going support and counsel are integral. The feedback, brutal at times, was critical. Thank you for the cover design and everything you add. We are not done yet! India, thank you for the beautiful bakes all through a summer where you lost your mother to her writing and put up with endless, boring discussions under our walnut tree. To Anna, for reading and cheerleading; you helped me to believe it was ok. Thank you to my young/new adult readers: Claire, Pia, and Imke. Your reactions were so important. My friends: Anne, Sarah and Pen who read early versions and were gentle and supportive. Thank you Sarah for the first cover design. Finally to Rachel who helped edit, guide and generally mentor. You taught me so much.

www.ingramcontent.com/pod-product-compliance
Lightning Source LLC
Chambersburg PA
CBHW021229060726
47590CB00005B/1681